The Perfect Daughter

Lynn Shurr

A Wings ePress, Inc
Historical Romance Novel

Wings Press, Inc.

Wings ePress, Inc.

Edited by: Jeanne Smith
Copy Edited by: Joan C. Powell
Executive Editor: Jeanne Smith
Cover Artist: Trisha FitzGerald-Jung

All rights reserved

Wings ePress Books
www.wingsepress.com

Published In the United States Of America

Wings ePress Inc.
3000 N. Rock Road
Newton, KS 67114

What They Are Saying About
The Perfect Daughter

"Shurr is a wonderful storyteller."

—The Romance Studio

"Very easy reads, well written, combined with conflict, believable plots and secondary characters that make the story come alive."

—Jane Lange, Romances, *Reads and Reviews*

"I love the picture the author paints of the town and the way of life, and the characters are strong and interesting.

—Joan Conning Afman
Author of *The Cheetah Princess*

"Lynn Shurr breathes life into the characters and allows each turn of the page to lead up to a pleasurable ending."

—Cherokee
Coffee Time Romance and More

"I love how deep and well-written the characters are."

—Juliette Brandt
Paperbacks and Frosting

"You can count on Lynn Shurr to deliver interesting characters and great romance."

—A.C. Mason
Author of *Deadly Bayou*

Dedication

For Trudy Patterson, librarian extraordinaire and long-time friend.

* * *

***The progeny of Pearce and Flora Longleigh,
Duke and Duchess of Bellevue, as recorded in
the family Bible:****

- James Logan Longleigh, Storm Cloud, born in the Ohio Territory, April 12, 1784?
- Thalia Amabel Full Moon Woman Longleigh, b. March 1, 1785.
- Iris Emily Doe Eyes Longleigh, b. October 16, 1787.
- Twins, Calliope Constance Corn Tassel & Clio Judith Small Turtle,
- b. June 22, 1789.
- Joshua William Big Paw Longleigh, b. January 24, 1791
- Jason Samuel Benjamin Rattler Longleigh, b. January 24, 1792
- Pandora Jane Black Wing Longleigh, b. September 15, 1794
- Euphemia Dorcas Little Dove Longleigh, b. December 31, 1795
- Justinian Giles White Bull Longleigh, b. July 10, 1800

And all made the lives of their parents very interesting.

<h1 style="text-align:center">One</h1>

London, April, 1804

Lady Thalia Longleigh, the Duke and Duchess of Bellevue's eldest daughter, acknowledged her assessment by the ton summed up in one word—perfection. She strove to live up to their expectation. Thalia possessed the same dark eyes as her father. They harbored an identical spark of passion in their depths, though she kept hers tamped down and modestly veiled by long, downcast lashes. Her mother's heritage accounted for their large size and the occasional glimpse of mischief quickly subdued.

A myriad of curls inherited from Lady Flora, the duchess, framed the exquisite oval of her face, but they grew as thick and black as the straight hair on the duke's head. Once his youth had passed, he'd always been one to disdain wigs and powder if at all possible, some said out of vanity, his own locks being so handsome. Thalia was rather fond of her own.

Of course, Lady Thalia ordered her maid to arrange her coiffure in the latest of styles *a la grecque,* piling it atop her head in two courses, each set off with gold cord, and allowing just the right amount of soft, ebony curls to frame her face. This particular evening, she wore a simple elegant gown, a draped white tunic bound beneath her breasts with the same cord and embroidered at the hem and sleeves in a Greek key design executed in gold thread carrying out the theme of antique simplicity. She owned the tall figure to carry it off superbly.

Long-limbed like her father, Lady Thalia had grown to a lofty height by her nineteenth year. This might have been considered disastrous had she not carried herself with perfect grace and a goddess-like demeanor. Any who suggested she would have been better off sharing her mother's petite form quickly learned they thought wrong, as even short men longed to scale her heights. That she had a noble bosom often at eye-level with her dance partners could not be denied. If those gentlemen managed to raise their gazes higher, they settled quickly on her full lips naturally ruddy in tone, another gift of birth from the duke. She did have Lady Flora's more aristocratic nose rather than his broad one, a fortunate present from nature. All in all, she enjoyed rising above others with her regal stature.

If Thalia owned to any flaw, her complexion might be a trifle dark. Those not conversant with the Longleigh family history received a quickly shared genealogy revealing an Italian great-grandmother, an opera singer wed by her duke after he proclaimed, "Damme, I shall marry whom I please!" When she told the story, she left out the 'damme.' Lady Thalia's rich soprano voice quickly became attributed to this long-gone ancestress, though many remembered Lady Flora as having a similar talent in her youth.

Those whom Thalia considered her competitors for the title of Perfection were all too willing to tattle that her darkness had a closer source as the current duke's father had a liaison with a Red Indian woman resulting in Pearce Longleigh, Thalia's father. She applied a bit of powder and simply did not give a fig. Any miss with a dowry of twenty thousand pounds could be dark as a Negro and still marry very well. The tint of her skin quickly lightened to a delightful burnished tone when discussed in tandem with this huge sum of money.

This ball began like any other, with suitors dogging her steps in such numbers Thalia frequently tripped over them, but another always stood handily nearby to catch her elbow and save her from embarrassment. They brought her more sweet insipid beverages than she could possibly drink between dances. She knew the patronesses blamed her for the condition of the dusty palms ornamenting Almack's ballroom, which yellowed from the amount of sugar they received as she disposed of the excess with a quick flick of her wrist. Her dance card filled so quickly she had need of two and began with the next already filled for the following occasion. Despite an over-abundance of male interest, she had not chosen amongst her beaux in her first year out and the start of her second season showed no more promise. The men who surrounded her were all so very much the same.

Thalia did not fret, however, secure in the love of her family. While the Duke of Bellevue sent his first-born son, James, Viscount Laughlin, off on a Grand Tour to encompass several years with no more than a paternal slap on the back, he often declared his six beautiful daughters need not marry, but should stay safely at Bellevue Hall for all of their natural lives rather than take on an inferior fellow. While Thalia did not intend to follow his advice, knowing she would not be forced to marry provided some consolation. She intended to take her time until lightning struck her heart and sent it thundering. So far, she hadn't experienced so much as a spark.

When her father blustered his viewpoint, the duchess always answered, "That is not the way of young women. They will go where their hearts take them." She had done so in following him deep into the wilds of America and eventually drawing him back to England to be her husband. The tale made Thalia sigh and wish for the same sort of adventure.

"True," the duke acknowledged, but still cast a fierce and savage eye on any man approaching Thalia, which did discourage a few but not nearly enough. Now in the second month of this second season, Thalia still showed no preference for any suitor, so none had drawn the full force of his scrutiny this evening. She always kissed her father's cheek and bade him not to worry. "The only danger of my marrying will come when I meet a man who measures up to you."

However, on this very bland evening, Lady Thalia looked over the heads of her clustered beaux, across the narrow ballroom, and immediately recognized the man she would accept as a husband. The complete opposite of her father in coloring, he possessed a similarly impressive height and massive bearing. She had utterly no idea of his name or when he had arrived amidst the guests. His eyes shone as large, gray, and penetrating as her mother's when Lady Flora suspected her offspring of misbehaving, but they were overshadowed by the masculine cliff of his forehead edged with nearly white eyebrows that matched the straight hair combed back from his temples. Not a single, fashionable white-blond curl strayed across his forehead in the latest style for men as if he had no time for such foolishness. Despite the color of his hair, he was not an elderly man. His pale skin stretched tightly over a strong jaw, a noble nose, and high cheekbones similar to her own. His lips compressed into a thin, straight line of mild annoyance. His eyes searched for someone or something in the room.

"Here I am!" she wanted to cry out, but those piercing eyes turned away and drew his face in another direction entirely to reveal a slight disfigurement, a thin, pink scar running from the corner of one eye all the way to his chin. That intrigued her all the more.

Resisting an unladylike urge to shake her mother's thin shoulder, she merely bent her head over the seated Lady Flora and inquired discreetly from behind her fan, "Mama, would you know who that striking young man might be? I have never seen him at Almack's."

In turn, Lady Flora moved her furled fan from side to side tapping members of the crowd surrounding her daughter and requesting, "Please step aside and allow me some air, gentlemen. Do take a short stroll and let me spend some time in private converse with my girl."

Since the suitors often curried Thalia's favor by doing small favors for her mother, they immediately sprang aside, cleared her view, and trotted off to make a circuit of the ballroom like Lady Flora's obedient lap dogs being put outside to piss. The duchess did not ask which man had caught her child's interest. He stood head and shoulders above the rest and that white-blond hair did attract attention. Many stared his way, and since staring was most rude, both women quickly lowered their eyes and retreated behind open fans.

"I do not recognize him, but I believe I do know who he is, my dear."

"Tell me," Thalia said with her voice avid and demanding in a way that had been schooled out of her in the nursery by a strict governess.

Her mother's well-defined brows rose. "I suppose I should have expected this. You are my daughter, after all. When I met your father as a child, I became instantly intrigued. That fascination did not diminish with the years, nor has it ever. The passion we continue to share—"

Thalia cut her off immediately before her mother could stray on to inappropriate comments on her father's attributes. She ascribed this terrible habit to Lady Flora's having come of age in a more dissolute century.

"This is nothing of the sort, Mama. I do find the man interesting as I would any stranger of his stature and appearance. We will seek an introduction, he will join the ranks of my suitors, and after a suitable period of time, I might show him some favor and listen to his very proper and expected proposal of marriage. Whether I shall accept or not, I do not know at the moment. Now, stop toying with me and tell me who he is."

The duchess gave her an arch smile with her little, bowed lips as if she knew better. "Let me see if I recall." She placed one small, gloved finger against an alabaster forehead nearly free of wrinkles and drew out the suspense. "Hmmm, the Earl of Danelagh passed away quite suddenly several months ago. A bad heart, I fear. His wife having died many long years ago, he left no widow. Sadly, his heir was travelling abroad and could not attend the service. The duke and I did pay our last respects since your papa enjoyed hunting with the man. We traveled all the way to York in very foul weather to do so. His only daughter received us at Battle Hill. How tragic to have but two children and one away in time of sorrow. That shall never happen with my ten. A large family is so much better."

"Mama! What has this gloomy tale to do with my question?" Oh, how she wanted to tap her foot with impatience, but that would be unseemly.

"I was able to help the poor, overwhelmed young woman locate her brother. You see, I had a recent letter from James, and he mentioned meeting Godric Erikson in Heidelburg. I wrote immediately, told your brother the tragic news, and requested that he send the man home at once to assume his duties and lift the burden from his very young sister. Godric, what an awful name to put upon a child."

As if Thalia Amabel Full Moon Woman Longleigh were any better! But Thalia merely said, "Your point, Mama," as sweetly as she'd been taught.

"Oh, I haven't seen the lad since childhood. Off he went to a rather dismal martial academy at a very early age. One would have thought his hair might have darkened by now, but no. I believe we are sneaking glimpses of the new Earl of Danelagh." The duchess peeked coyly over the rim of her fan, but her daughter hid a dusky rose blush behind hers.

"You will arrange an introduction, won't you?" she tried to say coolly.

"No need. Fold your fan. I believe the young man has found the person he sought."

"A lady?"

"For heaven's sake, he has only been here for mere minutes. Most people do not attach as rapidly as you and I. No, no, lower your fan. He is speaking to your father."

"Truly, I have not formed any instant attraction. You imagine it."

"Ah well, then no need to waste our time negotiating the nuisance of all these ropes they have cordoning off the dance floor to present you. Eventually, they will come to us."

Thalia's eyes flickered to the man's black crepe armband and took in his somber attire. She offered a hand to her mother as if the duchess were not as spritely as a shepherdess in spring most days—and nights.

"Allow me to help you arise, Mama. It is only proper that we offer him our condolences."

"Go gently, Thalia. You have very nearly pulled me out of my slippers. Glide, glide. Do not make haste. Your father has him cornered."

Knowing she tended to stride when agitated, Thalia slowed her pace and dropped small curtseys to the patronesses, nodded and exchanged a few pleasantries with dowagers as she went. But still fearing the Earl of Danelagh might move away, she made inexorable progress toward her goal, another Longleigh family trait. Upon reaching her father, she laid her hand lightly on his large forearm and delivered a smile known to bring callow youths to their knees.

"Thank you so for staying the evening, Papa. I realize how these events bore you."

"Why, I would not leave you unprotected amongst so many young men, dear child."

"Yes, young men can be a bother, but Mama is an excellent chaperone." She tilted her curly head slightly in the direction of Godric Erikson, in appearance a few years older than her brother who reached his majority before going off to see the world. Her father did not respond to the subtle hint, but her mother did.

"Who have we here? Why, little Godric Erikson grown to manhood. So many years since we've met, but I would have known you anywhere. I am simply sorry that only the sad occasion of your father's passing brought you home. My deepest condolences." The duchess offered her hand and the newly minted earl bowed over it most elegantly for a large man.

"Might I say, Lady Flora, you have changed very little with the passing years. As a child, I found you both beautiful and fascinating and envied the sheer size of your family. Your children did not lack for playmates as I did."

So, he possessed a glib tongue, telling Mama the very things she liked best to hear. She must beware of that, Thalia cautioned herself, but if he paid her such compliments, could she resist? The musicians returned from their intermission and began to tune their instruments again. Shortly, the dancing would resume and her card overflowed with names as usual. Her pack of suitors rounded a corner after sniffing about other delicate young flowers of the ton and would soon be upon them. She glanced at the next name on her list. Oh, surely that noodle would give way if she explained she must dance with an old family friend newly come from abroad and arrived just his minute, especially if she promised the rejected suitor two turns about the ballroom another evening.

"We ended with ten children in all. Our youngest, Justinian, will turn four this summer. I believe only five filled the nursery before you were sent off to school."

Her mother went on and on. Patience is a virtue, patience is a virtue. Thalia's governess made her write that many times over to curb her impulses.

"Oh, I do forget myself. Thalia is the eldest daughter of my brood. Thalia, may I present Godric Erikson, Earl of Danelagh?"

She dropped and arose from a curtsey smooth as cream. "So pleased to meet a friend of my brother, James. Mama mentioned that you met in Heidelburg." She focused the full force of her dark eyes upon his face as he stood from his bow.

"Yes, he gave me the scar that you stare at so unblinkingly."

"I—I am so sorry. You were not friends then?" Had she been staring? The scar excited her, speaking as it did of combat and valor, but surely, she had meant to meet his eyes. Thalia swore the world tilted slightly beneath her feet at the prospect of losing him to a family quarrel. The duke would take James' side as always, perhaps going so far as to call Danelagh out to duel at dawn.

The earl answered her with a wry, thin-lipped smile. "Quite good friends, actually. Unacquainted with the rules of mensur fencing when first we met, he initiated me into the student society with an excellent slash that I endured with unflinching fortitude, the whole point, really. Later, I returned the favor."

The duchess put a hand to her heart. "My son is scarred!"

"Not so severely, I assure you. He has but a small mark high on one cheekbone which only serves to make him more dashing to the ladies. I swear I have never known a man untrained in the military way to have such a grasp of all sorts of weaponry. I came here tonight primarily to bring you word of your son as he loathes to write."

The duke's broad chest expanded. "His prowess is my doing. I saw he had the best masters and taught him much myself. Did you know James can bring down a stag with a single arrow?"

Oh dear, they were about to divert into hunting stories. She must prevent it. Thalia called up an even better smile far brighter than the first and made certain her eyes strayed nowhere near the scar. "Did my brother speak often about our family?"

"Most certainly. He had some nursery tales to tell about you that I would never repeat. Starting your second season, aren't you? No takers first time around, eh?"

Glib tongue, indeed! What had James said about her? Had Danelagh just insulted her? Neither her father nor mother seemed unduly perturbed. He did speak the truth, but why didn't they rush to her defense and say she'd turned down many men. Very well, she could defend herself.

"I accepted none of my numerous offers. I believe one should wait for the person who makes one's heart beat most strongly. Do you not agree, Lord Danelagh?" Her heart thumped so violently under her maidenly white gown she wondered if he heard.

"Oh, I agree entirely. When I meet that person, I am sure I shall know." He turned to her father again. "A single arrow you say—from a blind or on horseback?"

"Let us adjourn to my club and have a long chat without having to speak over this blasted music. Flora, do keep an eye on Thalia's pack of puppies. Here they come now. Daughter, you know what to do if any act improperly." With that admonition, the duke slung his thick arm over Danelagh's broad shoulders and moved the younger man off to discuss slaughtering deer while her own doe eyes filled with tears of frustration. How could Godric Erikson turn away from perfection?

Two

Godric Erikson let himself into his lodgings. He'd told his valet, Bascom, not to stay up, but noting the stout-bladed mensur sword resting on table where he discarded his hat and gloves, knew his servant lay in wait somewhere on the premises. Bascom, a dour giant of a man and a former sergeant in his Majesty's army, made an unlikely valet. Only the recently deceased Earl of Danelagh would have hired him for such a post when the man inquired about work at Battle Hill after mustering out of the Yorkshire regiment when England very briefly found itself between wars. Battle-scarred and adept with armaments, Bascom appeared to know nothing of fashion or fine manners, but he did keep both clothing and weapons clean, shining, and entirely up to military standards. Admonished to look out for the heir and to challenge him in every way to excel, Bascom took this direction literally. Now, where did the man lurk?

Staying near the wall whenever he was able, Godric moved quietly across the small parlor. A man of Bascom's size could not hide easily, but he knew how to blend well with the shadows cast by the single oil lamp illuminating his out-held blade. Not crouched behind the settee, nor pressed behind the open door leading into the bedchamber. Bascom might have removed shelves from the large wardrobe holding the earl's clothes and doubled himself over, but that seemed a lot of work for this late in the evening. Expecting to find nothing, he lifted the bedclothes with the tip of his sword. Anyone hiding under a bed put himself at a great disadvantage, though best to be sure. A suddenly out-thrust blade might trip him. No, no one there.

So, the heavy draperies, designed to keep out the light and noise of a London morning when a young man out carousing until all hours and needing some rest, must conceal his valet. Bascom had to be standing on the sill as not even his shoe tips showed. Yes, the upper portion of the curtains bulged. Godric struck the brown velvet with the side of his sword. The dust released nearly blinded him, a clever if unexpected ploy. With the moonlight streaming through the parted curtains reflecting off his massive shaved head, Bascom sprang out and shouted, "*dummer Junge!*"—Silly Boy, a mild insult the students of Heidelburg used to provoke a match. They did not strike, advance, and retreat in the French manner, but rather parried blows with neither giving ground.

At last, the Earl ended the combat with a scratch under his valet's chin. He hadn't intended the slight wound to be quite so deep, but the long evening had taken a toll on his energy, and he wanted his rest sooner rather than later. His father would have said exhaustion was no excuse for sloppy execution, but Bascom could not draw blood from his master and had to keep fighting until his employer ended it. As usual, Godric issued no apology to the man who meant more to him than his father ever had. He tossed Bascom a piece of spotless white toweling from the washstand to staunch the blood. Removing the crepe armband, he turned to allow the servant to help with his coat. Towel tucked under his chin, the valet did so, pausing to inspect the garment for stains or other damage before folding it neatly and placing it in the wardrobe.

"Might I inquire if you found the Longleigh family, milord?"

"I did. The butler at Bellevue House directed me to Almack's, the duke, his wife and daughter having repaired there before my arrival. I should have waited for normal calling hours, but curiosity got the best of me." Godric loosened his neckcloth and tossed it aside. He unbuttoned his black waistcoat and divested himself of a gold pocket watch, a small purse, and a heavy signet ring.

"Were they all Viscount Laughlin claimed them to be?" Bascom took the waistcoat and conducted the same inspection before putting it away.

"That and more. I could and did listen to the old man's tales of his life among the Shawnee all night long. Some might find him a bore, but I found him entirely fascinating. We parted from his club only when he felt he must leave to see his wife and daughter safely home from the ball. The duchess is as delightful as I recall from my early childhood."

"And the eligible daughter?"

"James gave her far too little credit. 'Not ugly, fairly attractive,' indeed! She is a raving beauty with men falling at her feet. Somewhat stiff with manners and good breeding, however. What did James call her during their childhood? Thalia, Queen of the Nursery, or Queenie for short. He still does call her Queenie simply to nettle her, I believe. She is very regal, and I suspect rather superior with most people. He did warn me not to let her get the upper hand and admitted he mostly handled her childish demands by ignoring her. I took care to heed his advice."

He envisioned James Longleigh, Viscount Laughlin, as he'd last seen him slouched in one of the heavily carved chairs around a table illuminated by a single candle stuck into a wine bottle in the darkness of a *Kellar* frequented by students. Straight, dark hair fell over the man's bronzed forehead and the darkness of his skin only served to bring out the startling lightness of his gray eyes. He possessed the duke's strong features, marred only by the small nick Godric had given him. Such was their skill with the mensur sword, neither had added another scar, but they'd given many in their short acquaintance.

"Wiping the foam of a dark beer from his lips, the fellow advised, 'If you must return home and set up a nursery, you might have a go at my sister, Thalia, though I do pity any man who must settle down to the drudgery of a wife so soon in his life. She's not ugly, fairly attractive, I suppose, but I warn you, she likes to rule. Queenie I've called her since our nursery years.' He went on to tattle on his sibling as only a brother can."

Bascom knelt to remove his lordship's shoes. "With a dowry of twenty thousand and the promise of having her mother's fecundity—ten living children, is it?—she does appear to be a prime candidate for the position of Countess Danelagh. You should lose no time in securing her and getting an heir. With the Erikson family down to only you and your sister, no time should be wasted."

The man might look like a thug, but Bascom had learned his role well, aping his betters until his lower-class accent vanished and his demeanor shone like the brass buttons on a dress uniform. His mind did not lack brilliance either. In Napoleon's army, he would have risen to be a general.

Godric pulled the tails of his shirt from his breeches. "I am unsure."

"Unsure you want a rich, beautiful, and fertile wife connected to one of the most powerful families in England? What ails you?" He drew the shirt over his lord's head and offered a fresh nightshirt in its place. Beneath the nightshirt, Godric dropped his breeches, drawers and stockings.

"She lacks passion. I saw no spark I could fan into a flame, except when I implied she'd been unable to find a husband in her first season. She did not hesitate to tell me of her many conquests. She said she waited for one who made her heart beat the strongest, so I suppose she has some slight possibility of pleasing me."

Bascom snorted through a nose flattened in a battle or a brawl. He never said which. "There now, that's a symptom of those damned romantic notions you are so taken with. Wealth, beauty, and connections should be your only concerns in seeking a bride. Passion, bah!"

Sometimes Bascom forgot himself, but Danelagh allowed it as the man always had his best interests at heart. He took himself to bed so both could have their rest.

"Her dowry might go far toward making a comfortable home of that pile of stone I've inherited much too soon," he admitted. "James, his father and mother would make superb relatives, but I fear Lady Thalia is too rigidly perfect to interest me."

"In your dreams, milord, in your dreams. Sleep well."

~ * ~

"Do tell," Flora insisted as she nestled in her husband's brawny arms, a small, white Persephone in the clutches of Hades some would say. She considered her present position to be more akin to the Elysian Fields than a dark underworld, especially since they'd recently finished making love.

Earlier, the Duke had allowed his manservant to envelop him in a shirt for the night and see him to bed. As soon as the valet took himself off, he'd gone to Flora's chamber and shed his nightshirt because he preferred sleeping *au natural*—as did she. Flora laughed as he'd stripped her out of the night robe that smelled of roses. In the morning, he would observe the proprieties and return to his own bed for the sake of keeping up appearances before guests, servants, and the children. Flora insisted on feeding this fiction. She felt it added zest to their perfectly legal marital assignations, though her duke told her clearly and often he did not care who knew he doted on his wife. Yet another reason to love him so.

Tonight however, Flora had more on her mind than intercourse. She poked his chest above the red thunderbird tattoos with one delicate finger. "Tell me what you discovered about Godric Erikson. James wrote he is likely a better man than any in London."

"I would agree. Truly, I thought I could never approve of any man who would take away one of my daughters, but I believe Danelagh is capable of protecting her and has infinite patience as well as suitable rank and fortune. He listened to all my old tales without once making an excuse to leave the club."

The duchess stretched her slender neck to place a kiss on his cheek. "Your stories are enthralling, but some youngsters do not appreciate them. I am glad to hear this of Godric, but he did not seem very interested in our daughter. I am sure Thalia's affections are already engaged with him, however."

"I suppose I could buy him for her by upping the dowry, but one would think twenty thousand plenty for such a perfect bride. Most of her followers would take her for half that."

His own bride of many years pinched his stout pectoral muscle. If it hurt, the duke gave no indication. "Don't you dare!" she said. "Thalia must win him, or she will be forever miserable in her marriage."

"She hasn't much time. He indicated he would soon remove to Yorkshire to see to his sister and Battle Hill. Being in mourning, I would not expect him to stay in London dancing, drinking, and dicing the season away."

"We must act swiftly then and invite him to dinner and a quiet evening in our home. Thalia can perform for him, show off her accomplishments that are sure to impress. Her voice is far superior to mine in my best years. My range has diminished with age."

Her duke clasped the finger that had poked and pinched and kissed its tip. "Yet still it thrills me. I will send an invite around to the boy tomorrow. If Thalia wants him, she shall have him."

Three

Naturally, he'd accepted the invitation to dine with the Duke and Duchess of Bellevue and their fair daughter. A small, family affair simply to welcome the son of an old friend back to England, the summons read in the duke's own bold but inelegant hand. Supposedly, they'd invited no other guests out of regard for his mourning. They ate *en famille* in a small day room at a round table. Placed between the duchess and Thalia and across from the duke, Godric had no choice but to make conversation with one lady, then the other, as well as Bellevue.

As they ate their way through a simple meal of soup, fish, fowl, game, mutton, pudding, fruits, nuts and cheeses with the appropriate side dishes and beverages for each course, Thalia engaged him in polite conversation. Was the weather very different in Germany? Did he have a favorite horse or hound at Battle Hill? Would his sister care to visit Bellevue Hall in August when her mourning period was half over?

"Colder," he answered in a chilly voice. "No, I've been away from home too often to form attachments to animals. Yes, my sister would be honored to visit the Longleighs once her grief abates." He politely stifled a yawn behind a large hand more suitable for grasping goblets or steins than fine stemware and noticed Thalia's desperate glance at her mother.

"Tell us of your travels," the duchess said. "Leave nothing out."

"Yes, do," Thalia breathed. "I have never been abroad."

"A pity. Initially, my father sent me to Europe to study current military strategies. He believed Napoleon would present a challenge to England, and I did find their army much superior to that of Prussia. Sadly, the days of Frederick the Great are no more. Though I spent quite some time among the Prussians, their weaponry and battlefield techniques are far inferior to the French. They had best beware."

"How so?" the duke asked. An hour passed in discussion of rifles and cannons, drills and maneuvers. By the time her father cracked walnuts with his fist during the last course and offered the meats to his wife, Thalia's long-fingered hand fluttered to her ruddy lips and suppressed a sigh.

"So sorry to bore you, Lady Thalia."

"Oh no, I find all this military exposition very...educational."

"Well, I do not. Shame on you, my dear, for allowing this discussion to go on so long in the presence of ladies." The duchess laid the blame on her husband, but Godric appreciated her outspokenness. If only the daughter had half the old gal's fire.

"We could all do with some music, and Thalia will provide it. Coffee and tea in the drawing room once we have all refreshed ourselves. Come along, child." She swept from the room, and he heard Thalia's low, frantic appeal as they went. "But Mama, I tried my best to engage him properly."

Godric felt he must apologize to the duke—but not to Lady Thalia. "I am sorry if my conversation upset your daughter. I often get carried away with military talk because of the way I was raised. Well, you knew my father."

The duke waved his words aside with a flick of thick fingers. "Young ladies are easily upset. I have three more to introduce to society in the next few years and dread the very thought of it. Then some relief as the next two are boys, more simple creatures altogether, before the other two girls come out. Simply tell Thalia you enjoy her singing, and she will be all smiles again."

Godric made a mental note not to do that lest she think him snared. He enjoyed the last of his wine with the duke, took time to relieve himself, and went to join the ladies in the drawing room where Thalia was already stroking the keys of a pianoforte. Her long fingers gave her a great deal of reach capable of striking tremendous chords, but instead, she played a pleasant, bucolic melody without much force.

"Very...nice," he said as she finished the piece.

"Yes, she does play very well, but our girl excels at singing. Thalia, please indulge us," the duchess said as she beckoned to Godric to sit next to her and take coffee while the young lady entertained their guest.

Thalia stood tall in the curve of the piano, knotted her hands at her waist and sang to them in Italian. Each note released had perfect form and duration, but not an ounce of emotion. The duke in his arm chair leaned toward Godric seated beside his wife. "Don't understand a word of it myself, but she does it well, don't you think."

"Yes, of course." Thalia finished, and he rewarded her with a tepid "Brava."

Distress that she had failed to impress showed in her tight smile and curt nod of thanks. She grasped the neck of a guitar propped against one leg of the piano as if she would strangle it. Taking a deep breath, she seated herself on the end of the piano bench, relaxed her fingers and began to play while singing a light, Spanish ditty.

Remaining unmoved, Godric nodded at her effort and said, "Do go on."

A second song followed with more demanding lyrics, chords, and finger work. A fine sheen of dew collected across the top of Thalia's breasts and several locks of her raven hair shook loose and cascaded down her back. She chafed her lips with her fine, white teeth and the color rose in her cheeks. For a moment, Godric envisioned her as one of the light ladies he'd met in a Spanish brothel. Carlotta had not performed nearly as well with voice and guitar, but then, her specialty did not lie in music but what came after, where fire and technique really mattered. The thought brought the blood to his pale face, and he knew his scar darkened with the memory of desire. Now, if only Lady Thalia… The duke cleared his throat loudly. The song had ended, and Thalia stood waiting for his judgment as she put the guitar aside.

"By far my favorite piece of the evening," he said, holding his coffee cup in such a way to hide any sign of arousal.

"Thank you, mine also."

She looked too pleased with that glowing smile. "I don't suppose you know any compositions by Herr Beethoven?" he asked.

"No. Miss Wentworth, my music instructor, felt German works to be too heavy for young ladies and said they were best left to concert halls and professional musicians."

"A shame. I had the privilege of hearing his work often and regard it as the finest music of our era."

"I am sure it is," she said, quick to be agreeable. "I will order some of his sonatas for the piano, and you must visit again when I have mastered them."

"Then you must be quick as I am soon off to Yorkshire."

"I assure you, I am a very quick study."

There, a flare of annoyance, a hint of temper in her voice, but the duchess intervened before he could prod her further. "Do come over here into better light and view some of Thalia's paintings," she urged.

Lady Flora rose from her seat, and he had no choice but to follow. Thalia drifted to his side as he pawed through a portfolio of her artwork conveniently left out on a side table directly beneath two wall sconces. Watercolors of pretty shepherdesses with their lambs, charming kittens, a basket of puppies, pleasant prospects, and flowers of all sorts passed beneath his fingers. "Hmmm, pretty," he said without enthusiasm.

"I can see you do not care for pretty," Thalia answered sharply and drew an alarmed glance from her mother.

His hand stopped on a yellow rose. "Nicely executed."

The duchess smelled of musk roses, but her daughter, her performances having heated her skin and heightened her perfume, had a more tangy scent, not lilac or lavender or anything he could put a name to, perhaps citrus and cinnamon, but he would call it simply Thalia. James' words echoed in his mind. "Do not let my sister get the upper hand."

He turned the portrait of the rose over and revealed a unicorn obviously copied from an old tapestry. "True enough, I do not care for the sublime but prefer the gnarled oak and the blasted pine to the espaliered pear grown on a trellis or the carefully pruned cherry tree in full bloom."

Thalia's dark brows rose. Her full lips thinned. "Are you saying you prefer older women to young? Please speak plainly."

"Older women do have more character and experience which any man might find attractive while young women are still unformed." He turned to the duchess who tapped him playfully with her fan and looked beyond her to the burning eyes of his host.

"Lady Flora is taken," the duke growled, seeming to turn from man to bear in an instant.

"Indeed, I am very taken." Her eyes alight with joy at his jealousy, the duchess turned and touched her husband's arm. "Come, my dearest, walk with me in the garden. We have only a small space here in the city, but I must have my flowers," she explained. "The tulips and daffodils are up, and we can enjoy their fragrance in the evening air. It seems a fine night, but do I need my shawl?" she pondered as she moved toward a set of double French doors at the end of the room and an exterior staircase leading downward.

"I will see you are kept warm, my love." The duke hastened after his wife.

"Now you have made them amorous," Thalia said with exasperation. "We had better not follow them too closely."

"Is there anything wrong with that? They are man and wife."

"You have no idea how many times their untoward affection has embarrassed me and my sisters. I do not wish to speak of it." Cheeks turned dusky red, she closed the portfolio and opened another beneath it. "My sister, Iris, did these, and she is not yet seventeen. I do wish I had her talent, for that is what she has, talent not mere technique. I believe you will like them."

She revealed sketches that captured a face, an expression in exquisite detail, more of the visages old and wrinkled than young and attractive. The watercolors displayed craggy vistas and violent seas. "Iris should be allowed to take instruction with a master and express herself in oils without fear of getting her hands or dress soiled, but Papa does not trust artists, and Mama fears such training would be unladylike."

"You speak for your sister, but not for yourself. Your voice is..." He wanted to say extraordinary but held back the word. "Lacking in expression, but could be trained to rival any I have heard upon the stage."

"Really? I thought you did not enjoy my performance."

"I liked the last piece very much. It reminded me of my travels in Spain."

"Ah, so that is why your face became flushed. I thought you might be embarrassed because of my lack of skill."

"You do not lack skill, only emotion, but some did show at last."

"No matter, Papa would never allow me to go on the stage or even study in Italy. He also distrusts musicians and poets, writers and actors. All men should be warriors and hunters, according to him. It is the Shawnee way, and he has half their blood." Her large, dark eyes looked earnestly into his. He noticed a tiny dot of blood on her lips where she'd bitten them while playing. The tip of her tongue touched it and wiped it away.

"So he told me last evening. What do the Shawnee women do?" The urge to twist one of her black curls around his white finger became exceedingly strong. He raised his hand slightly and pulled it back.

"According to my mother who lived amongst them, they hoe corn, tan hides, and..." She stopped herself in mid-sentence.

"Go on." He felt she poised on the edge of telling him something surprising, maybe even shocking.

Basso laughter sounded in the garden and girlish giggles followed. "We must join my parents in the garden at once!" In swift, unconstrained strides, she crossed the room.

He caught her elbow at the open double doors. "Do your parents really require a chaperone?"

"Yes! Their carrying on is why my governess, Miss Thurgood, left to take a position in a more regular household. She said she could not bring me to the peak of perfection with their lack of propriety in her way, but that I should heed her lessons on exemplary behavior and do my best to reach that pinnacle without her."

"When did she make this profound pronouncement?'

"Why, three years ago. Iris and I were entirely tutored at home, but the twins proved to be too much for Miss Thurgood and for Mama, I suspect, and were sent off to be finished at a boarding school. Mama, Papa, we are coming to join you!" she called into the darkness beyond the lanterns set at the foot of the steps to illuminate the way.

The laughter ceased. The older couple emerged from behind a plinth that blocked the light and met them at the foot of the steps. The pretty tucker the duchess wore lay askew across her bosom. Her light blonde curls were disarrayed as if a large hand had raked through them. The pins being gone, she patted at them to no avail.

The duke greeted them with a pleased grin and quick, sly look at his wife. "Your tucker, m'dear," he prompted.

"Oh my, yes. Thalia embroidered this for me." Dropping any pretense, the duchess removed the tucker, held it out to Godric, and revealed the tops of her powdered white breasts. Some of the powder had been wiped away and exposed red marks on her pallid skin. The duke quickly ran a handkerchief embroidered with his crest across his lips to remove the evidence of dalliance while his wife pointed out the exquisite needlework.

"You see, she sewed it with all sorts of flowers, a tribute to my name, and gave it to me as a Christmas gift. Thalia is very clever with a needle. You should see her pillow covers."

"How could you humiliate me much more, Mama?" Leaving Godric with the tucker draped across his open hands, Thalia turned and fled into the house.

"I should go after her. Please excuse me," the duchess said with color highlighting her pale cheeks.

"No, allow me. I will assure your daughter I took your words in the best way possible and remain unoffended."

His host and hostess exchanged a hopeful glance, gave him the nod, and Godric set off, still clutching the tucker. He caught up with his quarry at the foot of the stairs as she struggled to light a candle with a spill from the fireplace. Her hands trembled so that he draped the tucker over one arm, took the twist of paper, and completed the task before she burnt her fingertips. He swore he could have lit the wick from the spark that passed between them. The sheen of tears only made her large eyes lovelier in the glow of the flame. She bit her lips again, a childish habit the redoubtable Miss Thurgood had failed to stamp out, he did not doubt.

"Thank you and good evening. I am going to my chamber now."

"Not yet!" He schooled his voice into careful politeness. "Allow me to return this. Your jonquils are superb." He offered her the embroidered scarf.

She searched his face for any sign of double entendre, but he kept his eyes carefully on hers, not allowing them to sink below chin level as they rebelliously wished to do. "You do not care for my singing, my playing or my watercolors, yet you admire feminine needlework? What sort of man are you?"

"Entirely natural," he hurried to say. "Your parents' actions did not offend me. I find their playful attachment very refreshing and most surprising. I relish the unexpected, you see."

Thalia dabbed her eyes with the end of the tucker and lifted her face to his in an almost challenging way. "I could surprise you. I could show you..." She hesitated.

"Tell me." He leaned closer to those chafed red lips. He would have to kiss them very gently.

Instantly, her long, dark lashes lowered, and she stepped back. "But I cannot. Good evening, Lord Danelagh." With a straight back and a great deal of dignity, she ascended the stairs with the candle lighting her way and the tucker trailing from long fingers. He followed her course until she turned a corner and merged with the darkness.

For a large man, the duke moved very quietly. Godric jumped when the huge hand clapped him on the back and cursed his inattention, distracted by a mere woman. How his father would have scorned that—but not Lord Bellevue.

"Stunning, ain't she?" he asked.

"Most beautiful, but she hasn't her mother's liveliness," he answered carefully.

"Do not believe that, son. She is Flora's daughter and only needs the right man to bring it out."

The duchess appeared from behind the duke's broad back. "I really must go to her, but you will visit again before you leave London, won't you, Godric?"

"If only to have the pleasure of your company once more," he replied gallantly as he bowed over her hand. A footman appeared from nowhere exactly as a well-trained servant should and handed him his hat and cane. He took his leave still pondering in what ways Thalia might surprise him.

Four

Thalia wanted to throw herself on the high canopied bed and beat her fists against the very pillowcases she'd embellished with her superb jonquils, but her maid dozed in a chair by the fire. It would never do to show so much emotion before a servant, according to the departed Miss Thurgood. A lady is a lady in public or private. Thalia hadn't thrown a temper tantrum since a very early age, but oh, how she yearned to do it now. Startled awake by the thud of the door closing, scrawny but efficient Balfour immediately rose to help her mistress out of her evening attire and into a dressing gown before taking down the mass of black curls. Hairpins pinged into a shallow china dish. All the while, Thalia held in her frustration.

She could have surprised and shocked Godric Erikson simply by lifting her skirts and showing him the stiletto strapped to her thigh. Her father insisted she wear a weapon to prevent any man from taking advantage of her. He'd taught her how to thrust it into vital organs by using a straw man marked with a red heart, a brown lung, even a pair of bean-shaped kidneys if she had to strike to the rear, and of course, a blue line that marked an artery in the throat for an instantly fatal blow. To please him, she'd learned to strike hard and fast, while gentle Iris fainted dead away at the mere thought and never managed to kill the dummy with any serious effort.

Danelagh might have been brought to laughter if she confided in him the debate between her parents as to where the weapon should be worn. Her mother favored the calf because wearing it higher might ruin the line of her gowns and the weapon would be more easily reached. Her father asserted that until her skirts were cast up to her thighs, she would not be in any real danger, and possibly she could be overpowered if she drew the stiletto too soon. Thalia wondered what the earl would look like when he truly smiled. She'd yet to see any expression on his face when he addressed her except mild boredom and that strange avidness when she'd played the guitar and stood close to him in the hallway. His heat reminded her to keep her fingers from the flame.

Certainly, Miss Thurgood had not found the stiletto discussion amusing. In fact, the mere thought of her charge raising her skirts thigh-high before a man, even without a weapon to show, would have brought on a fit of her palpitations. Poor Miss Thurgood, a wonder she had survived in the Longleigh household so long without her heart giving out. She stayed because in Thalia she'd created her masterpiece and told the girl so often. Iris, though lovely, would never stand out because of her shy and dreamy nature. However, that sister gave Miss Thurgood no trouble, unlike the twins and her abominable nine-year-old sister, Pandora, who trailed after her brothers and showed no sign of transforming from hoyden to lady.

Still, the numerous unruly Longleigh children had not driven off the governess. The *coup de grace* came when, while taking her daily constitutional on the extensive grounds of Bellevue Hall, Miss Thurgood stumbled across the duke and duchess indulging in a reenactment of a Shawnee courtship dance. While her mother wore a white buckskin tunic that covered her to the knees and farther if the long fringe counted, her father appeared in only a loincloth, his muscular bronze body well-oiled, his black hair wild down his back as he bent over the duchess in a very lascivious manner, their bodies nearly touching. Miss Thurgood's palpitations came on so strong she'd fainted immediately and made a great crash into the bushes. Her father resumed his clothes while her mother revived poor Miss Thurgood with the aid of a burnt feather held under her narrow nose and a brisk fanning with the wing of a wild turkey, part of the props in their Indian wigwam folly. The duke insisted on carrying the governess back to the house, but she'd kept her eyes screwed tightly shut the whole time.

"Almost as if I'd witnessed fornication," Miss Thurgood told the housekeeper later. Naughty Pandora, only six at the time and given to spying, repeated the whole conversation she'd overheard while hiding under the long skirt on the housekeeper's table as that good woman administered restorative hot and very sweet tea to the shocked governess. Though she'd stumbled over the word 'fornication' and did not know its meaning, Pandora's mimicry of Miss Thurgood delighted the younger children still in the nursery, especially her vile little brothers who quickly figured it out.

While Thalia, being so much older, was conversant with the word, she realized her mentor's tenure had neared an end after this appalling display so cunningly told by her abominable little sister. How could anyone as cultured as Miss Thurgood continue in the loose atmosphere of Bellevue Hall? Never could her governess appear before the duke again without clutching a hand over her heart. She soon allowed herself to be lured away by a countess hoping for the perfection of her own daughter, leaving Thalia without the strong moral guidance she'd come to rely on, in contrast to her parents.

The duchess was not unduly upset. "Humph, I provided her with the best of raw material," she said. "I should have let her go sooner as she was not a good fit in this family."

If only Miss Thurgood were here to counsel her favorite charge now. Just look at her face with its puffy eyes and bitten lips. No wonder Godric Erikson despised her. Thalia wanted to hide from her reflection in the mirror of the dressing table, but could not do so until her maid finished bushing her hair and gave her some peace. Someone scratched on the door and entered without waiting for an invitation, her mother naturally, clad in her own dressing gown, pale hair down but covered modestly with a nightcap.

"You may go, Balfour. I shall finish Lady Thalia's hair. How many strokes did you complete?" The duchess held out her hand for the silver-backed hairbrush and received it.

"Forty-five, your Grace." Balfour backed from the room and left mother and daughter alone.

"Forty-six," the duchess said, drawing the bristles through the black tresses. "You owe its marvelous thickness to your father but your curls to me."

"So you've often said," Thalia replied coldly.

"When you were very small, I often combed out your tangles because you cried when the nursemaid did it. Always in disarray they were."

"Until Miss Thurgood came and taught me that if I sat quietly and minded, I need not suffer the pain of having the snarls combed out. No need to snip out gummy bits if I did not try to scale pine trees with James or wash it so often because I'd gotten away and played in the muck of the stables with the dogs."

"Yes." Over her shoulder, her mother's fine-boned face tightened in the mirror. "I should have let her go far sooner. She schooled the spirit right out of you and made you unfit for a man such as Lord Danelagh. Fifty," her mother said decisively.

For a moment, her lips formed a pout, but Thalia quickly forced her face into passivity again. "I am all a young lady should be and yet he seems to prefer you, Mama."

"Nonsense, he flatters me by buttering me all over." Her mother's reflection took on a thoughtful mien.

Undoubtedly, the duchess would now order a crock of butter to be sent to her bedchamber, and heaven knew what Mama and Papa would do with it. The possibilities shamed her. Why couldn't they be normal aloof parents who went their own way and allowed people like Miss Thurgood to raise their children properly?

"Why, why did you and Papa have to carry on so in the garden? Why can't you simply leave each other alone as other parents do?" Tears gathered again in Thalia's eyes.

"There, there, Godric did not take it amiss. I think we amused him."

"How could you tell? He never smiles."

"Certainly he does."

"Not at me."

"Sixty." The Duchess drew the brush through the thick curls once more. "Your father and I were simply trying to give you some time alone with the man. We hoped he might speak to you less formally with us out of the way. Unfortunately, your father never misses an opportunity to show me his adoration."

"Yes, I am well aware."

"Neither here nor there. What did young Danelagh say when he returned the tucker?"

"That I had superb jonquils."

Her mother's face lit in the mirror. "Excellent! I wondered when he would succumb to your beauty. He fought to keep his eyes from you all evening."

"He meant my embroidery!"

"Whatever you want to call it, dear, but I know men. He has no interest in sewing or jonquils. At least, I hope not, or you have set your cap for the wrong kind of man. I do see progress in this. Anything else?"

"He said he likes surprises, prefers the unexpected."

"Then he has come to the right family. We excel at the unexpected." A tiny crease marred her mother's forehead. "So much so, I often wonder if that old Shawnee hag, Snakeroot, put a curse on us. No matter, the Longleighs are up for anything. We prevail. If you want Godric Erikson, you shall have him. Ninety."

"I don't see how, Mama."

"Would you mind missing part of the season in order to travel to Yorkshire to assist the earl and his poor, bereaved little sister in setting their household in order? Why the girl is but seventeen and had the burden of planning her father's funeral service with only the aid of his solicitor. I would have stayed longer to help but had to get ready to move the household to London. They can hardly refuse the offer of a duchess. Once at Battle Hill, we will find a way to surprise Godric that will bring him to your feet."

"Truly? Let us go! I am already bored by dancing and adoration."

The duchess smiled at the hope blooming on her daughter's face. "Yes, but you might have to learn to be less than perfect. Perfect frightens men whether they will admit it or not—a problem I never had—being too perfect. Knowing no other way, I sought to raise you as my mother wanted to raise me. She failed. I succeeded too well. There, one-hundred strokes completed. Sleep well, dear child. We will find a way to make Godric Erikson smile upon you if you are sure you want so stern a man."

"I am sure. Did you not say Papa rarely smiled in his early years, and now he does so all the time?"

"Your father is a happy man, and I have made him so." She planted a kiss on the top of her daughter's head and left for her own chamber.

As Thalia snuffed the candles on her dressing table and moved to get under her covers, she heard her mother ordering a handy servant. "Bring a crock of butter to my chamber, would you?" She could not help but wonder if being less than perfect would involve odd uses for butter and if such uses would make Godric Erikson smile.

~ * ~

Godric opened the door to his lodging very carefully. He called out to Bascom, "No attacks or swordplay tonight, if you please. I have much to think about."

In the darkness of the small salon, his manservant sheathed a sword and lit a lamp. "Very well, milord. How was your evening with the Duke and Duchess of Bellevue and their perfect daughter?"

"Sit and listen to my thoughts." Godric threw his hat and cane aside and stretched out on the settee with his hands behind his head and his feet propped on one carved arm of the furniture. Bascom's large form overwhelmed a matching parlor chair nearby.

"I doubt Lady Thalia ever tried so hard to please anyone as she did me this night—except her draconian governess. I could not let on how she pleased me. I slipped at the end and admired her jonquils."

Bascom's stern visage split with the grin of a pirate. "You mean her…"

"Yes, of course. What else do men notice? Superb jonquils. I had to pretend an interest in embroidery that nearly unmanned me in her eyes. But I won't have a woman gain ascendency over me. Yet, I do not want a marriage as cold as the one my father and mother shared, however briefly. You have seen my mother's portrait at Battle Hill?"

"Yes, a beauty, the most perfect woman of her time, the other servants say."

"The fairest in the land, my father called her, and he bought her with his title and fortune. Once he had me in the nursery, he was done with his wife until the thought occurred, he might need a spare after I had the audacity to disappoint him by coming down with a fever and nearly dying of it. And so he got another child. My mother died bearing my sister, another severe disappointment for Lord Danelagh. The only soft and gentle part of Battle Hill gone and myself shipped off to the academy to be trained for a war I might never engage in because my father overexerted himself bathing in a cold sea and dropped dead on the beach after his swim."

Bascom's grim face grew even bleaker. "I would not worry about a lack of wars, milord. Another one always comes along, and Napoleon swells with ambition and conquests. You will have your shot if you want it. Also, I am quite sure your father did not mean to discommode you by dying. He was to all appearances hale and hearty."

Godric stood and began to pace. "Then he could have remarried and had his spare if he wanted me to be the warrior. How I envy James Longleigh with so many younger brothers he may do as he pleases, marry or not, die pursuing his interests and pleasures with no care about assuming his duties or getting an heir. His parents are a treat, so mad about each other they still steal kisses in the garden like young lovers. If only Lady Thalia had that fire."

"It is my observation that women with superb jonquils are usually good breeders. Wrapped in a pretty, golden package, that is all you need. Buy the well-bred mare and get on with your business. I merely counsel you as your father would."

"Yes, I know. But would I purchase a mare that lacked speed and spirit simply to ornament my pasture? I did see more hopeful signs tonight."

"Her jonquils," Bascom leered.

"Enough with jonquils! She showed some real affection for her sister and admitted the girl excelled her in art. Perhaps she could conceive an affection for my sister, too. Krista sorely needs another woman's attention, or at least she did when I left home. Also, Lady Thalia is not perfect. She bites her lips when distressed, causing them to swell and redden, even bleed. I noticed when I lit her candle and swore something passed between us."

Bascom gave his master that lurid, pirate's grin again. "Swollen red lips, hardly a flaw. I can put a name to what passed between you. In my day, we called it lust."

"Nonsense! A mild attraction, maybe. No matter. I do not have time to explore Lady Thalia's perfection any longer. I have paid my respects to James Longleigh's family and must be off to Yorkshire shortly."

"You may want a faster and more spirited filly, but this one won't be on the market much longer. She might want another year of frivolity and frolic, knowing she can have nearly any man available, but no young lady wants to remain unmarried as she creeps up on her twentieth year. I don't think you will find any better. Sleep on that, milord. Bascom wants what is best for you."

Five

She left the townhouse early and directed the carriage to the most likely destination offering German sheet music. By one in the afternoon, turning away all visits from her suitors, Thalia sat at the pianoforte and began practicing the Beethoven's *Piano Sonata No. 14 in C# minor*, said to be as beautiful as moonlight, until her fingers ached. Her father left the house after the first four renditions and went for a long, long ride in the park. At four, her mother insisted she cease to take tea and refreshments. The duchess sipped a tisane for a pounding headache while they shared a tray of small sandwiches, tiny cakes, and other dainties.

"Are you sure Lord Danelagh will dine with us again tonight, Mama?"

"Yes, yes. I sent a note inviting him as soon as was decently possible. He had our servant wait for an answer and replied that knowing few in London, he had no other plans but would have to make an early evening of it since he departs for Battle Hill in the morning. As we shall be doing once he invites us to his home tonight. Now, I feel you have practiced enough. The opening movements are lovely, but I believe I have heard enough of the last."

"The last is the most difficult and the only part giving me trouble. Those ascending arpeggios are quite challenging. I must run through them several more times in order to perform them perfectly."

The duchess shook her head. "I do not think Godric is looking for perfection. I believe he is seeking emotion in your playing, judging by his previous comments. Infuse passion into your performance, and he will not notice a few missed notes. Ah, your father has come home."

The duke joined them and snatched a handful of dainty foods from the tray. His wife supplied him with tea well-sweetened and doused with cream as he liked it. "Did you have a pleasant ride, my dear?" she asked.

"Very. Fine spring day. Have you finished your piano practice, Thalia?"

"I feel I need to rehearse the final movement a few more times if I am to impress Danelagh."

"He is a fool if he is not already impressed by you. As I said, a very fine day. I believe I will take my tea to the garden and dine among the tulips. They remind me of your suitors, nodding and bowing on their spindly stalks. Danelagh is a good choice for you. He stands out like the plinth in the center of the yard." The duke gathered a selection of fruit tarts and biscuits onto a plate and started for the door.

"I have not chosen him, Papa. I am merely intrigued by him," Thalia called after him.

"As you say. Leave it to your mother. She knows how to hunt a man down."

"I am not chasing a man! I would never; I have no need to..." But her father had already made his retreat.

The duchess patted Thalia's aching hands. "If you are going to resume practice, I believe I will have a lie down before dinner. Please, give yourself some time to rest before Godric's arrival."

She promised, but first she would master this piece as she would later master the Earl of Danelagh.

~ * ~

Dining with the Duke and Duchess of Bellevue remained as before: the intimate setting and seating, the parade of fine foods starting with a lobster bisque, then oysters, roasted cockerel, jugged hare, a roast of beef and so on to the puddings, fruits, nuts and a Stilton cheese. Only the dinner conversation varied. Skillfully directed by the duchess, they talked of Germanic music instead of cannons and battlefield tactics. All except the duke lauded Bach, Mozart, and Handel who had come to England to compose for the first King George. Not interested in music other than his wife's voice and his daughters' recitals, the duke nearly dozed off on several occasions, but Lady Flora sat near enough at the small, round table to give him a nudge now and then.

Thalia spoke with animation about her morning's purchases. "I have secured several of Mr. Beethoven's sonatas for piano and have practiced one you might enjoy, Lord Danelagh, the Number fourteen in C-sharp minor."

Trying his best to appear bored when her eyes sparkled like moonlight on dark water, the very essence of the first movement of that sonata, he replied, "Yes, I have heard it performed many times, quite popular in Europe. Did you know Herr Beethoven wrote it for his pupil, the Countess Giulietta Guicciardi? She was seventeen at the time, and it is said he loved her."

Abruptly, the duke joined the conversation. "You see why I will not allow my daughters to have any but female instructors."

"Oh, Papa! Though it is true Miss Thurgood and Miss Wentworth only approved of Bach and Mozart for me, and none of these new innovations in music, I found working on the piece exhilarating."

"I am sure I will find your performance—adequate," Danelagh said. There, he'd killed the light in her eyes and would have given away his mensur sword to have it shine again.

Thalia's back went very rigid. Seconds before his comment, she'd leaned toward him like a daffodil in the breeze. She wore pale yellow tonight which only brought to mind her jonquils again.

"I believe, sir, I can do better than adequate. Mama, are we finished here?"

"Quite." The duchess stood and indicated to the men they were to follow at their pleasure.

~ * ~

Going immediately to the piano, Thalia sat on the bench, flexing her fingers nervously, rehearsing each note without touching the keys. The men did not linger behind long. Good, very good. That meant less time for her dear Papa to mention her daylong practice and how it had driven him out of the house. Instead, he rose to the occasion and said, "Now we shall have a treat, Danelagh. Please begin, daughter."

She depressed the sustain pedal as the composer indicated and launched into the *adagio sostenuto*. The opening was a poem written in music. The duke commented to Danelagh, "Lovely, eh?"—thereby proving music can soothe the savage beast. She could not hear the earl's less stentorian reply. The flowery *allegretto* went well, but then she approached the last movement, the *presto agitato,* the tempest that raged on the calm waters and crushed the blossoms against the earth. She let the ascending arpeggios run from her fingertips. So, Danelagh thought her singing and playing lacked feeling. Let him hear this!

Hairpins flew as she tossed her head. The yellow ribbons threaded through her stormy, black curls unwound and fell to the floor like bolts of lightning. A capped sleeve slipped from her shoulder, but she did not let that stop her for one second. There, done! Take that Godric Erikson and dare to criticize! Thalia stilled her hands and took a deep breath. She shoved her sleeve into place and with her hair tumbling down her back, turned to face her audience.

Her father jumped to his feet and applauded. "Brava! Brava, Thalia! I do not think I've ever heard music so fierce."

Lady Flora rapidly fanned her heated face. "My dear, that was—so stimulating."

Their eyes turned to the earl. Their ears awaited his remarks. Thalia noticed his scar had darkened as it did when she'd played the Spanish song. He seemed to be choosing his words carefully, perhaps not wanting to insult the daughter of a duke. Out with it, man! Out with it!

"Not perfect. I've heard it better done by masters of the piano in Germany, but very good for an English girl."

What hurt he had inflicted with his blunt honesty. A tear coursed down her cheek. She flicked it away with one long finger and straightened her shoulders.

"I am glad you found it adequate, Lord Danelagh. Mama, some tea if you please." She took a seat on the far side of her mother and turned her head away so he could not see her face or notice that she'd bloodied her lip again.

The duchess took charge. "Tell me, does your sister play the piano, Godric?"

He considered for a moment. "I have no idea, but I suppose so. All English girls do. There is six years difference in our ages, and I've been gone most of her life. My father did not care for the finer things in life. We had no instruments in our house, not even a harpsichord for my mother, though I'm told she excelled at playing one. Krista probably had some instruction at her school."

"Poor dear child, to grow up without the love and guidance of a mother to see to her education. She will come out next season, I assume. Who is to help her choose her wardrobe, teach her proper deportment to the patronesses of Almack's, guard her from the ruffians of society?"

"I thought she would run my household until one of us marries."

"Just like a man to think no farther than tomorrow and not next year. A girl of seventeen will be cheated by her servants and taken advantage of by fortune hunters if she lacks the support of more experienced women. I believe I shall take her in hand, poor little dove. We will travel with you to Yorkshire and see to her training. Thalia can act as her big sister, a perfect example, as she is to Iris, the twins, and even our tiny Phemie."

"You forgot Pandora," the duke prompted, referring to his most troublesome daughter.

"Pandora has chosen other models," the duchess answered briskly. "How did you plan to go, by sea or road?"

"As my boxes have been sent ahead, I've rented hacks for me and my manservant, but I would not dream of curtailing your *second* season, Lady Thalia." Godric peered over her slight mother's head, deliberately not making eye-contact, after making this provoking and insulting statement.

She intentionally singed him with the fire in her eyes and let the heat of anger dry her tears. "I tire of it already. Surely, we will be back to London in time for me to choose a husband from amongst my many beaux before it ends. If I can be of assistance to your sister, it is surely my Christian duty and the right thing to do."

The duchess clapped her hands. "Then, it is settled. Godric, you will give us another day to pack. We shall use our carriage, though the duke often prefers to ride. My, how safe I will feel with two such men guarding me."

Lady Flora had come up on him stealthily like General Washington on the Hessian soldiers at Valley Forge, a bravura performance by Mama! He had no choice but to surrender at once. "My sister and I would be honored by your help."

~ * ~

Later, as he made his way back to his lodgings, Godric wondered if his easy capitulation came about not from Lady Flora's machinations but from his own wish to part Lady Thalia Longleigh from her admirers. His desire had not one ounce of Christian charity in it and was certainly not the right thing to do. Tonight, she'd shown herself capable of incredible passion, and he wanted her all to himself.

~ * ~

Urgent rapping at her bedchamber door forced Lady Flora to remove from her husband's embrace and answer the call. "A moment, Flora." The duke groped for his discarded nightshirt.

"Oh, simply pull the covers over you while I see what it is." She drew on her own night costume crumpled on the floor and padded to the entry. Thalia's maid, her brown eyes wild as a hunted hare, stood before her when she opened the door.

"Pardon, your Grace, but Lady Thalia is having some sort of fit. Never has she been harsh to me and now she assaults me with pillows, and berates me because her hairpins fell out tonight while she played the piano. I cannot calm her."

"You may go to bed, Balfour. I will see to her."

"Daughters!" the duke said with his deep voice muffled by the bedclothes covering his head.

Balfour pretended not to hear. "Thank you, your Grace." She backed away.

"Keep the bed warm, dearest. I doubt this will take long."

Lady Flora drew on a dressing gown and slippers and set off along the hall to Thalia's room expecting to find her child in tears over Danelagh's callous lack of appreciation for her efforts to impress him. A few comforting pats and a "Now, now, all will be well," should do it. She did not anticipate finding Thalia's always neat and tidy bower full of floating feathers from a burst pillow and a broken pin dish in shards amongst the mess. She judged Godric Erikson had destroyed several years' worth of Miss Thurgood's training. Jolly for him!

Thalia stood in the midst of her self-created chaos with her hands fisted and her hair wild as a turbulent night. "I played that sonata perfectly. I did! Tell me, just tell me, what he said to Papa as I played the first movement. Some paltry, lukewarm compliment to appease him, am I right?"

"On the contrary, Godric repeated Mr. Beethoven's description of the piece, *Quasi una fantasia*, almost a fantasy. You know your father has no facility for languages as I do, but he repeated it for me to translate and did observe our young lord never took his eyes from you. An encouraging sign of his interest, I believe."

"I do not care! I played every note correctly and with great feeling. Either Danelagh has no ear for music, or he is a liar. I hate him!"

"I take it you no longer have any interest in Godric," Lady Flora said calmly. "Shall I tell him we won't be accompanying him to Battle Hill after all?"

"No! We will go. I shall ensnare him, then kick him aside with the toe of my slipper."

"That's the spirit. Now mind. Do not cut your feet on the broken glass. Balfour can clean up in the morning. Get into bed and let me stroke your brow. There, there, my darling. Rest knowing your father and I found your performance very stimulating indeed."

Six

Battle Hill, living up to its name, loomed starkly over the ducal coach. Thalia gaped at its gray eminence as their vehicle ascended the twisting drive passing the remnant of a hill fort, an old Roman tower, and at last crossing a bridge over a crescent-shaped pond, all that remained of a moat. Never had she seen such a dour place still inhabited. Certainly, she had no desire to reign over it as Danelagh's countess.

Her mother, having been there before, simply remarked for the hundredth time on the journey that she had never felt so safe on the roads of England as she did now with the duke, Danelagh, and the ominous Bascom riding before them. Not that the coach lacked other protectors, having three armed footmen and a driver. The duke never took chances with the welfare of his ladies when traveling.

The earl had cautioned his guests to bring their own servants to see to their needs as his father had maintained a masculine household with only enough women about to keep down the dust, cook the food, and do the laundry. Whatever comforts and niceties his mother once provided were long gone...tapestries, carpets, soft cushions, and artworks stored in the attics. He doubted if anything had changed in his three years abroad and apologized in advance for any discomfort they might experience.

They pulled up before an entrance possessing two massive doors probably needing several men and a winch to open, but for modern convenience, two smaller apertures had been set within them. On each hung a huge brass knocker shaped liked a clenched fist, but they needn't use them. A woman clothed in black stepped forth to greet the travelers. From a distance, Thalia assumed her to be the housekeeper plainly dressed but lacking the apron such servants usually wore. Closer inspection revealed this person to be only a girl, if a rather towering, big-boned specimen. She wore her thick, fair braids wrapped around her head and fingered a clear glass locket hanging from her neck by a black velvet cord. Fitting mourning jewelry, it contained a lock of blond hair, presumably clipped from the head of the late earl. Godric embraced her briefly, revealing her to be sister. He led her by the hand to be introduced to the duchess and Lady Thalia.

Poor little Krista? Though she stood some inches shorter than her brother, she still topped Thalia's lofty height, and Thalia was unaccustomed to being looked down upon. Surely this overgrown child who appeared as if she had stepped out of a Scandinavian fairy tale would be cold and overbearing—like her brother. Thalia put on her most imperious expression and, unsmiling, stared into the girl's wide blue eyes set above high, broad cheekbones similar to Godric's. She would not be cowed or criticized by another Erikson.

With an immediately downcast glance, the young lady wilted into a curtsey. In a small, soft voice totally unrelated to the size of her body, she said, "Such a pleasure to meet you, Lady Thalia." Her shaking hands belied her words.

Krista quickly turned back to the duchess. "Oh, Lady Flora, I am so glad you have come to visit again. I tried to make the staff mind me, but the men here do not like taking orders from a woman. Hugh Grey did attempt to help me by putting them in their place, but he will soon be gone into the army. He won Papa's last commission." She wrung her large hands.

The duchess balled her small, gloved fingers as if preparing for a fight. "Never fear, we will soon have them jumping to your tune, dear child. Won't we, Godric?"

"Now that I am here, you need not worry, Krista. You have grown so in my absence." That brotherly remark brought the red rushing to the girl's white face.

"I mean you are now a woman, a young lady." Godric stumbled for the words to make his sister less self-conscious of her size and failed. "You were always a hearty child and now, and now...you have fulfilled your promise of—of—great sturdiness in the true Erikson tradition."

Krista's pink lips quivered as she tried to hold back tears. Thalia's hand shot out to touch her arm. "When a lady is taller than most, one must be all the more aware of good posture and the set of the head. If others cannot look into her eyes, let them get a footstool to stand upon. My governess, Miss Thurgood, taught me that."

"Humpf, at least the woman did some good," the duchess remarked. "So, head held high, let us assemble your staff and deal with them."

The duke put a restraining hand on his wife's fragile shoulders. "I think we should wash off the dust of travel first, dearest, before you go into battle."

"Very well. Godric, assemble your servants in the courtyard in one hour. Krista, show us to our chambers."

The girl nodded. Holding her head high as directed, she led them inside the fortress. A grand and gothic oil lamp probably looted from an abbey in the time of the eighth King Henry hung from a heavy chain in the ceiling and provided the light for the gloomy foyer paved in the same gray stones as the house. Once an entrance large enough for a carriage to pass through, the far side of the great arch now held a window edged in colored glass that provided a view of a bleak courtyard with a well at its center. Krista did not pause at this unappealing sight but proceeded to take two steps up to the right through another arch bored in the original walls to enter a single long room faced on one side with tall windows and ornamented on the blank inner wall by ranks of pikes and fan-shaped displays of antique pistols, enough for an armory. Suits of armor guarded both the entrance and exit door.

"This once served as a barracks for men-at-arms. My great-grandfather sought to turn Battle Hill from a fortress into a palace and added the windows, thus rendering the place useless if assaulted by an enemy," Godric remarked.

True, the faded and rotting gold brocade draperies flanking the windows did seem out of character with the rest of the room, along with the ornate curved pediments topping them which matched those on the outside of the house. What bizarre décor, Thalia thought.

The duke rubbed his chin. "It's not hopeless. If Boney should attack England, you could knock out the glass and use the openings as cannon bays. The height of the hill would give a defender a supreme advantage."

"Yes, of course! We could put our riflemen to fire out the windows on the second floor," Godric agreed.

Honestly, he might as well be courting the Duke of Bellevue, and perhaps, he was. Thalia moved on with Krista and the duchess while the men discussed more strategies for a war that had yet to happen. They passed into the next chamber to find more martial decorations: crossed swords of all types from broadswords and cutlasses to sabers and scimitars. Dirks, daggers, and stilettos represented smaller deadly weaponry. Here, family portraits interrupted the relentless march of armaments along the wall. Nearly every Earl of Danelagh wore armor of some type or other, even one of the women.

"Look, Mama, a female warrior. Wouldn't our rapscallion, Pandora, be pleased?" Thalia said, pausing before a picture of a lady wearing a custom breastplate allowing room for ample breasts over a draped red gown. A pointed helm sat atop her flaxen hair that descended in braids on either side of her imposing chest. A sword lay across one dimpled, white arm. Despite her costume, the armored woman had a full, warm smile and happy blue eyes that seemed to say she found her portrayal highly amusing. She faced a man similarly clad but bare-headed to display his huge, shoulder-length wig of fair curls. He possessed the stern gray eyes of the Eriksons but allowed himself the slightest of smiles which was more than Thalia could say of his descendant, Godric.

"Yes, that is Lady Kristiana Erikson, Countess of Danelagh during the Civil Wars. She held Battle Hill against the Roundheads until her husband could arrive and rout them. Sometimes, I fancy I resemble her," the big girl said wistfully. "She is my namesake, but the family calls me Krista. I would like you to call me that, too, Lady Thalia," their hostess requested as if she asked a very great favor.

"I will do that, and I shall be Thalia to you. We will be great friends. And yes, I do see the likeness."

Krista beamed as Thalia went on. "Never fear, Mama and I will see you have a season in London and escape from this dreary place."

"Leave Battle Hill? I do not imagine I ever could."

Before either woman replied, the men caught up and accompanied them into the last room filled with maces, broadaxes, and more ancestral portraits. Arriving at the last in line, Krista said merely, "Papa."

What a cold, unyielding visage stared out at them. He wore the scarlet jacket of a high-ranking British officer of the last century and it dripped with military honors. Beneath a small, tightly-curled powdered wig, his gray eyes looked down a long nose at his audience, and a lip lifted in a slight sneer.

As if making an excuse for the man, the duke said, "He served Lord Cornwallis with great honor during the American Revolution and could not be equaled as a hunter, except perhaps by me."

Godric did not share his father's thin, superior nose, Thalia observed. His was stronger and more blunt, possibly inherited from the other side of his family, which prompted her to ask, "Where is your mother's portrait, Krista?"

"We have none. Father said she was a weakling and did not deserve to have her likeness hung among his illustrious ancestors. This is all

I have of her, a lock of her hair clipped by the midwife when she died giving me life because—because I was too big." Krista fingered the glass locket again.

Godric placed his hands on his sister's shoulders. "Listen to me. Papa was often wrong-headed." That comment brought a small gasp from the girl as if the man himself might step from the frame and slap them both.

"I own a miniature Mama gave me when *he* shipped me off to school so early that I barely knew my ABC's. I've kept it with me always, but now it will be yours. You have her eyes, the kindest, most beautiful eyes in the world."

"Do I really?"

"Yes."

Always able to turn an awkward conversation with grace, the duchess gestured to another portrait. "Who is this merry gentleman?"

The body-length painting portrayed its subject in a full-frontal pose. Between his splayed legs displayed in tight hose, he held an ancient broadsword with the pommel at his crotch and the tip touching the floor. No armor for him but a great deal of scarlet ribbon at the wrists and elbows of his billowing sleeves and just above the knees as well. These were set off by a striking pair of shoes bearing high red heels. A slim blond moustache adorned his upper lip and a goatee his chin. Between them, he sported a wide grin that the ladies must have found very attractive, along with the rest of his muscular body. He wore the absurd large wig of the times matching his facial hair, but it made him seem dashing. Oh, how his large gray eyes laughed at them all.

"Ah, great-grandpapa, the Cavalier. I am afraid I cannot discuss his exploits in front of Krista as they were mostly of the amorous variety. A great friend of the second King Charles he was. To think his parents fought the Puritans for his right to dress that way. You must be tired. Let us move along." Godric motioned them toward a door.

Thalia tilted her head and regarded the randy earl on the wall. "Why, I do believe I see a great deal of him in you, Lord Danelagh."

"What! Never! That is absurd."

"There, I did surprise you, and I might do it again." With that, Thalia followed Krista to the door and up a dim staircase in the corner of the house to be assigned her chamber for their stay.

~ * ~

Thalia and Krista were required to witness the berating of the staff by the duchess, who lectured them on the duty and loyalty owed to their young mistress—or they would be out of a job before the Longleighs ended their visit. Krista stood wide-eyed and amazed while Thalia, more accustomed to her mother's force, made mental notes on how to handle laggard servants.

After that ordeal, all rested from their travels before supper, some more than others. The duke and duchess took to their bedchambers. Krista fretted over dinner preparations, and Godric worked out the stiffness of a long ride by engaging in swordplay with Bascom in the courtyard. Carefully concealed by faded draperies, Thalia, unable to sleep for several reasons, watched from a second story hall window. She'd been walking the hallway for exercise when the clatter below drew her to the glass.

They'd started with sabers doing the usual parry, thrust and retreat she knew from her father's sparring with James, which Miss Thurgood had forbidden her to watch—but she had on the sly. Papa always fought magnificently, and she hadn't minded when he took her brother down a peg or two. Then, Danelagh and his servant moved on to a different sort of sword with neither giving way until the earl drew a bead of blood on his valet's chin.

Stripped to their shirts and breeches, both men practiced until sweat soaked them through. The magnificent muscles of their chests and thighs showed clearly beneath their damp garments. No wonder Miss Thurgood declared this sort of sight too inflammatory for a young lady to witness. Not that Thalia ever thought of her brother or father in that way—but Godric Erikson was another matter entirely.

The opponents finished their exercise, drew up a bucket of water from the courtyard well and doused themselves. The stream of water darkened the earl's white-blond hair and carried it down across his high forehead, what Miss Thurgood would have called a 'noble brow.'

The governess approved of noble brows but little else when it came to men. A husband should be chosen for rank, wealth, gentlemanly manners, and a lack of foul habits, according to her, not his physical attributes. Still, Thalia's eyes followed the stream into the opening of his shirt where it plastered the fair hair on his chest flat onto his muscles and farther down to...

"Ain't that a pretty sight, Miss?"

Thalia startled and hastily removed herself from the draperies. "What do you want?"

"Just bringing her Grace a pitcher of hot water as requested," the servant replied. "Her maid said she'd be wanting it after her nap. Could I do the same for you?"

Thalia touched her heated cheeks. "No, the cool water in my basin will be fine. You are called...?"

"Gracie, the upstairs maid. Not that my duties have been very heavy under the old gentleman. Slept in a camp bed he did and would allow no women in his place. Mostly I dust a few of these chambers every day, and there are quite a few of 'em, you mind. I hope yours is satisfactory, milady."

"Yes, satisfactory," Thalia answered. "And the view is very fine."

She hurried to her room. What would Miss Thurgood say about her spying on men in undress like her wretched sister, Pandora? That she had not raised a lady, certainly.

~ * ~

At the evening meal, the servants unceremoniously set the various dishes on the table and retreated to the dark corners of the dining room where they stood stiffly as if holding up the edifice with their brawny shoulders. The footmen certainly were a striking lot, every one of them looking as if they'd recently stepped off a Viking longboat, but far more elegantly clad in the black and gold livery of Danelagh. Thalia could understand entirely why they intimidated Krista, but thought in the same predicament *she* could make them mind. Of course, she'd had the advantage of watching her mother order servants about for years. "Firm, but never cruel or capricious," the duchess always instructed.

Krista's hands trembled as she attempted to ladle a thin soup into shallow bowls and hand them round the table. The duchess spared the young lady the effort. "I do find dining *en famille* delightful. Might I serve the soup?" She took over before the girl could bungle the job.

"I did ask Cook to prepare something finer than our usual fare as guests were expected, but..." Krista gestured helplessly to the offerings on the table.

Large loaves of fresh bread flanked a tureen of thick mutton stew. A hastily wrung roasted goose sat awaiting carving in front of her brother. Its skin glowed with a luscious, greasy brown sheen, but the bird had been badly plucked as singed pin feathers stood up here and there on the carcass. A large steamed flounder, its tail flopping off the end of the platter, stared up at Thalia with one cloudy eye.

"Nothing wrong with good plain food," the duke said, patting the hand of his hostess as if she were one of his daughters. "Your father certainly had a fine cellar," he added as a footman poured wine into their glasses from a dusty bottle wrapped in a linen towel.

"Yes, that is what Papa always said about food. If we had no company, there would be only the stew and bread and a bottle for him. He said I must not be allowed wine until my eighteenth year and then only sparingly." She'd not been served from the bottle, the old rules still being in effect.

When all had finished the soup with its floating morsels of onion, carrots, and perhaps diced chicken, Thalia pried a piece of fish from the flounder's skeleton at her mother's bidding and passed it round. Godric showed his skill with a blade when he stood to carve the goose and portion out the meat on the plates. They ended with the stew and bread broken from the loaves before the servants cleared the table and brought in several heavy puddings. Thalia swore she saw one of the footmen give Krista a nod and a wink as he lifted the soup tureen. How utterly improper, but the gesture seemed to settle the girl enough to serve the desserts.

The dinner conversation went poorly in Thalia's opinion, very poorly. Krista asked if their accommodations were satisfactory. "I did have fresh linens put upon the beds and every speck of dust removed from the furnishings. The guest chambers are so seldom used as Papa did not entertain."

"Do not fret. The duchess and I have slept on the ground, in wagons and in wigwams," the duke told his hostess.

"All is well," the duchess assured her. "But the bed ropes are in need of tightening. I doubt if that has been done since your mother passed away. Why, when we lay down—I mean when I laid down to rest—I rolled immediately to the center of the bed. We must take care of it this evening."

Thalia hoped Godric hadn't caught that faux pas. One reason she had been unable to sleep besides an unaccountable restlessness was her parents rollicking in the next room. When they crashed together in the center of the bed, her father boomed, "Flora, I do believe you will have to go on top."

"Delighted, my dear," her mother replied. Delighted about what?

A hint of a smile lurked in the corner of the earl's mouth. Thalia hurried to change the course of the conversation. "I thought I heard some swordplay in the courtyard this afternoon. Is all well?"

"Nothing to be alarmed about, Lady Thalia. Bascom and I enjoy a brisk weaponry practice daily. We started with sabers and ended with the *Korbschlager*."

"*Korbschlager*?"

"Yes, one of the types of Mensur swords. The other is the *Glockenschlager* with a bell-shaped guard, but I prefer the basket type of the former. I brought both back from Germany with me to add to the family collection. I would be glad to show you my *Mensurschlager* after dinner."

The way he said those words sounded terribly like the way her father often spoke to her mother with a double meaning, and she lost her power of speech to answer. The duchess filled the gap.

"She would adore that. Did you know your father had a mighty Shawnee war club at one time, Thalia."

"Still do," her father said in that suggestive way her parents often used.

Heaven knew why her mother's hand moved under the table at that moment because at this small gathering, they sat side by side. Her parents should always be separated at far ends of the table if they could not behave in public! Was that a ghost of a smile haunting Danelagh's thin lips?

At that point, Krista, totally confused, asked," Shall I send for the pudding?" And so they reached the end of the meal with slices of plum pudding and hard sauce passed around.

Godric addressed his sister as he finished his portion. "Remind me to look up my old friend, Hugh Grey, tomorrow and thank him for assisting you in my absence."

Krista colored. "Why, he stands right behind you, brother."

"Hugh?" The earl twisted in his chair. "Step forward. When did you take my father's livery?"

One of the massive footmen moved to the table, but continued to stare straight ahead. He filled every inch of his black livery perfectly and his manly calves bulged in white stockings. With his pale hair heavily powdered and drawn back, he had no need for a wig to top another of those noble brows, Thalia thought. He could very well be Godric's younger brother, but perhaps not. She followed her mother's keen gray glance to Krista's flushed face and back to the stalwart footman, the same who had winked at the girl.

"My father died last year, and we were put out of the parsonage, milord. One must make way for the next to fill the position," the man answered without emotion or a trace of Yorkshire accent.

"The Thunderer dead and gone! I was not informed. I am so very sorry." Godric turned to his guests. "This man's father served as our village curate. He could give a sermon that raised the roof, very low church, but much to my father's liking with all that hellfire and brimstone and promise of retribution for sinners who lived impure lives. Papa did not attend when the vicar made his monthly visit to preach tepidly and briefly in order to get to his dinner faster."

The new lord addressed his footman again. "But why go into service, Hugh? With all the Greek and Latin your father stuffed into you, I would think you would join the clergy."

"I have no taste for the Church. Your father granted a commission in the army each year to the one in his household who did best in the drills and training he devised. I have won that prize and will soon go to join my regiment where I might advance quickly, given that Europe rumbles with war."

"I neglect my guests. Let me speak with you in the library after dinner."

"Oh, no. Do go on," the duchess prompted, resting her small, pointed chin atop her steepled hands as if she readied for a good story. "What of your poor mother, Hugh? She cannot be happy having you go to war. I do not want any of my sons in that messy business."

"No, your Grace. She is not keen on the idea. The previous earl saw she got a small pension to keep herself, but he felt a man my age should seek his own fortune in the world."

"Bah! My father wanted you in his personal army, and you have grown into your chosen role. You were a tall, skinny lad of fifteen when last I saw you."

"I have filled out, thanks to Lord Danelagh's rigorous training, milord."

"I see," said the duchess.

Krista, clasping her hands together, spoke up in that soft, girlish voice of hers. "Hugh was always a stout lad. When home on holiday, my brother led us in playing Robin Hood. Hugh played Little John and I, Maid Marian. Rick, being by far the eldest, always got to be Robin."

Thalia could not resist. "Really? I should have liked to see that. You call your brother Rick. I would have thought his friends would refer to him as God for short."

She drew Danelagh's immediate attention with that sharp remark. "Please feel free to call me either, Lady Thalia," he countered.

While the duchess seemed to enjoy this exchange, judging by the tiny smile on her lips, Krista appeared shocked. "No! That would be blasphemous. In our game, we called him Sir Robin, wore paper hats with cock feathers in the brims and carried wooden swords. Rick would have preferred to have more and older Merry Men, but had to do with us as my father did not allow married servants, and we had few playmates up here on the hill."

Forgetting himself and his lowly status, Hugh Grey spoke up. "Yes, Rick always wanted me to be Friar Tuck, but I refused." He caught himself. "Forgive the familiarity, milord."

Godric rubbed two fingers against a line forming between his eyes as if to erase it. "No need to apologize, Hugh. You will soon be on your way to protect King and Country."

Krista, lost in her childhood memories, continued as if her brother had not spoken. "Rick soon outgrew our games and came home less and less. Then, we played knight and lady. Hugh was ever my hero, completing any quest I asked of him. That ended when I was sent away to school, too, after my twelfth birthday." Sadness washed over her broad but pretty face.

"Your father allowed you so much freedom before that?" Thalia questioned.

"He cared very little what I did and left me to the governess, who cared even less except for making sure I knew my lessons. Actually, I think Papa would have preferred me to be more like Lady Kristiana and wield a sword, but real weapons have always frightened me. I never walked through the halls of arms if I could take any other way around. Since the house is really a big, hollow square, I did that easily enough, but one day, Rick lured me there by crying out that he'd gotten hurt. Instead, he was hiding inside a coat of armor and pursued me the entire length of the place. I never got over it."

"What a bad, beastly boy you were—Rick, exactly like two of my little brothers," Thalia said.

"James never tried to terrify you? Since I am now Rick to you, might I address you as Thalia?"

"I doubt if James *could* terrify me. I would have pushed him over and refused to help him up, armor being as heavy and ungainly as it is. When not at his studies, he trailed after Papa out of doors while I stayed inside perfecting my music and my embroidery."

"Your jonquils." Danelagh's eyes strayed to the smooth, tan tops of her breasts revealed by her eveningwear.

"Yes. A pity you will never see the best of my specimens."

"Ahem." The duke cleared his throat loudly. "Thalia showed great promise with a bow and arrow before that woman, Miss Thurgood, got hold of her. She wounded a buck enough for us to track him down and slit his throat."

"Not at dinner, dearest!" his wife declared.

"I believe we are finished eating, darling."

"You surprise me again, Lady Thalia." Godric's eyes showed a certain admiration, but her feat still did not earn a complete smile.

"Papa helped me skin it, but Mama insisted I treat the hide myself with its mashed brains as she did among the Shawnee. That cured me of any interest in the chase."

"Perhaps I can interest you in the chase again."

"I doubt it, Rick." Across the table, her mother drew her attention from the repartee by nodding her head and rolling her eyes in the direction of Danelagh. What had she forgotten? Oh, yes. "Please do call me Thalia."

"I am honored. Had James no other pet name for you?"

"None," she lied.

"As I recall, he used to call you..." her father answered.

The duchess stood and everyone at the table arose, too. "Time we went to the drawing room, ladies. Hugh, you may step aside. Krista, come along."

Seven

Thalia put a dark, hooded cloak over her nightdress, slipped into her shoes, and took the back stairs to the deserted courtyard. Still awake when a tall case clock in the hall struck one, she could not blame her parents this time. They were quiescent, possibly enjoying their tightened bed ropes.

Nothing untoward had happened after dining. Once the men joined the ladies, she performed a few pieces on her Spanish guitar, a beautiful inlaid instrument that Thalia had brought north in the carriage with them. After their banter at supper, Godric retreated back to his normal aloof self and gave her thanks for her effort to entertain, but no compliments.

Krista, however, begged for guitar lessons. "Papa saw no use in music or for spending his money on a piano and an instructor, but a guitar would not take up much room nor cost too greatly."

Obviously, the poor child sorely felt her lack of accomplishments. Thalia spent the remainder of the evening in a corner of the room teaching the girl a few easy chords to Krista's delight. The men spoke of sports and Bonaparte. Her mother observed everything with her perceptive gray eyes and talked little.

With the end of a long journey and a late night behind her, Thalia should have been able to sleep once everyone took a candle and lighted their way to bed, but she continued to be restless. Every time she closed her eyes, she saw Danelagh's face as they exchanged words over the pudding. Exercise, she needed exercise. A few turns around the courtyard should do the trick.

A full, haloed moon shortly to begin waning into May sat high in the sky like the goddess Diana clothed in a diaphanous gown. She threw down sharp spears of light that only made the shadows of the courtyard deeper. This far north a chill remained in the night air, and Thalia paused in the darkness by the carefully closed door to draw her cloak tighter and cover her head with the hood. *What a desolate place with its walls of stone, floor of slates, and all those inward facing windows staring down like empty eye sockets.* With the addition of a few comfortable benches and some jardinières to hold blooming plants, the courtyard did have possibilities as a pleasant sitting area— or a trysting place. Speaking of which...she found she was not alone.

Diagonally across the open space stood two tall figures casting only one shadow because of a tight embrace and oblivious to all else. Heedless of the lamp provided by the moon, they exchanged ardent kisses, Krista and her footman, Hugh Grey. Pressed against such a stalwart form, Godric's sister appeared much less ungainly, so completely feminine, as the couple paused for breath. She rested her head on his broad shoulder, her black gown merging with his dark livery.

"I cannot bear that you are leaving, Hugh, and might die in some foreign land."

"Come, Krista. This is the only way I might ever aspire to marry an earl's sister. I will rise in the ranks and return trailing clouds of glory if only you will wait for me."

"I will, oh, I will!"

Her words carried clearly in the cold, dew-laden air. Thalia wanted to put a finger to her lips and caution them to be quiet, but instead, she backtracked to the door, intending to leave the couple as they were. Tomorrow, she would seek her mother's counsel about the matter. What an entirely impossible, improper match, and yet she felt herself moved by their doomed love. About to give them their privacy, she shot one last glance over her shoulder before ascending the stairs and found herself shouting, "Watch out!"

Emerging from the doorway nearest the young lovers, Godric appeared fully dressed with saber in hand. "I heard voices in the courtyard, saw movement in the shadows, and came to attend to the matter expecting to find drunken guards or a maid with an assignation. I find this—a friend of my childhood debauching my sister! What else have you done in my absence? Stolen the family silver?" He wedged the flat of his sword between them and pushed the two young lovers apart.

"In your absence I took care of Krista and dried her tears after her father's cruel remarks, but where were you? Abroad, with no thought given to her." Hugh, a boy newly come into manhood, stood his ground.

"There was no debauchery. Our love is as pure as a knight's veneration of his lady," Krista claimed, wringing her hands before her breast.

Behind Thalia, the staircase door opened suddenly, pushing her into the pool of moonlight. Her father, holding the sword he always wore when traveling on horseback, barefoot and clad in his dressing gown, rushed across the courtyard. "We heard the uproar, and I come to the defense of Battle Hill! Oh." Taking in the young couple, he paused in disappointment. "Only a foiled elopement."

"We are not eloping. We know we are too young to marry, but I will wait for him until the River Ouse fails to run to the sea." After this dramatic declaration, Krista attempted to place herself between her brother and Hugh Grey, but Godric shoved her aside.

"Bellevue, toss the man your sword and stay to witness that I killed him in a fair fight," Danelagh requested.

"No, no, no!" Krista wailed. "Brother, haven't you ever wanted what you could not have so badly your heart breaks?"

"Never. Bellevue, your sword if you please."

The duke presented the weapon. The young footman accepted it with a firm hand and prepared to defend himself. The earl attacked him in the next second. Hugh parried Godric's first thrust successfully and each one thereafter. Moonlight glinted off the blades like small strikes of lightning as they moved across the slates. The footman defended himself well but made no moves to win the duel.

Thalia watched with rapt attention, no friendly sparring here but a matter of life and death. Beside her, the duchess spoke. "Thrilling, isn't it?" She'd covered her white nightdress with a huge shawl and wore a voluminous cap over her curls. Her bare toes curled against the chilly stone underfoot.

Krista bolted across the courtyard and threw herself into Thalia's arms, the duchess being too small to catch her without both of them landing on the ground. "Please, please make them stop," she implored.

"I have observed it is best not to get between two angry men. Never fear. The duke will not allow Mr. Grey to be slaughtered," the duchess said, squeezing the girl's cold hand.

"I do believe Godric Erikson has no heart at all," Thalia stated. "He should dismiss the man, not try to kill him."

The fighters began to tire. Hugh Grey slipped in a damp spot as they circled the well in the center of the courtyard. Krista screamed as the tip of Godric's blade whipped across the footman's cheek leaving a small, deep cut behind. Grey regained his footing and continued to parry as blood washed down his pale cheek. He did not attempt to kill Krista's brother, but merely defended himself. His skills were good, but in time he would fall before the earl's furious onslaught. Thalia had witnessed many a mock fight between her brothers after Miss Thurgood's departure, never meant to kill. Her heart thundered, whether for the safety of the lad or for Godric should he, too, slip and open himself to death, she could not define.

"Stop, I say!" The duke's deep voice reverberated off the walls of the enclosed space. "Blood has been drawn. Honor is satisfied. This duel is ended."

"Would you cease if one of your daughters had been ruined?" Godric asked, panting as he continued to pursue his one-time friend around the well.

"Well, I...um," the duke said, unable to lie.

"He would skewer such a man, cut off his genitals, and shove them in his enemy's mouth," Lady Flora murmured, but Krista heard.

"Dear God, no! I am not ruined, only in love. Have mercy, Rick," Krista pled.

"Enough!" The duchess used her shrill soprano voice to cut through the bloodlust. "If what your sister says is true, simply send the man on his way in the morning for presuming to reach above his station in life. Now, let's see to that wound."

"No. I want him to bear my mark," Godric forbade her. He lowered his sword. "Gather your belongings, Hugh, and be out of here tonight. The full moon will see you on your way. If you are still here in the morning, I will finish this as *I* want. The servants' stairs are over there." He pointed the way with his saber.

"I will return for you one day, Krista!" Hugh called out as he surrendered his weapon to the duke.

Godric cut the air with his blade just inches from Hugh's back to hurry him along. The duke wrested his weapon away. "Take your sister within," he ordered, glaring up at the windows high under the eaves where the old battlements had been roofed over, each one filled with pairs of eyes, and bellowed, "All of you back to your beds. The show is over. Come, Thalia. Come, my dearest. Why, your little toes must be frozen. Shall I carry you to your bed?"

The duchess looked up lovingly at her huge husband. "I would adore that."

He scooped her immediately into his arms and strode off. Thalia followed, knowing she would get no sleep now, not with Krista wailing like a forlorn ghost, her own heart still thudding from the excitement, and her parents doing...whatever. She lingered in the upper halls and explored until she found a front facing window.

Below, she watched Hugh Grey appear out of his livery and in a decent enough set of clothes suitable for the son of a curate. Whatever else he owned, he carried in a small casket balanced on one wide shoulder. He paused once to look back at Battle Hill. The pale hands of the moonlight caressed his swollen, injured cheek rinsed clean of blood but showing a dark mark that would remain upon it forever. He did not meet Thalia's eyes, and not finding the blue ones he sought, Hugh turned and continued on to whatever fate awaited him in battle.

Eight

Godric said, "I think Lady Thalia does have a warm heart beneath all those cold and proper manners. Last night proves it. Did you see how tenderly she held Krista during the evening's calamity?"

Bascom helped his master into his jacket. "I did notice their embrace from my vantage point."

"Do you think she admired my prowess with a sword?"

Godric straightened his lapels in the dressing room mirror. Not too pleased by his appearance, and it had nothing to do with his clothes, he shook his head. Nothing he could do about the dark circles beneath his eyes from lack of sleep, the curse of a fair man, as Krista's weeping had kept him awake until dawn. Even his scar seemed pallid this morning. Did Thalia find it attractive or repellent? He ran a finger down its length.

"I cannot say, milord. I find women very hard to understand. To me, her expression was one of slight anger."

"Proper as she is, she probably despised the uproar in such an ill-managed household. I will ask her and Lady Flora to help me set things aright. Women like to mend what is broken. I want to see how she handles Krista today. That is important to my happiness."

"Instead of all this observing and testing, why not ask the duke for her hand immediately while you have the lady all to yourself? Now, *he* admired your swordsmanship I could tell."

"I will not tie myself for life to someone until I have gauged the strength of her heart, the depth of her soul. That last night in London, she played for me with such passion that it nearly broke me to seem indifferent. I do believe I went along with Lady Flora's machinations only to part Thalia from her other admirers so I could study her further."

"More romantic rubbish, not much better than your sister falling in love with a footman."

"Bascom, you overstep just as Hugh did, and he was a boyhood friend. I am going down to breakfast."

Hoping to find Thalia, he discovered only the duke looking dolefully at the vat of gray porridge, the crock of butter, and a rack of slightly burned toast. His guest cheered a bit when a maid brought in a tray with tea and coffee pots. Spooning a large mound of the cooling cereal into a bowl, the duke dressed it with butter and crumbled a lump of sugar from the tea service across the top. Satisfied, he prepared his tea and sat to eat.

"My apologies, Bellevue. I thought my sister had left instructions about the serving of breakfast."

"This will do. The ladies are all taking breakfast in their beds. I believe the preparation of so many trays has put the kitchen in a dither. Some bacon would have been welcome, though."

He should speak to the man now about courting his daughter, but the moment he declared himself, she would have ascendency over him. Enjoyable as their conversation has been at dinner like the thrust and parry of swords, he did know Thalia would relish having him at her beck and call a little too much. Courtship made a man vulnerable. Before he could make up his mind, the duchess arrived, prepared herself a cup of tea, and took a seat beside her husband.

"Good morning, Godric," she said a trifle coolly.

"I thought you planned to make up for lost sleep this morning, my dear. Could you refill my cup?" The duke held out a piece of porcelain far too small for his big hands. "You know how I like it."

"Yes, with too much cream and sugar. I did break my fast upstairs and simply came down to take tea with you."

"While the young ladies are still abed, could I entreat you, Lady Flora, to speak to my sister and instill some good sense about her infatuation? If you might undertake the reorganization of my household, I would be eternally grateful," Godric asked as he scraped the char off his toast with the edge of the butter knife.

"I did note you have an abundance of footmen but no butler and seem to be lacking a housekeeper as well." She handed the duke his tea.

"My father left both a pension in his will, and they are gone. I believe he did not mean to expire so soon. I thought to promote Bascom into the position of butler."

"He certainly would be very intimidating," she agreed. "You must have his uniform custom made. I will interview the female staff and see if any would suit for a housekeeper. As for Krista, I shall do what I can, but the young take matters of the heart very hard. Only time and diversion will help there."

"Anything you can do to make her see her foolishness." Godric jolted when he heard Thalia's voice behind him.

"You who value emotion and blasted pine trees call love foolishness? You know nothing of it."

"No, but I am willing to learn all the ways of love." Good God, he had nearly declared himself right there in front of her parents. He switched quickly to the mundane. "Have you eaten?"

"Such as it was. Mama, I am going to sit with Krista. Will you come with me?"

"Certainly. She needs our comfort. Good day, gentlemen."

The duke nodded them on their way. "This porridge is not half bad if it has enough sugar on it. I believe I will have some more."

~ * ~

Krista's tray sat untouched on a bedside table. The girl curled beneath her covers like a calf burrowed in a heap of straw with only the top of her blond head showing. Although the women had tapped on the door and called her name, they did not hesitate to enter when they received no reply. Distraught young ladies could act very foolishly, the duchess declared to Thalia, and she would take no chances with this one. Gently, she found a hunched shoulder beneath the spread and peeled away the wrapping as if she were delivering a child into the world. Like many a newborn, this one cried and would not open her eyes. Lady Flora handled her as if the child were her very own.

"Come Krista, sit up and take some tea, then a bit of porridge and you will feel all the better for it."

"I will never eat again! I plan to stay in this bed until Rick must carry my bones to the grave."

"I would reconsider, dear child. Certainly, your death would wound your brother, but think...what if your young man should make his way in the world only to return and find you gone to the great beyond. Like Romeo, he might take his own life."

Krista raised her splotchy face and opened her swollen eyes. "I hadn't thought of that."

"No, because you are very young and all grievous happenings seem like the end of the world to you. But you have many years ahead that can be used well or poorly. You must make the decision how you will spend them. Here, eat."

The duchess handed the girl the bowl of porridge. The pat of butter in the center had melted and oozed to form a yellow ring around the gray mound like an ogre's eye. Still, she ate a few spoonfuls, gulped a cup of tepid tea, and accepted a piece of cold toast. Meanwhile, the duchess laid out plans for the day, the week, even the next year of Krista's life.

"Today, we will tour Battle Hill from top to bottom and see how it can be made more hospitable. How long have you been returned from school and dealing with this staff, Krista?"

"Since the Christmas holidays. Papa sent notice to Miss Ridgeway's Academy for Young Ladies that I would not be returning. He suffered from chest pains and believed them to be brought on by having to deal with the petty details of the household as well as his other interests. I was to take over as lady of the house. While the butler and housekeeper stayed, they told me what had to be done, but once they left..."

"That is in the past. I am here to guide you now. Miss Ridgeway's Academy...I do not believe I have ever heard of it."

"Papa selected it especially because of Miss Ridgeway's policy of not coddling the girls. We wore gray uniforms, slept on hard beds, and dined much like this." Krista bit into a piece of the hardened toast and sent crumbs dropping into the bedding. Hastily, she tried to brush them to the floor. "We never ate in bed at Miss Ridgeway's unless we were very ill and certainly not at Battle Hill either. Lazing about was not my father's policy."

"Leave the crumbs. Your maid will take care of them when she makes the bed. No wonder I never heard of Miss Ridgeway's Academy. It sounds very much like an orphan asylum."

"Truly, not that bad. We had our lessons, practiced fine penmanship in writing letters home, worked diligently on our sewing and good manners, and participated in an excellent choir as well as vigorous walks. Papa would not expend the extra money for art, piano, or riding lessons. He considered that frippery."

"Then your education is incomplete. Ah well, we have an entire year to correct that. Tomorrow, we go into York to replenish your wardrobe. No one says a lady must mourn in sackcloth and ashes. Black can be very becoming to a girl with a pretty complexion such as yours."

"Do you really think so?" Krista raised a hand to her cheek.

"Absolutely, once you have put some cold cloths on your face to take away the blotches. None of my dark daughters wears black at all well. We must also get started on your wardrobe for your coming out next year. I will present you with my own daughter, Iris, and I am sure Godric will not want you to appear shabby beside her. Iris must show you how to do watercolors and Thalia is splendid at music. It is perhaps too late to become accomplished on the piano, but I think the guitar is more easily learned. Once you see the wider world, you may not be so heart-broken over losing Mr. Grey." A misstep, the duchess realized it as soon as those last words left her lips.

"I will love him always! I will have no other." Those round blue eyes welled with tears again.

"You are very young, Krista, and sometimes women—and men change with time. What seems wonderful to a child might have no appeal to an adult. How old is Mr. Grey?"

"Eighteen, one year older than me."

"He is entering a man's world and cannot come back the same boy you knew, but let us not argue about it. Concentrate on becoming the kind of woman Mr. Grey would admire if he returns to Battle Hill. Well then, call your maid to assist you in dressing and off we will go to dismiss the cook."

"Oh, she has been here so many years and always prepared what my father wanted."

"Then a pension. After all, Battle Hill is not an orphanage, but the country seat of the earls of Danelagh. Today, you start to reclaim it."

Leaving the girl to ponder these new thoughts, the duchess beckoned to Thalia, and they left the chamber. Once down the hall, Thalia began her protest.

"Mama, you know I look very well in black. How could you say that about me?"

"Of course, you do, but the child needs puffing up after so many years of deflation by her father and probably this Miss Ridgeway."

"Haven't you always said you fell in love with Papa as a child and never cared for anyone else? How could you suggest Krista's feelings are not as strong?"

The duchess countered her daughter as if they also thrust and parried. "I am sure Miss Thurgood never taught you to think that way, the stiff old board. I was ten when I first saw the half-savage Pearce Longleigh, thirteen at the time. I never forgot him, not even during my brief first marriage. When my husband died, I went to find him. You know the rest, but my point is, I, too, was an earl's daughter and your father held the title of Viscount Laughlin, heir to the Duke of Bellevue. We were as well-matched in rank as you are with Danelagh. Not so with Krista and her Hugh Grey."

"You always *said* you would have taken Father if he had not a title or penny to his name. You would have lived with him in the American wilderness if not for James' sake. As for Godric Erikson, he is a callous man who could have handled his sister's tender feelings in a better way than dueling with a man not this equal."

The duchess regarded her daughter with a tilt of her head as if to gain a new perspective. "I believe Krista is not the only one who is doing some changing, my dear child."

~ * ~

Since the duchess insisted, Krista led the ladies up the crude, stone steps to the servants' quarters under the roof. Thalia took in all its bleakness. Bellevue Hall's staff certainly fared better, not luxuriously, but with small comforts allowed such as a favorite pillow or a quilt brought from home.

One long narrow room with stone walls front and back and small inset windows where the crenelations of the old battlements allowed for them provided space for the household staff to rest. Each had a cot with a chest at its foot for belongings and a chamber pot beneath for bodily functions. A small table held a bowl and pitcher and left space for a candlestick. A mirror square hung above allowed each woman to check the set of her cap and the arrangement of her hair in the morning. Clothes could be hung on ample pegs. A stout wall with no door separated the males from the females.

"The other side for the men is much the same. Papa dismissed any man found on the women's staircase and vice versa," Krista explained.

"As if that would stop anyone bent on pleasure." The duchess gazed out one of the small windows. "Though I must say one would have to walk some way to find so much as a tree or bush for a tryst. Not a garden or plantation for acres."

"To offer the enemy no chance of concealment," Krista revealed.

"Is it very cold up here in winter?"

"Not so much as the chimneys from the kitchen provide some warmth, and Papa did believe in good wool blankets for all."

The thought of scratchy wool blankets made Thalia's arms itch. Perhaps she was overly used to fine linens.

"Generous of him," the duchess remarked.

"Really, you must not think him stingy. He and his father spent years recouping the family fortunes after Derek Erikson, the one you called the merry lord, spent nearly all he inherited on making this old keep into a palatial country home. Because of their thriftiness, I do have an adequate dowry set aside, Papa said. Enough, I thought, for Hugh and me to live on." Tears again and wobbling lips.

"I see," the duchess said quickly. "Moving on then."

They explored the chambers on the second floor, full of antique furnishings of good quality but in need of reupholstery. What a job the next countess would have making this place hospitable, Thalia thought. Good that she had decided she no longer wanted the position.

One large corner room remained locked against their explorations. "I wasn't given the key and have never been inside. Papa said its contents were not for a maiden's eyes."

"My curiosity is aroused. I must ask Godric if I can have a look," the duchess said. Thalia, not without her own curiosity no matter how many times Miss Thurgood told her it killed cats, hoped to be invited along for the mysterious viewing.

They passed on to the family wing where Krista showed them her father's room, Spartan in its severity. He'd slept on a camp cot and had a portable writing desk set upon a table for his use. None of the chairs, all straight-backed, offered any comfort. A large, plain wardrobe held his clothes. Krista opened its doors.

"I should pack his things away or give them to the poor. All I wish to keep is his uniform from his days with Lord Cornwallis. He valued it so."

A dressing room away sat the deceased Lady Danelagh's room. Krista's mother had lightened it with dainty and elegant furnishings. Newer toile fabrics covered the chairs and the bed. She'd had her share of small ornaments, some of them amusing like the collection of small enameled boxes shaped like animals. A press on the lid and a frog opened its wide mouth to receive a tiny treasure. A lily unfolded to show its contents. The back of an elephant sprang up to reveal a space inside.

"I would sneak in here and play with them as a small child. I always thought I would find a hidden treasure, but my mother had none. Papa said she was a spendthrift as she redecorated this chamber to please herself while he fought in the colonies."

"I do not think that of her, Krista. A woman should have a place to call her own," the duchess assured her. "Why don't you move in here and enjoy what your mother created?"

"Oh, no! This chamber will belong to the new countess. I hope I know who she will be." She smiled at Thalia, and Thalia had not the heart to say any infatuation she might have had for Danelagh had flown, partly because of his treatment of his sister.

The girl's own room could only be described as dreary with its walls the color of unripe olives and a mustard yellow trim, both dulled with age. No lightness, frills, or fancies, but only heavy brocade drapes and hangings in the same colors with dust deep in their creases. "We shall have to brighten it," the duchess declared.

"I would be glad to help with that endeavor," Thalia said, heartfelt.

They inspected a long-abandoned nursery at the corner of the long hallway where the wooden blocks, lead soldiers, a hobbyhorse, and old primers gathered cobwebs and moved on to the ground floor where the girl's mother had made some small inroads at creating a comfortable home with a pleasant sitting room and a small library rather short on literature. Military tomes in various languages filled the shelves. A small section held the works of Schiller...his plays, poems, and philosophy, and of Goethe in the original German.

The duchess ran a fond hand over the spine of a copy of *The Sorrows of Young Werther*. "We have this in translation at Bellevue Hall, but I find it much more moving in its native tongue. Have you read it, Thalia?"

"No, Mama. Miss Thurgood did not put it on my list." For a moment, she regretted having pursued only French, Spanish, and Italian, the last to improve her singing. Her governess had not approved of languages with guttural sounds, saying they were as unseemly as a young lady contorting her face to play the flute. What did it matter? She no longer sought to please Danelagh.

"These are Rick's books. He sent a box of them home, and I arranged them on the shelves, as we have room to spare," Krista said. "Papa did not approve of frivolous reading, though we do have Mr. Shakespeare's histories and tragedies, but not the comedies."

"Naturally," the duchess sighed.

"I see you have found my additions to the Battle Hill library, Lady Flora." Godric Erikson stood braced in the doorway. "I developed a fondness for Schiller during my time in Heidelburg." He offered her a quote in German.

"Ah, yes, I know that one. 'Against stupidity the gods themselves contend in vain'." She countered with another.

"Would you care to translate that one, Thalia, or should I?" he asked.

He made her cheeks burn as if she suffered from the stupidity mentioned in the first quote. "I am sorry I have no German—merely French, Italian, and Spanish. You will have to do the work yourself."

"Your mother said, 'Deeper meaning resides in the fairy tales told to me in my childhood than in any truth that is taught in life'."

"I like that one," Krista piped up. "I have only a grasp of French." Her face saddened again.

"Here is another from Herr Schiller in English just for you, Krista. 'Stay true to the dreams of thy youth'," the duchess quoted. The girl brightened. "Now, is there anything else we should see before inspecting the kitchen?"

"The dungeon," Godric said, with a spooky inflection in his voice.

"It's a terrible place. I never go down there, not since childhood," Krista informed them.

"What did your brother do to you there?" Thalia asked.

"How did you know?"

"While Bellevue Hall lacks a dungeon, my own brothers make good use of the one at Castle Laughlin, our holding in Scotland, to terrorize their sisters whenever they can."

"It was nothing. I left her in the dark in the chamber of horrors and pretended to be the ghost of a tormented prisoner—all in good fun," Godric protested.

"Beastly, just as I thought."

"Are you coming to see it or not?"

"Oh, we are! I would not miss it," the duchess exclaimed. "Krista, dear, remain here if the place unsettles you."

"I shall."

"Good, then off we go. Lead the way, Godric."

Stopping only to light some splints in the library's fireplace, he took them to the rear of the house where the staircase for the male servants climbed above a thick, oaken door situated beneath it. Godric took a ring of crude, antique keys from a wall hook and opened the dark maw. Allowing the heavy key ring to dangle from his wrist, he applied the splints to the wicks of two oil lanterns, handed one to Thalia, and took the other for himself. With the duchess between them, they descended into the most ancient part of Battle Hill where the walls pressed close and oozed with moisture. The downward steps ended in a room where guards once passed their watch over prisoners. Through another heavy door and they stood in a larger room well equipped for torture.

Stout bolts held manacles for hands and feet to the walls. An iron boot for the crushing of ankles and toes lay atop a pile of thumbscrews. The brazier to hold coals and heat nearby pokers for the putting out of eyes still stood in a corner, but the place of pride went to the stretching rack, a long plank table equipped with a wheel at one end. The rotting ropes that once bound the feet in place while others held the victim's body to be broken by the winch still hung from its sides.

"You lack only an iron maiden," Thalia said as Godric shone the light around the room.

He held the lamp up to her face. "Perhaps we have one now."

"You call me maid of iron, when for all your pretty quotes from Schiller you would not allow your sister to marry her choice, a good-hearted and brave young man."

"If only he had waited for my return and asked my help, I might have gotten him a position in the church or a commission in the military, but instead he took my father's livery. How could I allow Krista to marry a servant and one who took advantage of her innocence and timid nature? Hugh was always a promising boy. If he had given it some time, waited until she was older and he could support her in some way..."

Almost forgotten, the duchess spoke from the darkness. "Youth is ever hasty. I can vouch for that. What lies beyond the next door?"

"The cells, more chains, and the occasional visiting rat."

"Then, I believe I have seen enough for the time being. Now to inspect the kitchen and we are through for the day. Thalia, you have a lantern, show the way out."

As Thalia raised the lamp, she caught the gleam in her mother's eye and a faint whispering of the word, "Perfect."

~ * ~

Not really within Thalia's range of knowledge, the kitchen appeared to be very clean and well-organized but grossly understaffed, in her view. The cook herself performed the second kneading of the bread for the evening meal. A scullery maid scraped carrots, while a boy turned a roast of beef and a haunch of venison on a spit over the fire. The main courses were sure to be overcooked by dinnertime. Beneath the meat, a pan caught the drippings for the making of the famous Yorkshire pudding, nothing more than an egg batter mixed with the greases from the roasts. The evening sweet, a fruitcake doused in a great deal of preservative brandy, already sat on its pedestal plate. Not sophisticated fare, but Thalia was sure her father would enjoy it.

Mrs. Gunderson, the cook, wore a vast white apron over her wide body and a cap covering most of her iron gray hair. She dropped her curtsey to the duchess with her flour-covered hands held wide, then moved back to her table to pinch off rolls from the dough as if to show she knew more than one way to serve bread.

"Tell me, Mrs. Gunderson, have you served here long?"

"Aye, since I were the scullery maid like her." She spoke in a Yorkshire accent as thick as her arms.

"Such long service should be rewarded, don't you think?"

"The earl, the old 'un, dint think t'leave me no pension, your Grace. My leg veins is about to pop I've stood so long on these slate floors, but he dint remember old Iva Gunderson in his will and left me ne wiht."

"An oversight, a gross oversight. I do see how hard you work to feed everyone with so little help. I shall speak to young Lord Danelagh about your retirement personally."

The cook's round face went from sullen to smiles in a flash quicker than fat hitting the fire. "You'd do that for me, your Grace? What a fine and kind lady you be."

"I believe long and faithful service should be rewarded. We will have you out of here in under a week."

Thalia watched the duchess and marveled how smoothly the deed had been done. She vowed to follow her mother's instructions in all ways from this time forward.

Nine

The following morning, Godric entered the breakfast room and to his surprise found all the women gathered there. They chattered like sparrows feasting on a surfeit of crumbs, and no wonder. The offerings on the sideboard were remarkably improved: eggs with a side dish of bacon, tempting sweet rolls bursting with black currants, perfectly browned toast accompanied by a choice of jams and jellies, and hot tea and coffee being served by one of the maids. Best of all, Krista's blue eyes had cleared of tears and refilled with excitement.

"Ah dear boy, here you are at last," the duchess said as if he'd been terribly tardy. "Now, I have promised the cook a pension and to have her out of here by the week's end. We are taking the coach into York to see to Krista's wardrobe, and I shall also inquire about a French chef. Plenty of them to be had since their bloody revolution, all claiming to have cooked for Marie Antoinette or some other grand family long gone to the guillotine. If Bascom is to be your butler, should we take him along to be measured for his livery? I have also observed your staff and believe the upstairs maid, Grace, might make a decent housekeeper. She should be outfitted accordingly."

Feeling as if he'd been run over by that same ducal coach, Godric filled a plate and sat at the place reserved for him at the head of the table. "But why? I mean Cook seems just now to be getting the hang of making a decent meal, and Krista, being in mourning, will not be attending fetes and dances."

"Even mourning can be made attractive, and you do want your sister to be attractive, don't you? As for your cook, she is old and weary and was overlooked in your father's will. She deserves her rest and you a better table. I am sure you will be generous." The duchess held up her cup for a refill of tea.

"I would like to be, but must consult my father's banker about his assets. I intended to ride into the city today to see both him and the family solicitor. We have farmland and tenants in the vale, but I know Papa had heavy investments in shipping. I must see how our finances fare."

"While you are about that, please inquire about the amount of Krista's dowry. If I am to bring her out next year, we must know what comes with her. While I understand your father had an amount set aside for her, I am certain you will augment that if it is not liberal enough to attract the right sort. Are we all finished, ladies?' The duchess stood and led her small flock from the room, giving Godric a last glance of Thalia's black curls and Krista's blonde braids as they went.

He hadn't so much as gotten in a "good morning," let alone some conversation with either of them, but Thalia had regarded him with a curiously arch smile as she broke apart her currant bun and ate it bit by tiny bit. The duke poked his head around the door jamb.

"Are they gone?"

"Apparently to prepare for a trip into York to obtain a new cook and clothes for Krista."

"I've learned when my wife is on the march, it's best to stay out of the way or be trampled. She is relentless. Should have been a general. If she spies me, I will be carrying packages for her all day. I thought it best to escape early and went for a morning ride to whet an appetite for whatever might be served this morning." He eyed the bacon. "A great improvement from yesterday."

"I thought so, but still I am to pension off the cook."

The duke heaped his plate with meat and eggs and balanced a currant bun atop it. "Watch your purse, but otherwise, let them have their way with the household. Women can make your life a paradise or a bloody hell. One never knows what goes on in their minds."

~ * ~

In the end, Godric accompanied the coach into York but took his own mount. Bascom did not get off so easily. Ordered to escort the ladies and get his measurements taken at the tailor's establishment, he rode glumly with the women. As his master turned off for the solicitor's abode, he was dropped for his fitting with instructions to meet the duchess and the girls at the shop of a certain seamstress. Obviously, they would be far longer than he. Thalia nearly laughed at the man's discomfort and Godric's transparent excuse not to carry their packages due to his urgent need to speak with the solicitor, probably true but amusing nonetheless. After a brief stop to leave the duchess's requirements for a new cook at an agency, they moved on to the shop of a dressmaker Krista knew of but had never entered.

Seeing two ladies of style and wealth trailed by a large maid in a baggy black gown pause beneath the sign that read *Madame Cuthbert – Haut Mode Parisien,* the proprietress hurried forward to welcome them inside her establishment. Credit went to her for not attempting to assume a French accent, but she had schooled herself away from the local patois and aped her fine clientele. Her curtsey was elegant and her manor unctuous. Although an older woman, she had adopted the looser ringlets worn by the young and the modish. Though gray in color, they bobbed along with her. Her pale blue eyes gleamed with the prospect of a large expenditure.

"How may I serve you, miladies? Let me assure you, we can duplicate any pattern in the finest of materials and have available illustrations of the latest fashions directly from Paris."

The duchess acknowledged her with a nod. "Something for..." She drew Krista forward, and the woman's delight faded.

"Ah, your maid. Of course, we can do a proper uniform as well."

With the red rising up her neck, Krista fingered her locket and stared at her feet. Thalia thought she spied another lock of blonde hair mingled with the dead countess's fair curls but said nothing of it. The poor creature had suffered enough embarrassments.

"For Lady Kristiana Erikson of Battle Hill. I am the Duchess of Bellevue," Thalia's mother replied icily.

Not a tall woman to begin with, Madame Cuthbert shrank before their eyes into another low curtsey. "Do forgive my misunderstanding, your Grace. I believed the young lady to be away at school, not that the late earl ever allowed her to have an account with me. Today that will change. I assume you desire something less...less..." Words failed the proprietress. How Thalia enjoyed watching her mother in action.

"Exactly. Unfortunately, we must cleave to black for the moment, but let us plan for several day dresses and at least one or two gowns for eveningwear. We will be dressing her for her coming out next season and will leave her measurements with you, as well as choosing some becoming colors and fabrics for the spring, but let us wait to be sure of the latest styles before making up the gowns."

"Certainly. Only the best for Lady Kristiana. Step into our fitting room."

The gleam in her eye returned as the proprietress found a measuring tape and began to calculate what wide swaths of material would be needed to clothe a girl of such Amazonian proportions. She brought out bolts of superfine wool, muslin, silk and satin, draping swags of them across Krista's broad shoulders. Seizing a wide sash of black satin, she tied it beneath the girl's well-developed bosom.

"You see how the breadth of the sash gives her form more definition. The current styles may call for loose drapery, but we are still able to show off a lady's best feature. We can dress each gown differently, with dark lace and dotted or sprigged netting. Beading and embroidery will take longer of course, but I do have some pieces made up that may be used to make a smart border. Piping is always in good taste as well."

"Two of wool as Battle Hill is rather drafty, five of muslin for the warmer months, and one each of silk and satin properly embellished. That should be enough for now. The young lady will not be in mourning forever," the duchess said decisively. "Now, have you another room where we might discuss special attire for my daughter? Krista, do look at the illustrations to see if anything catches your fancy and pick out swatches of your favorite colors. Fair as you are, pastels of any shade will look marvelous on you."

Overwhelmed, the girl gave her only an open-mouthed nod. The duchess herded Thalia to another private dressing room and had her step up upon a low pedestal for measurement, which Madame Cuthbert did personally as she had for Krista.

"Now, tell me your desire. A gown for a special occasion? A London ball? A wedding, perhaps?" the woman hinted. "I have heard our young Lord Danelagh returned in the company of a most beauteous brunette. All your secrets are safe with Madame Cuthbert."

"As well they must be, or Lady Kristiana will be purchasing her coming out attire elsewhere," the duchess threatened. "My daughter is in need of a special costume for a fancy-dress ball."

"I am?" She'd had no notice of this affair before they deserted London.

"Yes, we received the invitation shortly before leaving London to assist Lord Danelagh in setting up his household. No one must know of her disguise. To begin, we shall need a black satin corset of the last century. Edge it with lace. From the bottom, extend a skirt of fine midnight gauze to the length of her knees and fill the bodice with the same material."

"Mama, am I to go in my undergarments and with naked limbs?" Alarm sounded in Thalia's voice before she could prevent it.

"No, no. Riding boots will cover you to the hem of the gown. If Miss Thurgood hadn't discouraged such exercise, you would own them already."

In defense of her old governess, Thalia said, "She believed riding sidesaddle deformed the buttocks unless the saddle was switched from side to side every day. She did not wish to take any chances with me and stressed that ladies should ride in carriages for good reason."

"Miss Thurgood again. She certainly would not approve of this costume. I like it more and more."

"Is it some sort of lady pirate you aim for, your Grace? We could make the hem jagged in that case. Spangles, would you like to add some spangles?" Madame Cuthbert offered enthusiastically.

"Why not? Go fetch some samples."

The proprietress hurried off to get her box of embellishments, and Thalia turned to her mother immediately. "What do you intend?"

"I believe you want to bring Godric to his knees, so to speak. This costume will certainly weaken them. I once had a maid named Chanel who went on to establish a business of her own."

"As a seamstress?

"No. She caters to very special tastes. I saw such a costume at her establishment where I confess your father and I occasionally spend a night enjoying each other's company, keeping our love fresh, so to speak. If this outfit does not astound young Danelagh, nothing will."

"It certainly astounds me. Where am I to wear it?" Knowing her mother, Thalia had reason to worry.

Madame Cuthbert bustled in with her array of spangles. The duchess selected a few to enhance the skirt and bodice and one to affix as an accent to the waist of the corset. The seamstress lauded her good taste.

"We are in need of a mask in black satin as well."

"I can recommend a milliner who has a selection for just such occasions as this, your Grace. It is not far."

"Excellent. I leave the gown in your good hands, Madame Cuthbert. Might we have it in a week's time or less? I am unsure when we shall leave for London and do want to take it with us."

"Most assuredly. Your order will take precedence over all others. Your daughter will make an utterly charming lady pirate, especially with her dark curls worn down."

"I believe so. Now to see what colors Krista has chosen."

The duchess approved the girl's choices of primrose, pale pink, lilac, apricot, and light blue. "Of course, we must have an array of white gowns as well and gloves and sashes, all a young lady needs to make her debut."

The wideness of Madame Cuthbert's smile would have cracked her aged face if they had stayed any longer. She escorted them to the door, glanced outside, then pulled back with apparent shock.

"Have you no male escort? A most brutish man stands without. He has the look of a cutpurse."

"Never fear. He is our brute and the earl's new butler." The duchess stepped through the doorway, and Bascom stood at attention. "Come along. We are going to the milliner's and will need you to carry our hat boxes."

Bascom did not flinch nor bat an eye. The duchess considered him. "Yes, you will make a very fine butler. Be grateful the Danelagh livery is black and not puce or orange as some I have seen."

"I am, your Grace, very grateful."

Thalia stifled an unseemly giggle. Bascom fell into step behind the ladies and took up his post outside the next shop.

They found a bonnet with a velvet ribbon and a black plume curling along the brim to replace the plain and unbecoming bucket of a headpiece Krista wore. The duchess bade the milliner to take the old one away to the dustbin, then she inquired about masks. The milliner laid out a selection. For the sheer fun of it, all three ladies tried them on, laughing and giggling at their appearance in the mirror. The duchess insisted Thalia take the black satin with a long feather rising rakishly from the side. She purchased one of pale blue and gold lace for Krista and another made of purple silk with a silver edging for herself, as well as a few extra plumes to adorn the hair. Whose hair she did not say and made Thalia wonder.

Lightly burdened with an empty hatbox and a parcel of feathers and masks, Bascom trailed them to the tearoom where the duchess dismissed him for an hour, telling him to find the coach and bring it forward. Refreshed with tea, small sandwiches, scones, and iced cakes, the merry trio eventually spilled into their vehicle and moved through the narrow, crooked streets of ancient York to a shoemaker Bascom recommended. After Thalia's measurements were taken for black leather boots and several new pairs of slippers ordered for Krista, they piled into the coach again, moved past the King's Fishpond and beyond York's walls to return to Battle Hill.

"Oh! I did forget to purchase a riding crop for Thalia. Bascom, could we have the loan of one?" the duchess asked.

"Certainly, your Grace, but I am in doubt if we have a sidesaddle, since Lady Kristiana does not ride, or a properly gentle mount for a lady."

"Never fear, we need only the whip."

Thalia's dark brows rose. Whatever did her mother consider? A whip but no saddle. Was she to ride bareback?

"And a light sleeping draught. I find I have been restless since the disturbance I witnessed the other night. Honestly, if I do not make a list, the details elude me." The duchess feigned a feebleness her daughter knew to be untrue.

"The village has an apothecary that can provide such on the way home."

Krista's joy over their excursion faded from her face. The duchess was quick to notice.

"What is the matter, child? Did I distress you?"

"I am sorry my antics have caused you unrest."

"Nonsense, women my age often sleep poorly. Anything might be the cause. Tell me, did you enjoy our excursion?"

"I have never had such a jolly time," Krista exclaimed, brightening.

Thalia thought the same but did not voice it. They had certainly put a dent into Godric's fortune, no matter what its amount.

"The first of many is my hope for you," the duchess said.

From his corner, Bascom nodded and offered what passed for his smile.

~ * ~

Godric returned to Battle Hill long before the women. He and the duke shared a pipe, a bit of cheese and crackers, and a good vintage in the library since they need not stick to tea and good manners with the ladies gone. They discussed the Danelagh estate.

"My father lived so frugally and invested so wisely, I find myself left with a very secure fortune. I suppose I must consider a dowry for Krista now. She still seems such a child to me, but Lady Flora insists she must make her debut next year. Is ten thousand pounds too much or too little? My father left her five thousand."

"Ah, daughters do grow up so fast. One minute they are riding on your shoulders, the next they are acquiring the admiration of young men. Mine are to have twenty thousand upon marrying, but that is an extravagant amount insisted on by my wife. She wants each to have enough held in trust for them to live as they wish, and I indulge her. Ten thousand is a handsome amount and should ensure your sister of a wide selection of excellent prospects. I do worry that mine will attract the wrong sort, not a man after my own heart, a strong man who can protect and care for them as I would."

The duke took up his pipe again and exhaled a small cloud into the air between him and Danelagh. He seemed to be waiting for Godric to declare himself by stepping through an opening wide enough to accommodate a coach and four, but got only thanks for his sage advice. He would not be tricked or subtly coerced into making an offer.

Obviously believing he had not put it plain enough, Bellevue asked, "Have you no interest in Thalia? You do not fawn over her like the others...weaklings, all of them."

"I will not say I have no interest, but..."

Bascom loomed in the doorway precluding any more intimate conversation. "The ladies are returned, milord."

"Did they load you up with parcels and make you take tea with nothing to eat but tiny little cakes that barely fill a hand let alone a stomach?" the duke inquired with a chuckle.

"No, your Grace. I was allowed to seek my own sort of refreshment and their parcels were few, but I believe there will be much pick up and pay for in a week's time... gowns, bonnets, shoes and such."

"There goes the family fortune," Godric groaned. If taken on as a wife, would Thalia be extravagant in her demands for luxuries? Yet another aspect of her to consider. Finding a mate, what a conundrum.

"Her Grace did request the loan of a riding crop for Lady Thalia, and I will fetch it for her immediately. We also stopped for a sleeping draught to ease her nights."

"Thalia never rides, and my wife sleeps very soundly. Ah, I see. The duchess can be very playful and inventive. She means to throw me off the track by saying the whip is for Thalia. Of course, I can easily overpower her if I wish, but we will have a bit of sport first. Perhaps, Thalia is the one she means to put to sleep." The duke leaned back and quaffed the last of his wine. "Bring the crop to me, Bascom, and I will deliver it personally."

Godric admitted to being intrigued but had no chance to ask the duke to be more explicit just between the two of them. Bascom returned with alacrity, carrying the desired item.

The duke took the crop and whacked it lightly against his thigh a time or two. "I believe I will rest before supper, Danelagh. I assure you again, for all her polish, Thalia is her mother's daughter." He left them with a huge smile on his broad, bronze face. What exactly did he mean by that? Playful and inventive? Thalia didn't seem so to Godric. Beautiful and strong, yes, but not possessing the other attributes.

"Did you ask his permission to court Lady Thalia?" Bascom pressed. "I cannot see them staying for much more than a week if you do not declare yourself soon. The prize of the season will return to London and all the beaux who await her." He punched the rotten curtain draping a window and it half fell from its moorings. "With twenty thousand pounds you could refurbish every drapery in the house."

"No, I did not. If only I could be sure she does take after her mother, but Thalia knows I seek passion in a woman. She is highly intelligent and could be feigning her emotions to entrap me," Godric answered.

"He who hesitates is lost...strike while the iron is hot," Bascom quoted.

"Do not spout maxims at me! I must make up my own mind on this and will not be hurried."

"As you wish, milord. But mark my words you have no more than a week or so at your disposal."

~ * ~

The duke took the stairs to his wife's bedchamber two at time. He noted Thalia's skirts just disappearing into her own room as he arrived. Excellent. Her door wide open, Flora sat removing her hat before the mirror on the dressing table.

"I brought the riding crop you requested." He laid it across his wide palm and held it out to her. "May I ask why you want it?"

"For Thalia. I think Godric might prefer a woman who rides. I also ordered boots for her." She did not meet her husband's eyes, but busied herself with fluffing her curls.

"Truly? You want it for no other purpose. I am disappointed."

With a coy smile and a light in her eyes, the duchess said, "If I intended other uses, I would use your own." She opened a small package, took out the purple half-mask, and held it up to her face. "What do you think?"

"Let me tie it for you, and I can give a better opinion."

She stood and offered the mask. He handed her the crop, but instead of going behind his wife to tie the ribbons, he pressed close to her body and did the service from the front. The duchess delivered a smart slap of the whip to her husband's buttocks. "Naughty," she said.

"I see I must disarm you and give you a spanking for that," he answered. And the chase was on around the room with a chair overturned and a scramble across the bed as Lady Flora, laughing, defended herself with an occasional snap of the whip. On the second pass, the duke kicked the door entirely shut with one mighty blow from his boot.

It slammed in Thalia's face as she came to retrieve her own mask and question what her mother intended her to do with a scandalous costume and a riding crop. The little she viewed before the door shut gave her some idea. Oh, surely not!

Ten

The following week passed pleasantly and productively with the duchess interviewing cooks and chefs and the girls making excursions to York Castle and the great Gothic cathedral in the center of the city. They explored the narrow Snickelways between the old half-timbered houses with the duke and Godric going before and after them. Having traveled so very little other than to London and Scotland, Thalia enjoyed the excursions and felt perfectly safe with her stalwart escorts. Often, she dreamed of going to foreign places, but only men were allowed the Grand Tour. Oh, for the canals of Venice, the plains of Spain which Godric had seen, or even his favorite, the dark walls of Heidelburg. Would he allow his wife to accompany him on his journeys or expect her to wait at Battle Hill working on her sewing?

By week's end, the duchess was free to join them in retrieving their purchases from the shoemaker and Madame Cuthbert. She had hired a man certainly too young to have been a head chef in any noble French household, but possibly an underling who had honed his skills in several great houses since coming to England and now looked to getting his own kitchen. He accepted the position with great French flair and went on to demand an instant doubling or more of the kitchen staff and a considerably larger budget for the purchase of provisions.

At the last, Mrs. Gunderson, having nowhere else to go, proved reluctant to leave. The duchess kept her on at half-pension to make the bread, buns, and Yorkshire pudding at which she excelled. Upon their return from York, the new chef would serve his first dinner, a grand occasion. That caused almost as much excitement as their exploration of the castle. Thalia certainly looked forward to more elegant fare like that served at Bellevue Hall.

The ladies stopped first at the shoemaker where Thalia tried her high-heeled boots until they felt comfortable enough and Krista exclaimed over having so many pairs of slippers and their great variety. At Madame Cuthbert's, the so-called lady pirate's costume had been completed as well as a few of Krista new gowns. As a small coterie of seamstresses helped Krista into dress after dress to make sure all fit well, the duchess led her daughter aside to another fitting room for the display of the black costume.

"My, my, it has been some years since I've seen a ladies' waist. You do look splendid, Thalia," her mother declared.

Thalia had her doubts. "Mama, I feel naked. I cannot go out in public this way." She turned this way and that, considering herself in the several mirrors lining the room. The tall, black boots came up to her knees and met the triple layer of filmy gauze cut with points along the hem. Small spangles peeped out of its folds and glittered as she turned and the larger one accented one side of her slim corseted waist. Sufficient black gauze filled the bodice to give only a hint of what lay beneath. Both her shoulders and arms remained bare.

"We will get some long, black gloves to give you more coverage if you insist. Remember, we expect this outfit to bring a certain young man to his knees."

With shock at her immodesty, Thalia supposed. Could she possibly wear this outrageous garment in public even if masked? She'd be ruined.

"Lord Danelagh?" Madame Cuthbert questioned, inquisitive nose twitching.

"I believe this would work on any man," the duchess replied, giving nothing away. "Wrap it up for us and Krista's gowns as well. We want to keep the element of surprise."

Krista balked about not wearing one of her new gowns home, but the duchess persuaded her to wait and show herself at dinner after her very own maid arranged Krista's hair more becomingly. After a stop at the glover's shop, they returned to Battle Hill to prepare for what the duchess declared would be an extraordinary evening. Thalia hoped that did not mean disastrous.

~ * ~

Thalia watched Krista's transformation as Lady Flora's very adept maid combed out her heavy braids and snipped a long fringe around her face, then applied the heated iron to make curls where none had been before. The rest the hairdresser lifted, coiled, tucked, pinned, and threaded with black ribbons until the young woman resembled a delightful confection rather than a dowdy girl.

Madame Cuthbert truly knew her business and made Thalia wish she had ordered more frocks of her own instead of the questionable black gauze. When her new gown with the wide satin sash was tied into place, Krista herself seemed amazed with the results. While the cut of the bodice with its edging of dark lace showed off her milky white bosom, it also minimized the breadth of her shoulders. She fingered the locket at her throat and murmured, "I wish Hugh could see me now." Thalia squeezed her shoulder in unspoken sympathy.

As they joined the gentlemen in the drawing room, Godric's eyes widened when he saw his sister's transformation, and he offered his first real smile, but not to Thalia. It shone wide and very white and abolished the scar alongside his face with its folds, but it was not for her. She'd worn the very becoming jonquil-colored frock he'd seemed to admire in London. She should have gotten a new gown instead of that absurd costume. She felt like the plain

Yorkshire pudding sitting next to the prime roast of beef as he held out his hands and beamed at Krista.

"You truly are a beautiful young lady and not a little girl anymore, my dear sister." He clasped Krista's hands and kissed her cheek. Krista answered him back with such a very similar smile it left no doubt they were kin.

Thalia was happy for the girl, truly she was. She greatly hoped her disappointment in not gaining any similar compliment did not show on her own face. They went into dinner with Godric escorting her mother and her father taking Krista's arm while she walked behind like the last gosling in the gaggle. At table, Godric continued to gaze at his sister and marvel. He had thanks enough and compliments for her mother, but none for her.

At least all the courses came well-sauced and Mrs. Gunderson, feeling the competition, had outdone herself with the lightness of her rolls and the variety of pies and tarts coming at the end of the meal. After the first satisfactory meal since their arrival, the rest of the night proceeded as usual with Thalia performing on the guitar and singing. While Godric did not issue any compliments, he did not disparage either, a very nice change. Afterward, she gave Krista another lesson, and her brother promised to buy a guitar forthwith. All in all, they passed a very pleasant evening, leaving Thalia to wonder when or if it would ever become as extraordinary as her mother had promised.

Abruptly, Lady Flora arose, pulling everyone else from their seats as courtesy demanded. "Ladies, I believe we should retire. We have had a long and eventful day."

"Oh," said Krista. "The hour is early. I had hoped to stay up longer."

"Beauty rest," the duchess explained. "We must keep our glow and long hours take their toll. Come, come."

Something strange but certainly nothing extraordinary in this, Thalia believed. Her mother could stay up with the best and generally made up for that with late mornings. She tested by saying, "I believe I will sit with Papa a bit longer."

"Thalia, you are already nineteen and need your beauty rest even more than Krista."

Godric smirked and Thalia frowned. What did Mama mean, insulting her like that?

"Frowning causes wrinkles, Thalia. Come along. Shall I send Bascom in with some brandy for you and Godric, my dear?" the duchess queried her husband.

"I should like that, but I will not be long to bed myself," he answered. Anticipation seemed to tinge her father's words.

Shooing the girls ahead with their candles, the duchess issued the order for a nightcap for the gentlemen to Bascom, uncomfortable in his new livery and wig. She went a few steps up the stairs and waited for the man to pass with his tray, then followed on his heels into the drawing room. Thalia turned from her path and trailed that of her mother while Krista went obediently onward. The duchess had never been a woman to wait on her husband hand and foot. She had servants for that. Thalia wondered what she truly intended. She lurked just outside the door to find out, spying as her mother had been wont to do as a child.

The duchess went into her act. "Silly me. I forgot my fan. I become addled with age. Here, allow me to pour, Bascom. I do know exactly how much my husband wants. You are dismissed."

The duchess turned to the tray resting on the table where she had left her fan. She tipped the sleeping draught concealed in her sleeve into the bottle, poured, and swirled the brandy around in each glass before delivering them to the two men already deep in a discussion about the Americans and their challenge to the Barbary pirates.

"I admire their refusal to buy the beggars off as the rest of us do. We should be fighting these corsairs as well," the duke said as he accepted his drink.

"I agree. The Bashaw of Tripoli is a greedy bastard," Danelagh countered.

"What would be your strategy to deal with them?"

Knowing the duchess would stay and express opinions of her own on the bashaw and what should be done about him, Thalia stole away on silent feet before her mother left the men to their conversation. She gained her chamber with just enough time in order for her maid to help her disrobe and take down her hair before her mother appeared.

"You may go, Balfour."

Were they to have another long discussion over the brushing of hair again, Thalia wondered? But, no. Her mother took over briskly, "Out of your undergarments and into your costume, Thalia. I will lace you up."

"No undergarments? But Mama, I had them on at Madame Cuthbert's."

"No use for them now. Don't be modest. My, how I wish my body were still so firm, my breasts so high without a device to hold them up." The duchess sighed wistfully.

Thalia stepped into the costume and turned to allow her mother to do up the laces. Unaccustomed to being bound, she winced as she said, "You are still a beauty, and always will be in father's eyes."

"That is what I wish for you, Thalia dear. Eternal love."

"Not with Godric Erikson. We are going to punish him for his insults!"

"Of course. Now the boots."

She sat and drew them on with some effort. Lady Flora handed her the riding crop. Thalia held it limply at the end of one hand.

"No, no, no. Wield the whip as if you mean it. Stride to the bed and give the mattress a few whacks."

Putting her back into it, Thalia complied.

"Very good. Now, you need not worry about hurting Godric. He and your father are large men. The sting is no more to them than it is to a war horse. It merely gets their attention and spurs them on. But, don't go near the privates. We wouldn't want any injuries there."

Aghast, Thalia said, "His privates? I should not be viewing his privates. What if someone should find out and tell?"

"You did say you were willing to set propriety aside in this venture. Never fear. No one will bother you. The servants are abed, and I've put my sleeping draughts in the brandy. I thought it best to double the dose as I am quite petite compared to them. Still, we don't want the men to sleep all night, just a brief time."

"You drugged Papa as well?"

The duchess took up the hairbrush and stroked Thalia's dark curls around her shoulders. "Liberal as your father is, he can be very protective of his daughters. Much as he likes Godric, he might not approve of my scheme. Best he never knows of it. Now put on the mask. Oh stunning!" She busied herself affixing another black plume in her daughter's hair. "Shall we add another? No, I think I will keep this one for myself. Now look at yourself in the mirror."

"Mama! You can almost see some of the most intimate parts of my anatomy."

"Yes, but Lord Danelagh will not be able to get at them because he will be chained naked to the wall of the dungeon so you need not fear as long as you do not release him."

"I am to torture him in his own dungeon—naked?" Glad she sat at the dressing table again because her knees had gone weak, Thalia found she had second thoughts. True, she wanted Godric to regret his treatment, but surely snubbing him might do that. However, she had assured her mother she could set aside all propriety, and Longleighs did not back down from a challenge. They overcame them. She'd learned that from both parents. To waver now would be to show herself a weakling. She stiffened her spine. Godric would, after all, be chained and at her mercy. She did enjoy that idea no matter now shocking her mother's scheme to bring him to heel.

"Only in a manner of speaking. Once he comes to, you torment him a bit with the crop, then you remove the feather from your hair and slowly, slowly, draw it over every part of his anatomy—his ears and lips, his chest and nipples, between his thighs and over his genitals until he is a quivering mass of desire. Do you think you can do that, confront a naked man so?"

Thalia flailed the whip in her agitation. "I've seen my little brothers naked. That is not what bothers me. Exactly what is the end result of all this?"

"Believe me, daughter, grown men and little boys are nothing the same. The result we desire is to make Godric lose all control, to want badly what he cannot have. This will do the trick, I assure you. After all, he values surprise. Now he gets it."

"If he should repeat this to others, brag at his club…"

"Not Danelagh. He would never admit to being captured by a woman and tormented. Besides, he is far too much the gentleman to tell. Are we ready to go, then? Cover yourself with your dark cloak in case we should come across anyone in the halls."

Thalia complied and followed her mother back to the drawing room where they found her father snoring gently and Godric in a light sleep. "Let your father be and lift Danelagh by the shoulders. I shall take his feet," the duchess ordered.

They struggled getting the large man out the door and through the dining room to the long, unfurnished chamber at the rear of the house. Once a ballroom, Krista had told them, but now recently only used to drill her father's footmen in military formations on days of inclement weather.

"A moment," the duchess asked, clearly winded.

"He certainly is heavier than I thought," Thalia said.

"All muscle like your father. I do wish they had ended the evening in the library. It is closer to the dungeon door. Give me a moment." Lady Flora raised her eyes to the chandeliers with their stubs of candles as she thought.

Moonlight filtered in from the courtyard windows and washed across Godric's strong, pale face in repose. Thalia studied him—Cupid, Apollo—no, some scarred Norse god fallen to earth. How could she possibly overcome him with a feather? The sound of ripping scattered her thoughts. Her mother laid out a piece of moth-eaten vermilion curtain on the floor.

"Help me roll him onto it, Thalia."

She did. "Now what?"

"We drag him along as I sometimes transported things on old deer hides when among the Shawnee. Easier than carrying."

"Just what do we do when we get to the dungeon steps?"

"Why, one of us will go ahead with the lanterns, and the other will give him a mighty shove and propel him down the stairs on the curtain. I think you had best do the shoving. I will attempt to stop him at the base. That's our plan then."

She took up one corner of the drapery and Thalia took the other. The floor being well-waxed, they made fairly good progress and approached the dungeon door. Ceasing their exertions, Lady Flora worked the large key to open it. "Drat, we need a candle to light the lanterns. Daughter, go back for one and allow me to rest."

Thalia turned to go and ran straight into a dark, massive form. She stifled a scream with a hand to her mouth. Papa? No. Bascom. The butler opened the shutter on a dark lantern he held and the light burst out upon the scene. Thalia imagined what the man must think of two women, one in outlandish dress revealed by the opening of her cloak, and a man unconscious at their feet before the open maw of the dungeon. He'd do his duty to rescue his master and tell Godric of it in the morning. Danelagh would oh so coldly ask them to leave. Their scheme was foiled.

"Will this be of use to you, your Grace?" He offered the light. "I was making my nightly rounds, making sure the footman on duty at the door did not sleep and no servants were engaging in improper activities when I heard female voices near the men's staircase and came to investigate."

Secure in her authority, the duchess answered, "Yes, it will help. Light the other lanterns for us." She offered no explanation to the servant. Thalia admired that.

As he did so, he regarded his master asleep on a red curtain at their feet. "Might I ask what you are doing with Lord Danelagh?"

"We understand he likes the unexpected, and we are doing our best to provide it. By morning, I suspect he will offer for Thalia's hand in marriage."

"Ah!" Bascom nodded. He had left off his wig and the light glimmered on his bald head. "I have been urging him to do so for some time. He can be stubborn. Might I assist you in any way?"

"Would you help carry him down the stairs? Then, we must strip him and put him in the manacles on the wall."

"When my lord awakes, he will be very surprised indeed." Bascom squatted. A faint tearing sound occurred as his tight satin breeches split. He ignored the mishap and raised his master across his massive shoulders. With Lady Flora leading the way, they made the descent beneath Battle Hill. The ladies hung their lanterns on hooks on either side of the chains where they proposed to imprison Lord Danelagh.

"Now to strip him down. Bascom, will you assist?'

"In the presence of Lady Thalia?" he questioned.

"Right. Dear child, your presence discommodes Bascom. Please step back into the cells and when we finish, you and I shall have a little talk. From there, you will be on your own."

"As I said, I've seen my baby brothers *au naturel* many times when they escaped from the nursery and ran through Bellevue Hall. Papa seemed to think it a grand joke when he chased after them and carried them back without a bit of punishment. Miss Thurgood said they would turn out poorly."

The duchess sighed deeply. "Not now, Thalia. Please forget all Miss Thurgood ever taught you and listen to me. Go to the cells and wait until I call."

Reluctantly, Thalia entered the darkness through the next great door, but did not close it. Intrigued, she might at least listen to their preparations.

"Do you require my assistance with his boots?" the duchess asked.

Bascom's basso voice answered. "I have done this many times. Allow me to proceed."

"Is he a tippler, then?'

"No more than most young men who must test their ability to hold their liquor. Generally, he dislikes losing control of his faculties as it interferes with his prowess. I meant I disrobe him nightly and prefer to proceed in a certain way."

"Hurry, Bascom, into the chains with him," came her mother's urgent voice. "He is shivering and will wake."

Thalia heard the grate of iron as the rusty manacles fell open and then, the loud metallic snap as they closed again. They'd done it—subdued Lord Danelagh!

"Bascom, you may go to the top of the stairs now. I assure you your master will come to no real harm. If I could have your assistance in getting the duke to his bed first, you may return and wait until Thalia calls for you to take him down. I do not think he will feel the cold once she starts, but none of us wants him to take a chill. And, as you have torn your new livery in our service, bring it to me tomorrow, and I shall mend it personally. Go. I must speak to my daughter a moment."

Bascom trudged heavy-footed up the dungeon stairs. Once gone, Lady Flora stepped into the cellblock and nearly collided with her daughter who stood at the very edge of the lantern light from the other room.

Thalia observed Danelagh's garments neatly folded and his boots side by side under the stretching rack, which was covered with the red cloth as if set for fine dining. She purposely kept her eyes averted from the main dish hanging on the wall behind her as she stepped into the torture chamber.

"Really, I should be doing this on the night before your wedding, but this occasion calls for more information immediately. Just an item or two that I omitted," her mother schooled. "You see when a man becomes aroused, well, the result is most impressive, and I must say Godric Erickson is a very fine specimen of his sex. If a male remains in that state of excitement for some time, he will—ah—erupt, spill his seed in a most dramatic way. Do not be startled. This is perfectly natural. He remains unharmed, very relieved, but unharmed. He might ask you to free him. He could even beg, but if you do exactly as I say, you will leave here, perhaps no longer an innocent, but still a virgin. Thalia, if you are afraid to do this, say so now and I will call Bascom to take him down and carry him to bed. Danelagh will never know the difference."

Thalia took a deep breath that strained her tight, black corset. "I am a Longleigh and unafraid." She focused entirely on humbling

Godric and paid little attention to anything else. "Do you really think he will beg? I would like that, after all his slights."

"How can I know for certain?" The duchess stood on tiptoe and kissed her daughter's cheek. "Now if you are ready, go surprise and delight Lord Danelagh."

Thalia turned and gasped at the sight of the man, but her mother tossed the keys on the rack and kept going directly up the stairs and out of sight. She leaned back against the rack and studied the naked man before her. With his white-blond hair partly covering his face, Godric's head lolled against his chest. His pale body bore other scars hitherto unseen...thin pink welts, some of them puckered, that he had acquired in living a strenuous life. None repelled her. The honed muscles of his arms stretched taut in the chains. His legs, spread-eagled, were delineated as perfectly as God made Adam and what hung between them—she could not avert her eyes from the sight. A lightly-furred sack held two ballocks so weighty she wanted to cup them in her hands like a purse full of gold. No boyish dangle sat above them. Slightly arched, thick and long, his manhood possessed a delicate pink head. Curiosity made her want to touch. She approached and put out a black-gloved fingertip.

He groaned, and she stepped back, bumping into the rack again. Godric shook his head trying to clear the effect of the sleeping potion and raised it as if his thoughts were very heavy indeed. Thalia retreated farther into the shadows behind the table and waited. His gray eyes opened, blinked. He spoke in a dry voice. "I am locked in my own dungeon—naked. Can anyone tell me how this came about?"

Thalia strode into the light and shed her cloak, letting it slip to the stones like the black chrysalis of an exotic butterfly. She watched as his eyes took in the sight from leather-booted toe to the tip of the plume in her hair. He lingered on the dark patch of curls between her legs and the tops of her dark nipples beneath the gauze. Strange how they hardened beneath his gaze. His penis executed a joyous flip. Immediately, Godric turned his attention to her eyes revealed only by the mask she wore.

"What shall I call you?" he said with an arch smile.

"I told you to call me Tha..."

"No, no. When one wears a mask, the names are always assumed—Brunhilde, Boudicca, or some other nonsense. You are very bad at this, are you not?" Now, his smile mocked her.

Thalia slashed at him with the riding crop and raised a red welt on his ribs. She almost dropped her weapon at the sight, but steadied her voice and replied imperiously, "You may call me Queenie, and I am perfection."

He laughed at her, rich and full. She gave him another blow on the opposite side. He did not allow so much as a wince.

"You can do that all evening long, and I will not cry out nor beg for mercy any more than Godric the Bold, my ancestor, did when he was racked in this very dungeon by his enemy."

"I am surprised your family has no portrayal of that gruesome scene in its gallery."

"Not our finest hour, but he did die bravely. His son returned the favor when he retook the castle. You know, you had better get on with what you intend. Bascom will miss me and come looking."

"Bascom will not be a problem."

"Did you drug him, too?"

Thalia started to say her mother had done the drugging and Bascom aided them, but realized that would make it seem as if she could do nothing for herself. Instead, she drew the feather from her hair, ran it through her fingers, and said solemnly, "Yes. We should begin."

"I am not one who finds pleasure in pain, but know I can withstand any torture you devise."

"Really." She stepped very close, close enough to feel the heat of his body, and ran the edge of the plume around his ear, down the length of his facial scar, and across his lips. They quirked as it passed. The feather continued down the side of his neck.

"Truly, that is all you have, a feather?"

"I want to see you smile. I want to hear you laugh." She continued working the feather around one of his nipples, then the other. They puckered and reddened. Interesting. She gave them another pass, stirring the light patch of hair between them with the tip of the plume.

That part of his anatomy which always betrays the mind began to rise. "You do not move me, Queenie, not at all."

"I believe I do." She glanced down between them and saw what rose against the layers of her gauze skirt as if it wanted to nest there. The head of the serpent was no longer pink but more purple in color. Would it erupt now on her very nice costume?

Thalia stepped back a pace and regarded him with some alarm. Even the scar on his face darkened as it had once before when she played her Spanish song.

"Use your whip, Queenie," he ordered as if he desired pain.

Viewing her rather fine results, she replied, "But I am not finished with the feather."

The plume moved down his centerline, then between his thighs, tickled across his testes, and fluttered up the length of his shaft.

"I say, give me a good thwack with your crop!"

"Are you begging me to strike you? I thought you did not enjoy pain."

"No, I am not begging. If you continue as you are doing, you might not like the result."

"What, the eruption? I am most curious about it. If I continue doing this, will it happen?' She ran the feather around the edge of the engorged head of his organ and peered closer at a droplet forming on its tip. "Is it weeping for me?"

"Yes. Please thrash me. I deserve it for all the times I have insulted your performances, your art, your..."

"What do you think of my performance now, Godric? I am more curious by the minute. I cannot resist the temptation." Thalia peeled off one of her long gloves finger by finger, tossed it aside, and touched the droplet. She rubbed it between her fingertips. "Silken," she said. "As is the tip, and yet the shaft is so hard." She watched a blue vein throb at the base of his erection with fascination and wrapped a hand strengthened by the playing of the pianoforte around his prick.

"Look at me, Queenie!" he demanded.

"I am."

"In the eyes."

She raised them slowly, but did not release her grip. In fact, her thumb fondled the tip making it release more of the lubricant. "So fascinating."

"You must not continue this, or I will embarrass myself."

"I think I should like to see you embarrassed for a change and not me."

"We would both enjoy this more if you released me. I could show you the way it should be between a man and a woman. I could give you pleasure, if only you will let me go."

"A trick. You will push me aside and leave me here looking like an idiot."

The feather left his groin and traveled up his side, deep into his armpit, tickling all the way. His stern lips trembled. He began to laugh, great gusty laughs that had almost the same effect as being whipped. The betrayer between his legs began its descent.

"I like hearing you laugh." Thalia tormented his other side with the feather, and his laughter boomed forth again. "There, I have triumphed over you."

"Not so," he claimed. "I have regained my control."

Her eyes scanned his body. The pleased smile on her red lips faded. "It's gone. What have I done wrong?"

"Nothing that cannot be remedied if you release me and give me release. Queenie, I beg you!"

"You do?" She had achieved all she wanted, but her victory came with unexpected consequences. A warmth grew low in her belly, and her naked thighs slicked with the same sort of moisture he exuded. Beneath her bodice of gauze, her brown nipples puckered much as his had done. She wanted more than his laughter, more than his pleading. She wanted everything he had to give.

Her hands felt for the ring of keys tossed onto the rack by her mother. Their coldness brought her momentarily to her senses. "Mama said I should not release you."

"Do you always do everything your mother tells you? Do you still obey the words of Miss Thurgood? Think for yourself, Queenie. Think what you desire."

"Yes, my desires, no one else's." She knelt and unbound his feet.

Just her proximity made him grow hard again. She stood to free his arms, but in his eagerness, he wrapped both legs around her waist and pulled her close against his erection.

"It's come back to greet you, Queenie. Lift your skirt and feel *my* desire."

She raised the gauzy layers and pressed her softness against his hardness. A throbbing very similar to his took up a rhythm between her legs. She rubbed against him wanting more.

"Wait, we must wait. I should not have done this. Free me entirely."

"I doubt either of us will ever be free again after this night," she said, but did insert the key into the last of the locks.

His legs slammed down and his arms came around her, binding her to him. He backed her against the rack where the red cloth lay neatly draped and lifted her onto the table of torment. Freeing her breasts from their gauzy wrapping, he suckled each distended nipple in turn. Her breathing quickened. He worked below her skirts with his hands and stroked where she throbbed. Moaning, she arched against him. He entered her with one forceful motion. She gave a small cry and bit it back.

Giving her time to adjust to his size, he stroked her breasts and reassured her, "The rest will come easily."

"I am unafraid," she said, but unsteadily.

Placing his thumbs to massage the pink pearl nestled in the dark curls between her legs, he began to move over her, slowly, then faster and faster. She raked his back with the nails of her ungloved hand and beat a rhythm with the crop on his buttocks with the other as if urging him to more speed. Thalia cried out, "Oh God, Oh God!"

"Exactly what I wanted you to call me."

Too far gone for a retort, her muscles began to clench around his cock. He withdrew rapidly and spilled his seed in one hot gush on her tawny thigh. Bowing over her, he rested his head on her breast. Beneath the mask, her eyes had closed. Gradually her breathing slowed. She stroked his white-blond hair and asked, "Why did you withdraw?"

"I would not get you with child." He came to lie beside her and drew the red cloth over them both as the chill of the place began to make itself known. "I will speak to your father in the morning."

Her eyes opened wide. "No! He must not find out what I've done."

"No reason to mention it. He has tried to bring me to the question several times."

"If you are sure I am not with child, I would like to wait a while."

"What?"

She heard the shock in his voice and felt the tensing of his muscles. "Once an engagement is announced, there will be preparations and parties. We will never be left alone to do this again until our wedding night—and I would like to repeat it sooner rather than later."

"You are remarkable." Godric leaned over her to kiss her lips. She'd bitten them again, but he kissed her gently and smoothed them with his tongue. She answered in the same way. A quick study, as she'd said when speaking about music. Tonight, they had outperformed Beethoven with their passion.

"You must continue to feign indifference, and I will continue to show my frustration with you. My parents will want us to spend time together. We can easily elude them."

"Perfection," he said.

"Exactly," she replied.

Thalia raised herself on her elbows. "I should go now."

Godric tenderly wiped her thigh free of his seed with the red cloth and helped straighten her bodice and her skirts. Gallantly, he stood to cover her with the cloak, leaving behind the touch of his lips on her neck. "If I were clothed, I would escort you to your chamber."

"Look beneath the rack."

"Ah, Bascom's work. I would know it anywhere. He colluded with you to bring me here? I wondered how you managed." He began shaking out his garments and dressing.

"He intercepted us and wanted to help for your own good, he thought. Do not punish him."

"I have no intention of that. I might even reward him for forcing the matter. There, do you need my help in walking, Queenie?"

Thalia tossed her black curls. "I am Lady Thalia Longleigh, not some country lass ravished by a cowherd. Of course, I can walk—Rick." She went up the stairs and her black cloak merged with the darkness.

~*~

Godric carefully folded the red cloth holding the proof of his possession in the small, dark stain where she had lain and the stiff splotch where he had wiped his ejaculate. Tucking it under his arm, he took down the lanterns and followed, but not wanting his assistance, she had already gone the length of the old ballroom and turned the corner.

Bascom stepped from his hiding place deep beneath the stairs. "Milord, you are well?'

"Could not be better, old man."

"I was prepared to intervene if necessary but heard only laughter and the sounds of—copulation. Is there to be a wedding?"

"Not immediately, but certainly. What else can I say? She is her mother's daughter."

Eleven

On the way to a late breakfast, Thalia passed Godric dressed for riding. "Good morning," he said with a formal nod. "And also to you," she replied. He glanced about, saw they were unobserved, and gave her the smile she had always wanted from him, the kind that made his scar disappear, solely for her. He moved on, walking in great, free strides. Evidently, men suffered from no soreness between the legs after their exploits. She harbored some tenderness below but would be careful to keep that to herself. Only her mother and a maid occupied the dining room. She raised the lid on a server sitting in warm water.

"Coddled eggs and a sauce to accompany them. Marvelous. I am ravenous this morning."

"Are you?" the duchess said with an undertone of suspicion. "I must say since Mrs. Gunderson is no longer overwhelmed in the kitchen, the toast is not burnt. I heard you speaking to Godric, a very formal exchange considering." Before continuing with the conversation, she sent the maid on an errand for more hot tea and to deliver her compliments to the chef.

"Now that we have some privacy, did you go through with the deed or flee after I left and leave Bascom to free him?"

"Papa, Krista?" Thalia asked, unwilling to say more until she was sure of their whereabouts.

"Your father is meeting Godric in the stables. Later, they plan to drill the footmen and practice their swordsmanship. Those two get along so very well. Since we put Krista to bed early, she is already out and about. Says she will pick some flowers, though where she will find any on this barren hillside, I do not know. The place needs a garden. Now speak before the maid returns." The duchess leaned close to her daughter's seat at the table.

"You should know I would not retreat," she chided her mother. "I made him smile, laugh, stand up and beg."

"Did you bring him to his knees as you wished?"

"Oh, yes." Literally, as he moved over her atop the rack, but she would not divulge it. Now that she had knowledge of a naked man, the two coddled eggs on her plate put her in mind of...never mind. "He wanted to speak to Papa today."

"Good. Now that you have astounded him the question is: Will you have him as a husband or kick him aside as you wanted? Playing the devil's advocate, I'll say you won't find many like him in the ballrooms of London. Once most gentlemen strip off their clothes and the padding that goes with it, they disappoint. Godric and your father are exceptional."

Why that last comment made her blush after all she'd done the night before, Thalia could not precisely say, except that she had no desire to see her father naked. "I asked him to wait while I considered. I have not decided yet what to do with him."

"Excellent! He will never disparage you nor take you for granted again. But don't let him dangle too long. That would be cruel."

Just hearing the word "dangle" increased the color in her cheeks. "When do we return to London? I will decide by then."

"I have determined to promote the upstairs maid to housekeeper. She has been in service here since a child, knows every corner of the place, and is bold enough to keep the other servants under her thumb. She is not afraid of Bascom, who gives even me chills on occasion. In fact, I think she finds him rather attractive. Gracie will do, but I need some time to train her, perhaps two more weeks."

"That should be enough time for me as well." Only two weeks to explore her newfound sensuality. Thalia pierced an egg and let the liquid yellow yolk spurt out across her brown toast.

~ * ~

On the surface, nothing had changed. Godric did not compliment either her accomplishments or her beauty, though he refrained from insults. In turn, Thalia no longer tried to impress him and treated him coolly. Unfortunately, opportunities to escape together were few with Krista trailing Thalia wherever she went and her father occupying so much of Godric's time in arms training. When a message came that Krista's other gowns were ready at the seamstress and she needed to come for a final fitting, Thalia feigned feeling unwell and asked to stay in bed. But how to get rid of Papa? Her mother took care of that all unknowing by insisting he escort her and Krista in order to see some of York before they left. Or did she? The duchess had a very devious mind, she'd learned.

Regardless, Thalia did stay in nightdress lying her bed and sent her maid away in order to have quiet to subdue a raging headache, she claimed. Balfour went to chat with Grace, and finally the carriage and its occupants left for York. She did hope Rick understood what she had contrived. A quiet scratch on her door confirmed they were of one mind.

"Enter." She held her arms wide for him, and he eagerly crossed the chamber, ending his short journey with a passionate kiss.

"Possibly this is the first time a woman has feigned a headache to have intercourse rather than avoid it," he said. "But not here. I want to show you something. Put on your dressing gown and slippers and come with me."

They fled down the corridor of the guest wing toward the last room in the corner of the building. Thalia found herself giggling, something she had always felt beneath her dignity previously. "The locked chamber," she said. "How exciting!"

He turned the key, let her move inside, and quickly closed the door again. Thalia took in the sight of a huge canopied bed draped in light blue brocade and edged in gold fringe. Delicate white furnishings with gilded curlicues adorned the room, really more of a generous suite taking up half the back hallway. This allowed for the inclusion of several large windows offering a view of the distant moors from a sitting area. Thalia peeked into two additional doors at the end of the chamber to find a dressing room and a bathing facility.

"Fit for Madame Pompadour," Thalia proclaimed.

"What I really want you to notice is the bed."

"As if I did not know that."

"We will get to that, but first lie down and move to the center. Look up."

"Oh, my, the Princess Europa being carried off by Zeus in the form of a bull, a very virile but peculiar bull, a yellow hide and a large gray eye."

"To honor Derek Erikson. He kept his mistress here and his wife in the family wing and also put up a thick wall between this suite and the nursery, lest any of his children find their way here." Rick joined her on the bed and slipped an arm around her shoulders. "At night or whenever he cared to, he would slip across the courtyard and come up the backstairs to visit Emmanuelle. I often wondered if they engaged in a *menage a trois* in this enormous bed. It's certainly big enough."

"A *ménage*....?"

"Ah, so you know your Greek myths with all that mayhem and rapine, but not your French frolics."

"We have always been allowed to read freely in the Bellevue library, and I adored the myths. Miss Thurgood did not approve. 'A true lady confines her reading to the Bible and books that edify and elevate the mind,' she would say, but she could not override Mama in this. I suspect my scurrilous little sister, Pandora, has already discovered the Greek stories, and she is only approaching nine. But back to the *ménage*, are you going to tell me?"

"Two women and a man, likely the case here, or two men and a woman, but I do not plan to share you with anyone at any time." Rick kissed her forehead. "I do love educating you, but I will admit your tickle torture was new to me."

"Mama suggested it as being harmless but very effective."

"Extraordinary, your mother, as are you. Do you see your resemblance to Europa, the ebony curls and large dark eyes, the voluptuous body? I suspect Emmanuelle posed for it, and you are she incarnate."

"How do you know? You have never seen me as unclothed as Europa."

"I am about to." He opened her dressing gown and removed her nightdress over her head.

Thalia resisted the urge to cover her privates like pictures of Eve, always shown with an arm over her breasts and one white hand splaying across her pubis if she lacked a fig leaf. She knew herself to be no pale, blonde Eve but a darker sister, a Lilith, Adam's first wife. Her breasts were full, her limbs long and perfect, her tawny complexion flawless, her curls dark above and below. But what would he think, he who had been so critical of her earlier? She bit her lip and turned her head to one side.

Light flooded the room from those tall windows. No wonder sexual activities usually took place at night under a layer of covers where flaws went unnoticed. Doing it here in broad daylight began to seem the epitome of improper. She started to say so, but her glance settled on a small bouquet of fresh flowers in a green vase atop one of the spindly tables near the bed.

"Jonquils," she said. "Did you put them here?"

"Yes. Krista brought a huge bouquet home from some glade she frequented with Hugh Grey when both were children. I hope they never went there recently. I did handle their affection for each other badly, but I could not think what else to do. They are too young. We were speaking of jonquils. I purloined a few from the arrangement in her chamber. They are lovely, but no more than yours.

He kissed both breasts and suckled her brown nipples. She forgot her self-consciousness and wrapped her arms about him. Without thinking, she raised her arms to stroke his back and her long legs came up around his hips, sealing him against her pelvis.

"Unfair that you are still clothed," she breathed.

"You have made a study of every inch of me already."

He rolled aside to begin that wondrous finger play between her legs. Before she gave herself over to him completely, she said, "Despite your flaws, I found you perfect."

He brought her to ecstasy so quickly and completely, she mourned that it had not taken longer.

"Allow me to disrobe, and we will go at it again, my dearest Thalia." She did not object in the least.

No servant stood nearby to fold his clothes into tidy bundles. They flew across the dainty chairs and fell by the wayside. He cursed at the difficulty of removing his boots, but at last came to her erect and ready to begin the dance of love anew with the same splendid result. Again, he withdrew quickly, soiling the spread beneath them at the last moment for her safety. As Thalia lay in his arms, an alarming thought occurred to her.

"The servants will know from the stain we've been in here."

"Only Gracie might suspect as she cares for this unused chamber like all the others, but I will turn the suspicion on your parents. I overheard her telling another maid that their bedclothes are always in great disarray, and she found a black plume deep within the covers. I'll tell her I lent them the key and that as the new housekeeper, she must learn complete discretion."

"Plausible. They would enjoy a romp here."

"Probably in the dungeon, too."

"My parents' antics have always been an embarrassment to me, to all of their children, but now I've come to appreciate them. Do you think your father and his wife ever used this chamber?"

"Never. He showed it to me as an example of the wickedness and temptation I might encounter when abroad and to beware of such places. I believe his true match might have been Miss Thurgood. Had he lived earlier, I am certain he would have sided with the Puritans. His father, a boy dwelling on the other side of that thick wall in the nursery, told him the scandalous tales as a moral lesson. He took them to heart."

"And you did not. Thank heaven!"

"A son does not want to be too much like his father. We should go soon, but stay there for a moment just as you are."

Godric rose and went into the bathing chamber. He returned with a cool, damp cloth scented with lemon and cleansed between her thighs. Thalia began to arch again, and he brought her along with two of his fingers substituting for his organ before he finished this task.

"Is this unusual, three times in one afternoon?" she asked with wonder.

"I suspect not for the Longleigh women, but it often depends on the patience and generosity of the man."

"Then, you are very patient and very generous."

"I am glad you think so." His erection poking him in the belly, he leaned over her for a kiss. She would have taken him inside again, but he stopped her. "Use your hand, and we will have less washing to do."

She played her hand up and down his shaft and teased its flushed cap as she'd done in the dungeon. He wasn't tardy in taking his enjoyment.

"Another way we can pleasure each other without your catching." he said.

"I want you to show me all the ways."

"Another cleanup and then we must stop this for today. I believe I will press Krista for the location of the jonquil glade, and I think the Roman tower is another possibility. My father had a door that can be bolted set into it in case Napoleon surges across the channel and lands in York someday. A lookout is to raise a red flag if he does. For the time being, I am leaving it unmanned."

"Is there a bed?'

"No, but you want me to show you all the ways. Up, up, and away to your chamber."

Rick checked the hallway for roving servants while she washed at the basin and sent her scurrying with a light swat on her hind cheeks.

~ * ~

Still a bit guilty about feigning illness, especially when Krista brought her an embroidered cushion filled with lavender from York to soothe her headache, Thalia did not want to use that excuse again anytime soon. She also observed as the girl sat by her bedside and inquired about her health that Krista had left off wearing her locket and instead had an onyx pendant, a gift from Lady Flora, in its place against her milky skin.

She squeezed Krista's hand and asked, "My mother noticed the second lock of hair?"

The girl nodded. "Yes. She said men are not as observant about such matters, but she thought I should put the locket away in case my brother noticed and took it from me. She said I should cherish it always as a first love is a special gift. Hugh took a terrible chance leaving the token for me. He knew I often took comfort in looking through my mother's possessions and left it for me inside the elephant box, so for once, I did find a treasure there—and a tiny note saying, *Remember me, H.* If Rick had found him prowling the family wing, he would surely have killed him."

"You *should* cherish it. Your brother mentioned that you also went to a secret place where jonquils bloom in the spring and said he hoped Hugh had not taken any advantage of you there." Deviousness truly did make Thalia's head pound now as well as her pulse. Whatever would Miss Thurgood have said?

"Oh, he never did. We found a tumbled down cottage when we were children out wandering and sought shelter from the rain. Once, its walkway must have been edged with jonquils. The rains over the years washed the seeds and bulbs downhill toward a little stream. It's a lovely sight right now. I would like to show it to you."

"I am sure to feel better by tomorrow. Let's walk there. The exercise will do me good. But for tonight, I believe I will take supper in bed to ensure my full recovery." And to keep her eyes from glancing at Rick's at the dinner table and giving their secret away.

~ * ~

Thalia and Krista set off soon after breakfast and took with them a basket of ham sandwiches, apples, cheese, biscuits, and a corked bottle of lemonade they could cool in the stream. They walked down the treeless hill and followed the road aways until they came to a brook running merrily downhill to join the River Ouse. From there following the stream upward, the way became more difficult with the faint path obscured by brush that caught at their skirts and filled with stones that bruised their feet. Two less sturdy young women would have given up long before they reached their destination.

In the end, their reward came when they found the glade in a notch of the wooded hillside. Truly the kind of paradise Thalia sought for herself and Godric. Its carpet of golden jonquils unfolded at their feet and filled the air with a strong perfume. They sat by the brook to eat their picnic, took off shoes and stockings, and soothed their feet in the cold, running water. Once done, they walked up to the old cottage with its stone walls broken and its thatched roof half-fallen, moving carefully so as not to crush the blossoms. Taking in the view of the vale below, Thalia said without thinking, "A magnificent place for a tryst."

This brought the scarlet to Krista's cheeks. "I lied. Hugh and I did more than pick posies here. We held hands—and we kissed very passionately. Am I ruined, Thalia? You are all a young lady should be. Please tell me."

"I cannot judge you, Krista, but your secret is safe with me. If no one knows, then how can you be ruined?"

"How I wish I'd had a sister like you to guide me, a mother like yours to give me advice."

"My own sisters do not hold me in such high regard, and only now am I coming to appreciate my mother. Let's pick a bouquet for her before starting back."

They filled their basket with the yellow narcissus, laying a damp cloth from their luncheon over the sappy stems to preserve them, and turned for home before the sun sank too low. Tired but bright-cheeked from the spring breeze and the exertion, the young women returned before anyone worried after them. Godric, coming suddenly out of the Roman tower, greeted them half way up the hill and walked along the rest of the distance.

Thalia reached into their basket and removed the two most perfect flowers. "Here, I know you admire jonquils, and I've found where they bloom in abundance."

He broke off the stems short and thrust them in a buttonhole of his jacket. The duchess appeared in the doorway, and Krista raced away to present her gift of flowers.

"Is it far off?"

"Unfortunately, yes, and too arduous a path to take horses."

"Then the tower must do. When can you meet me?"

"Tomorrow when everyone else rests before the evening meal."

The duke came to stand beside his wife who admired the basket of posies. He frowned at the blossoms in Godric's buttonhole and said sadly as if he'd lost a warrior in battle, "Wearing flowers like some tulip of the ton are we, my boy?"

"A gift from your daughter, Bellevue. She observed that I admired jonquils, and I do. They are beautiful, delicate, have a stirring aroma, and yet are able to flourish in the wild."

"What we do to please women. Just don't go overboard."

The duchess raised her eyebrows at her husband, a sure sign she'd heard that comment. The company went inside to take their rest before the evening meal. The hours churned away slowly until the same time the next day and offered only one amusing anecdote for Thalia to share with Rick. She'd overheard the new upstairs maid complain of the sticky mess in the duke's chamber where evidently the bedclothes had been strewn with heavily with jonquils crushed deeply into the sheets.

"Mama's revenge for Papa's comment about overindulging women, I am sure," she told him.

"I would roll in jonquils for you," Rick said as he took her into his arms. "I've been waiting an hour."

"I had to be sure my parents had ceased playing and moved on to a nap. What, no pallet? I thought you might have brought one here yesterday to accommodate us."

"There are other ways of making love than horizontally, and happily, you are a tall woman, my dearest Queenie."

He backed her against the rough wall, but prepared her with stroking and kisses before raising her skirts and finding the slit in her undergarments. He pressed himself hard against her while unbuttoning his trousers. She responded to his urgency untutored by wrapping her legs about his waist. When his flap opened and his erection sprang free, she rode upon it as he held her hips in his large hands. Fast, furious, and much too quickly, he had to withdraw and set her down, almost having to pry her legs from his backside and her grip from his shoulders.

"Why, why, why?" she asked.

"Because with discipline, forbearance, and imagination, we can do this quite a long time without endangering you. Recall, my own mother died in childbed."

"I understand, but I find compliance harder."

"No harder than I."

"So I see." She finished him off with a few strong stokes of her fingers and a care not to soil her gown. "I begin to understand why my parents seek out various places to meet. It does add zest to the game."

"Not a game, Thalia." Rick buried his white head in her curls and spoke into her ear. "*Ich liebe dich*, Queenie."

"I have no German. You must translate for me."

"You must divine my meaning."

"No. Repeat it for me again. If you won't cooperate, I shall ask my mother."

"If you remember the phrase."

He distracted her with his lips and fingers, bringing her to completion again. They sank to the cool, stone floor of the tower, and he held her close for a while. Though Thalia rested against his chest with the scarred cheek laid against her dark curls, she repeated the phrase *Ich liebe dich* over and over in her mind. She thought she understood its meaning, but wished him to say the words in good, plain English.

~ * ~

Tiptoeing past the chambers where her parents rested, she wasn't sure in which bedroom, Thalia went to her own and washed before calling her maid to help her dress for dinner. Balfour made no comment about the wrinkled condition of her gown or the disarray of her hair and yet still she felt compelled offer an explanation.

"I went for a walk instead of napping. The wind proved rather strong and I sat a while on the grass."

"I hope you enjoyed your outing, Lady Thalia."

She had to agree with her mother's preference for English maids over what Lady Flora referred to as devious, gossipy, flirtatious Frenchwomen for their complete British aplomb. Once prepared for the evening, she tapped on her mother's door, knowing her father would have gone to his own chamber by then as was their custom.

"Enter."

Lady Flora's maid struggled to rearrange the considerable tangles in her mistress's fair curls. Her own hadn't been nearly so bad, but then her parents had no reason to be cautious.

"The jonquils were a poor idea. I believe some of the sap has gotten into my hair and now it shall have to be washed, so risky in the early spring," the duchess muttered. "That's why rose petals are much better."

Thalia took a seat near the dressing table. "Are you giving me more advice, Mama?"

"Take it any way you like. You are here for a reason or you would already have gone down to sit with Krista. Speak up."

"It's a matter of asking for your help in translation. Godric said something to me in German and refused to tell me its meaning. I suspect it might have been very vulgar."

"Tell me."

"The phrase started with Ick and ended with..." No matter how imperfect she had become in the last week, Thalia could not quite bring herself to say the word aloud in the hearing of a maid, no matter how discreet. She cupped her hands and whispered in her mother's ear, "Dick."

Lady Flora's laughter trilled like lark on a sunny morning. "Thalia, *dich* is the German word for you, and *Ich* means I. Now if only you could remember the verb in the middle."

"It started with an L. He would not repeat it for me."

"Ah! Your father speaks only English, French, and Shawnee, but even he understands that when I say *Ich liebe dich* it means I love you." The duchess waved her maid aside and stood to embrace her daughter. "Godric has declared his feelings for you! He is truly at your feet. Will you accept him or deny him?"

Thalia doubted if she could deny Rick anything he suggested she'd grown so wanton, and yet he had not proposed to her in proper English. How easily he could use her and cast her aside. She would have no recourse unless she told her father who would then either force him into a marriage or kill him, whichever seemed best. The duke liked Danelagh, so probably the former, but did she want the man on those terms?

"I simply do not know, Mama."

"I sensed your anger with him weakening. He might be the right husband for you after all. Consider this carefully."

"What if—what if I wanted to do something else before I marry?"

"Such as?"

"Go to Italy and perfect my singing, a desire I have harbored for a long time. Papa would never allow me."

"You want to see more of the world. You want an adventure. I entirely understand that and so should he. Women's lives are so constrained after marriage and once the children start arriving there is little else for most. I will speak to your father. It might be arranged."

"Truly? I never thought so."

"Give me some time to bring him around, but in the meantime, if you showed some favor to Danelagh instead of your usual coolness, it would not go amiss with your father."

Lady Flora seated herself and turned once more to her mirror. "Oh, let's simply cover my hair with a turban. We will wash it when the weather warms. Jonquils, never again!"

~ * ~

That evening, Thalia played the Spanish song she now knew had aroused Rick the first time she'd performed it. Innocent then, she had not recognized the signs. This time, she sang it and gazed directly at his face. His scar darkened as did the gray of his eyes, and she knew he wanted her. Afterward, he made no pretense of indifference but came to take her hand and tell her of a town in Spain the song recalled to memory. The night being clement, he offered his arm for a stroll in the courtyard. The duke and duchess and Krista followed behind, but not too closely.

Thalia tilted her head toward Godric's shoulder and said quietly, "If we went on horseback to the base of the hill, the distance to the place of the jonquils would not be so difficult to attain. Not having ridden since childhood, I am not the most expert rider, but could manage with a gentle mount."

"I cannot believe you are not the best at everything, but if I have to go into York and purchase a mare and a sidesaddle, I will do it tomorrow!"

"Papa, would you mind if Godric gave me some riding lessons?" she said more loudly.

"Not at all. I have always felt you should show more interest in riding. Excellent exercise."

Excited, Krista spoke up. "Me, too! I want to learn to ride."

Exasperated, her brother answered, "I plan to purchase only one horse fit for a lady. It shall be yours after Lady Thalia leaves and not before."

"Of course! I do not mind sharing."

"Well, I do," he grumbled too faintly for his sister to hear.

Twelve

He'd been a fool about the horse. On the advice of his stable master, Godric sought out an Irish horse trader operating farther up the vale—as if the Irish or a horse trader could ever be trusted—and gone alone. The duke's advice would have been valuable, but somehow, he wanted this animal to be his decision alone. The dealer in horse flesh trotted one plodding hack after another before him. He recognized those too long in the tooth and rejected others whose confirmation promised to give future problems. A tall, rangy white gelding with a pink nose and eyes, but not an ounce of spirit would have done for Krista, but not his magnificent Thalia.

"I see nothing here fit for the lady I have in mind."

The Irishman's blue eyes sparkled. "Would ye be lookin' for a mount fit for a countess, then? I might have just the creature placed here on consignment from a grand lady fallen on hard times. The animal has been very lightly used, docile as they come, more a pet than a horse, really. Her name is Dark Fire."

The trader had him at the name. Dark Fire described all Thalia was. She must have a mount to match. The Irishman led out the horse he had held back all this time. The mare stood high, proud, and black as sin with a long, rippling mane and tail, Thalia in another form. He pulled himself together enough to ask that the horse be saddled. He put her through her paces and found her mouth to be tender, her gait smooth but lively, and her responses instant. How like Thalia.

The dealer named his price, enough to make all but the wealthiest walk away. "Ye see, there is my commission, and the dear lady is in great need and grieves to part from her pet and so has named a cost not to be negotiated."

At least, he had the presence of mind to demand her tack be included and as an afterthought, drove a hard bargain for the white gelding. He could see no one but Thalia riding Dark Fire and must do something for his sister. Silly young girls with romantic notions always wanted white horses. He left that animal behind for delivery in two weeks' time, enough for him to take Thalia to the glade without Krista tagging along, and led the other back to Battle Hill.

His guests poured from the house to see the new mount. The duke approved. Running his hands over the mare, he said, "If you have a mind to breed her, I've a black stallion that would do her justice. In fact, I'd buy any offspring for my daughter, Pandora. She sits a horse tight as a tick."

Eagerly, Godric turned to Thalia. "Will you try her out? We could go for a short ride immediately. Not very far."

They would simply go over the next two hills and out of sight of the family for a quick moment of passion in some hidden spot. She might have understood him and agreed, but the duchess intervened. "My, no. We must have riding habits made up for both the girls. At least you already have your boots and a borrowed crop," Lady Flora let slip with a twinkle in her eyes.

The tedium of waiting on a delivery from a seamstress knew no end. Godric worked off his desire to be with Thalia by crossing swords with Bascom and taking vigorous rides with the duke, the older man astride his own mount, a dapple named Bosworth big enough to bear a knight in full armor or a large man effortlessly for many miles. He used his father's favorite, a deep-chested, muscular beast gray in color, trained in cavalry warfare, and named Thor, who required a great deal of control. Little would he have believed that once out of his teen years and the military academy, he would still need to use exercise to subdue his lust.

Thalia drove him to madness and a cold swim in the river by declining another visit to the tower. She feared they might be caught. "What does it matter?" he argued when he got her alone for a moment. "Then, we will marry sooner rather than later."

"I have never said I would marry you. You have not asked me properly."

"You know my feelings."

"Expressed in a foreign language. Yes, I discovered the meaning of those words."

"Would you prefer I said them in French, the language of love? *Je t'aime. Je t'adore.*"

"Plain English would please me more."

"Marry me, Thalia."

"I will consider your offer," she'd replied. "I need some time."

In the back of his mind, Rick heard James warning that Queenie must always rule.

Finally, the riding habits arrived and had to be modeled and admired. Krista wore black, but beautifully trimmed. A dark blue with some gold piping gave Thalia's ensemble a martial flare. Even her hat resembled a soldier's headwear, except for the fetching little veil, of course. Godric praised the costume and wondered how he would get her out of it.

They set off the next morning proceeding slowly down the hill. He corrected her seat and how she held the reins for the benefit of her parents watching them go. Once out of sight, he asked if she could manage a trot and in answer, Thalia gave the mare a smart tap with the crop and took off at a gallop to the place where the stream met the Ouse. He overtook her easily on his warhorse, much more conditioned than the fancy pet whose sides heaved at the end of their race.

The long skirts of the habit proved to be an impediment to hiking up a stony hill. He handed her the saddlebag containing their refreshments and hoisted her upon his back. All along she playfully swatted him with the crop and gave him orders to go right or left, but he would have his way in the end. With the scent of her perfumed hair in his nostrils nearly matching the aroma of the jonquils, he tossed her off into their grassy leaves when they arrived in the glade and pounced.

"My hat," she cried.

He removed the hat and hung it on a branch, then pressed her head deep into the flowers with the passion of his kiss. "Be careful of my new clothes," she chided.

"Very well, if you cannot be mussed, I will have to give you another sort of riding lesson." Godric pulled her to her feet and marched her up the hill to the deserted cottage. He crushed the blossoms underfoot in his haste.

This saddened Thalia. "There are not so many now. The jonquils are at the end of their season."

"Remember, they return every spring."

He lifted her to sit on a tumbled wall and did a valet's service removing her boots and stockings, setting them aside as neatly as Bascom. Then, he found a spot padded deeply with old leaves inside the cottage and lay down, hands behind his head.

"Come spread your skirts over me if they are of such concern."

She took a seat exactly where he wanted her, atop his rapidly stiffening rod. Godric unbuttoned her jacket, covered her breasts with his hands, warmed and teased them until she groaned. He drew her down, kissed her lips, and taught her the French tongue play in depth. Eventually, his hands found their way into her undergarments and tested for her readiness. He raised her slightly and undid his buttons.

"Now Thalia, another kind of riding lesson." He set her on his erection and lowered her hips slowly until their bodies met. "You may go slow or fast, hard or gently. The pace is yours to set."

By the gleam in her eyes and the smile on her red lips, he knew he had pleased her. As smartly as she'd whipped up Dark Fire, Thalia started off fast. As his breathing grew heavier and his eyes closed, she slowed. She rose up and teased his tip, slid down and took him deep. He had to look at her. Her lids had lowered. Her mouth opened and her tongue ran across her lips as if she savored the most exquisite food. With her dark curls thrown back, she began to ride him again, faster and faster, panting like the mare in their race to reach this place. Withdrawal would be difficult, almost impossible, and he no longer cared. Her dark eyes opened, wide and wild. Suddenly, she raised herself at the crucial moment and flattened on his heaving chest.

"I will not be caught," she murmured.

"You knew when to stop."

"A look comes on your face almost of agony, and that is when you withdraw."

"And you, are you satisfied?"

"Some time ago, but I kept on."

"To think you said you did not ride well."

"As I child I enjoyed riding until Miss Thurgood came out against it. I was merely out of practice. One never forgets."

"Queenie, there is no other like you." That pleased her, too.

Afterward, they shared sweet wine, a bit of Stilton cheese and crackers, a packet of glazed fruits, then did a careful inspection of their clothes. As Thalia retrieved and reset her hat, she smirked. "I seem to have left a stain on you this time."

Rick looked down at a large damp spot on his trousers. Shrugging, he splashed the remainder of the wine on it. "Spilled my drink in a most embarrassing spot. I must change as soon as we arrive home."

He let her mount his back and carried her downhill without much effort. The horses took them to Battle Hill at a slower pace than they'd set going out. Godric assisted Thalia in dismounting before any groom could perform the service. He wanted no other man to touch so much as her hand. She rewarded him with a smile worthy of a queen bestowing a favor on one of her minions and walked away ever so stately with no hint of what they'd done earlier. He yearned to run after her and take her in his arms for all to see...My God, he was in danger of losing control! James had warned him not to let Thalia gain the upper hand, and she'd certainly been above him today. It was always she who walked away lately. Had his passion to show her all the ways of love put him entirely in her power?

~ * ~

Thalia climbed the stairs to her room to remove her habit. Her mother's door stood partly open, and Lady Flora called out to her. "Keep me company since I am having my hair washed. It could wait no longer, and the weather has gotten warmer this past week, much warmer."

Thalia entered and took a seat nearby. She hoped to hear one of her dearest wishes had been granted. The maid had already sluiced the blonde curls over a basin and was massaging them vigorously with a scented shampoo. A pitcher of lemon water sat to one side for the rinse. The fire had been built up to hasten the drying, making the chamber rather stuffy.

"Tell me about your riding lesson. You do have a healthy glow," her mother said, looking sidelong at Thalia and flicking a bit of suds from the corner of her eye.

"It went very well. Dark Fire is a dream to ride. A horse like that encourages me to do much more riding. I will hate to leave her."

"Your father might make an offer to buy the mare, then. I have spoken to him of Italy. He took a great deal of persuading, but I have convinced him. The *Nuovo Regio Ducale Teatro alla Scala* would be the best place to study. I plan to accompany you and see you settled with friends in Milan, which will make him worry less. He was loath to let me go, but I pointed out that Justinian is four and looks to be our last child as none have followed. Now, *I* would like to have an adventure or two. I will not stay the entire time, but plan to return once I have seen the sights and make sure you progress well. We must insist that James meet us there and escort you after I am gone."

"I cannot believe it. Another dream come true!" Thalia reached up to unpin her jaunty riding hat using her mother's mirror. She saw the duchess eyeing the back of her head in the glass.

"Sap," Lady Flora said succinctly. "You had better change into your dressing gown and have your hair washed, too. If your father suspects, you will never go to Italy."

Thirteen

Hoping to have a few private words with the duke, Godric went early to the drawing room. The time had come to speak of his intentions despite Thalia's coyness about accepting him. With his control slipping, their games must end until allowed by marriage. Once Bellevue gave his approval, his daughter would fall into line quickly enough.

He found the man alone and engrossed in a newspaper. Bellevue glanced up. "The ladies will be delayed. Seems they must dry their hair thoroughly, and Krista has gone to gossip with them. Other than that news, Napoleon has rewritten French law to his satisfaction, and the Americans plan an expeditionary force across their continent now that they own most of the land. What a fine adventure it will be. Makes me long for the wilderness where I was born."

"Yes, certainly." Rick took a deep breath. Might as well get it out at once. "Bellevue, I would ask your permission to marry your daughter, Thalia."

That got the old boy's immediate attention. "What? I thought you did not care for each other."

"Our feelings have warmed with proximity."

"I believed I detected a thaw, but this is the coming of spring. Have you made your intentions known to Thalia? While I am glad you have finally come recognize her many merits, I am puzzled. Recently, her mother petitioned me on my daughter's behalf to allow her to spend a year in Italy studying voice. The duchess can be very persuasive. She pointed out that a girl with twenty thousand pounds and great beauty may marry anytime she wishes, and so I said I would allow it. I will not force any of my daughters to wed where their affections are not engaged, and my eldest has given me no indication she prefers you."

"Italy? She would leave me to study voice?"

"I never knew such a pale man could become any paler. Sit down, boy. Let me pour you a brandy. Women, especially Longleigh women, can be very decisive about what they want in love. If she has conceived a tenderness for you, a year will make no difference. When she returns, you may resume your courtship and see how it goes."

The duke placed the glass in Godric's hands. His fingers did not tremble but had gone icy cold. He took a large swallow and let it burn down the length of his throat. Thalia did not intend to marry him, but had led him along with the intent of punishing him for his former indifference. The feather torture began her plot, and it ended in a field of jonquils. James had bid him to beware. No! She would not have her way in this. He had claimed her, and he would take her as his wife.

The duke's hand patted him gently on the shoulder. "I can think of no other man I would rather have for a son-in-law. Give her time and try again."

"We have no time! Bellevue, I have come to know your daughter in the Biblical sense." Rick saw his euphemistic words only caused confusion for the duke. The man's hand dropped to his side. He spoke plainer. "We have made love. I have taken her maidenhead."

Obscure terms might have been the better choice. The duke seemed to swell in size as he towered over the settee. The genial companion, the fond father, vanished. Behind the man's dark eyes, the savage who had taken a scalp in the American wilderness still lived.

"You are saying this to get your way. I will not have lies told about my daughter." Bellevue fisted his great hands.

"I do not lie. I have proof if you will allow me to retrieve it." Godric stood, man to man, and met the furious father's stark gaze. "I plan to do right by Thalia."

"Go!"

If a gun had been shot off at a lover escaping through a window, he could not have moved any faster. Rick raced from the drawing room through the many weapons chambers. The footman guarding the entranceway startled and came to attention. Godric passed into the family wing and took the stairs to his private quarters where he kept the red cloth folded in a cabinet. He had intended it for a memento to show his bride someday. She would be touched he had kept it. They would make love on the curtain again draped over their marriage bed. How foolish of him to think of it so sentimentally. Now the red cloth became his evidence. Tucking it beneath his arm, he retraced his steps. As he passed the guest staircase, he heard the light voices of the women coming to join their men.

The duke stood with his own brandy in hand. The good news: Bellevue had not armed himself in the meantime. Godric unfurled the cloth, laid it over the back of the settee, and pointed to the small, brownish smear in its center.

"Here is the proof of her virginity taken and here the place where I spilled my seed for her safety."

"Those could be any stains fabricated to have your way."

"Ask your daughter. Will she lie?"

"A Longleigh would never lie in a matter such as this."

The voices of the women came closer. Bellevue's huge fist thudded on the end of a spindly table. A leg collapsed. An amorous china shepherd and his matching light o' love crashed to their doom on the Persian carpet beneath a spray of dried flowers from a Chinese bowl. "Thalia!" he bellowed, the force of his voice making the crystal drops on the oil lamp clatter.

The three women appeared in the doorway. "Papa?" the lady in question said, but her gaze went directly to the red cloth.

"Have you lain with this man?"

Thalia's hand reached out to grip her mother's fingers, but the duchess did not speak in her defense. A quick glance told Godric circumstances did exist when Lady Flora had no dominion over her husband. The loss of all color in her face showed that plainly. How tiny and fragile the duchess appeared opposed to the duke in full wrath. Godric's chance of gaining his haughty bride increased with every tick of the ormolu clock on the mantle.

Thalia lifted her chin and met the duke's black stare. "Yes. I did so willingly, but I am not with child. We were cautious. Only the people here this moment know. I could still go to Italy and..."

"There will be no trips to Italy! Consider yourself engaged to this man, young lady."

Krista threw her arms around Thalia. "Sister!" she cried with joy.

Thalia gently removed the hug and appealed to her lover. "How could you? It was you who told me not to listen to others, but to follow my own will. I want to study abroad like James. I want to be free a while longer."

"You would leave me and might find another. Italians! I know how they are."

"I love no one but you, Rick, and will never take another. Please, don't deny me this chance." She held out her hands, imploring, but Godric remained where he stood right next to her father. His scar throbbed in time with the pulse in his neck.

"Flora, plan the wedding," her father said. He ground the china shepherdess underfoot.

The duchess regained her composure. "Dearest, people will talk if we act too suddenly. If there is no child, we need not make haste. Thalia can have a long engagement. She might even have her adventure if Godric will agree, since I will see she is well-chaperoned. We could plan a wedding for next spring."

"Rick?" Thalia questioned, though she had dropped her hands to her sides again.

He crossed the room, fell to one knee before her, and grasped her fingers. Looking up, he said, "Thalia, if you will consent to marry me, you may go to Italy wearing my engagement ring."

She raised him up, and leaning into his broad shoulder, answered, "I will marry you, Godric Erikson, when the jonquils come into bloom again."

Fourteen

The engagement announcement set the ton a-twittering. Much to Thalia's satisfaction, a green cloud of envy hung over the London ballroom as the duke stood on the musicians' low dais, called the young couple forward, joined their hands, and announced their intention to marry the following spring. Thalia accepted a ring possessing a large diamond of the first water and surrounded with smaller stones, the right of a nonpareil. When the couple stepped down, the ranks of those coming forward to give their best wishes parted them for a time. The young ladies, her former rivals in the husband-hunting game, crowded to see the ring up close. The young men, Thalia's former suitors, grudgingly gave Godric a shake of the hand and a pat on the back.

Lady Flora stood to one side of the crush valiantly deterring the men taking an interest in Krista. The child did look splendid in her black gown strewn with jet beads and sewn along the same lines that minimized the breadth of her shoulders and showed off her creamy complexion.

"She is not yet out and still in mourning. Save your breath for next season, dear sirs," the duchess repeated again and again. "Still, we could not have her miss the celebration."

Thalia joined them to help in Krista's defense and waved off the beaux who had hounded her but were now on the scent of ten thousand pounds. They left her presence like whipped puppies. "How do you think the news was received, Mama?"

"Splendidly. Your beaux are bitter at having been outdone by a newcomer after a season and more courting you. The young misses are relieved you are out of the competition, yet jealous you snared an earl the moment he set foot in Almack's for the first time. Their mothers feel we played unfairly by following him to Battle Hill, and their fathers regret the loss of your twenty thousand pounds. In other words, their reactions could not be more perfect."

Perfect, exactly the reaction Thalia wanted. "Wait until they hear about Godric's gift of a stay in Italy. What will they make of that?"

"Whatever they wish. The Longleighs pay no mind to the opinions of others for the most part. Let them talk. Meanwhile, I have dropped the word about Krista's ten thousand pounds and so baited the mousetrap for next year. Some of the wits are already calling her *Die Valkyrie*. Wonderful!"

Krista blushed all the way to her white-blonde hairline. "I do not deserve such a title."

"You will. We shall polish you to a fine sheen before next season. Nothing I like better than a good sobriquet to create interest so long as it is flattering. I was once called Little Yellow Flower among the Shawnee, and the duke uses it still as an endearment."

They waited until the end of the long evening of dancing to drop the other shoe. Within a month's time Bellevue House would be shut for the season as Lady Flora and her daughter left England to spend some time in Italy where Lady Thalia planned to study voice and her mother to see the sights. Greatly gratified, Thalia overheard more than one woman remark she wished she had a husband so generous or an intended so understanding, but Godric belonged only to her.

~ * ~

Godric insisted the ladies set sail on a ship in which he had invested because he knew the *Seahorse* to be sound of hull and guided by an experienced captain, Henry Belcher. He sent along as well two of his most highly trained footmen, blond giants named Wills and Geoffrey, for their protection. Thalia's heart warmed at his care.

"My, aren't they magnificent," Balfour said of their escorts as she placed a hand on her bony chest. Aged twenty-five, a thin woman with sleek brown hair knotted at her nape and nervous but nimble hands when it came to the creation of coiffures, Thalia's maid had volunteered to serve both women aboard ship when Lady Flora's older servant begged to be left behind secure in England, not wanting to brave the sea or foreign parts of any kind.

"Yes, very," the duchess said, agreeing with the maid's assessment of Wills and Geoffrey and smiling slightly at the woman's smitten expression.

Godric took Thalia in his arms at parting. "If I did not need to see the estate and Krista, I would be by your side, my love. *Bon voyage,*" he said before handing Thalia into the boat that would take her and the duchess to the *Seahorse.* He indulged in a farewell kiss too long to be decent, and Thalia reluctantly left his arms—but adventure beckoned!

Bellevue, not to be outdone, did the same to his duchess. The duke made it clear in parting he could not endure London without his wife by his side. He planned to return to Bellevue Hall to enjoy the company of his young sons and adoring daughters and rove the woods surrounding the estate, much more to his taste than any club or ballroom.

The merchantman sat offshore so heavy laden with trade goods she barely rose on the swell. Her figurehead, not a fragile sea creature, but a black horse with a fiery eye and the curled tail of a serpent, pointed out to sea, eager to be gone. Truth be told, so were the ladies, despite leaving their men. Ah, the start of an adventure, nothing better! Now Thalia understood what her mother had experienced in leaving England to follow her love to America.

They waved their lacy handkerchiefs until they were taken up onto the ship and stayed on deck until the anchor was lifted. The sails of the *Seahorse* billowed with the prevailing wind and joined two other merchant ships bound for the Italian peninsula. They had the good fortune to be escorted by naval frigate going to Gibraltar, a sure way to ward off Bonaparte's rapacious privateers. Godric and the duke had seen to that.

May proved to be a fine month for sailing. As they strolled the deck for exercise, Lady Flora said, "I did not suffer from *mal de mer* on my first voyage and am glad to see you are also well, Thalia. Longleigh women are very hardy."

Her words issued from deep in the veils she wore to preserve her white complexion and ward off sunburn. Despite her mother's warnings to preserve her skin, Thalia, already dark-complexioned, reveled in the sunlight off the sea. The wind that filled the sails toyed with the curls that escaped her bonnet. She delighted in the wonderful sense of freedom she'd had since giving herself to Rick and doing her own will. With Miss Thurgood's teachings cast aside and striving for perfection in the past, a whole new life lay ahead to enjoy to its fullest.

The ship put in at Lisbon and then Gibraltar where they lost their mighty escort and encountered a strong gale deep in the Mediterranean Sea that pushed the *Seahorse* away from the other ships and closer to the coast of Africa than she'd ever been intended to go. Thalia and her mother sat in their cabin and sang hymns to the accompaniment of Balfour's sobs and sea water seeping through the battened hatches. Longleigh women did not panic or cry, Thalia repeated in her mind as she embarked on another verse of the Reverend Augustus Toplady's popular *Rock of Ages*. Mention of the water and the flood caused Balfour to cry harder.

After the passing of the storm, Captain Belcher commended their calm demeanor and assured the ladies he had only to make a course correction south of Sicily to bring them safely to the Italian shore. Unfortunately, Thalia soon learned that turn was not executed in a timely manner. Before noon, a boat appeared on the horizon, a small, swift Moslem xebec by the looks of her triple lateen sails, Captain

Belcher informed them. A bit pompous and fusty she thought, he did run a tight, immaculate ship and enjoyed showing off both his knowledge and his experience at sea to the women.

"Nothing to worry about, my ladies. The corsairs will want to come aboard and make sure we carry a passport signed by their pasha. The British government has paid the beggars off in advance. We should come to no harm, but these ruffians are on edge right now with the Americans blockading Tripoli. Their captain might suspect our flying of the British flag is some Yankee ruse. Still, it is best you go below, keep to your cabin and bar the door until we are done with them. One never knows what a pirate might fancy, my hat, your silk gown. It is best not to tempt them to bad behavior, wrong-headed heathens that they are."

The ladies assented and sat nervously on the edge of their built-in beds while the two footmen sent along by Danelagh to keep them from any seafarer's insults guarded the door. Balfour huddled in the rear of the cabin. Calmly, Thalia freed her stiletto and hid it in the folds of her skirts.

The hulls of the two ships knocked together with a solid boom as the corsairs came aboard. They could make out the deep voice of Captain Belcher, cordial at first, then raised in anger, but not his words. Crewmen ordered from their duties shouted out protests. Feet thumped down the steps to their quarters, and their footmen called out a challenge followed by a sharp cry and an ominous thud against their barred door. On the other side, someone tried to force entry. Lady Flora armed herself with a substantial chamber pot and climbed atop one of their traveling boxes. She raised it high and waited. Thalia stood and held her weapon as her father taught her, close to the body and ready to dart out hard and fast.

The door gave way, and the first corsair, armed with two scimitars and another held in his teeth amidst a black beard, stumbled in when it burst. The duchess brained him with the chamber pot and scrambling down, picked up one of his weapons and tossed another to Balfour, who sadly preferred to shriek rather than scoop it up and defend herself.

"Useless woman!" the duchess cried. "Thalia, prepare."

Her daughter already held the third scimitar out before her and kept the dagger near. Outside the door, one of the rapacious pirates stripped an unconscious footman of his black and gold livery. Another engaged the second footman in a swordfight, difficult in such confined quarters. A third, a huge bald Turk sporting two long mustaches hanging down either side of his face, leapt over his fallen comrade and charged the women. If he expected them to cower from his ferocity, he grossly underestimated their spirit.

Using two hands, Lady Flora stroked down on his left arm burying her blade in the meat of his muscle. He batted her aside like a fly buzzing around a bloody side of beef. Thalia parried his blade with hers, but he used his superior strength and skill to shove her weapon aside and grab her by the hair. She drove her stiletto hard into his side, but knew she'd failed when the tip hit bone and slid sideways, opening some flesh but not penetrating the lung. With her enemy's cutlass at her throat, she had to surrender amid what she assumed were many Arabic curses aimed at recalcitrant women. Balfour screamed and screamed. The duchess, not willing to risk her daughter, threw her weapon aside and surrendered. Their captor made it plain by a jerk of his head that she and her maid were to precede him through the door where the second footman still held off his assailant.

"Wills, lay down your sword," Lady Flora directed. "I am afraid we are defeated for the moment."

It pained him, Thalia could tell from her dangerous and awkward position, but he did as ordered. "They came on us sudden and coshed Geoffrey on the head, your Grace. Don't think he's dead though."

"Good, very good. Carry him topside, then. I suppose we must go with these scurvy fellows."

Thalia expected to see the deck red with blood, the dead and wounded littering the boards. Instead, she found the crew, including their portly captain, lined up and wearing only their undergarments. At the sight of the ladies, a few of the less hardened turned red beneath their tans. With the cutlass at her back, Thalia's captor pricked her forward.

"Avert your eyes, Thalia," the duchess ordered.

"Mama, I have seen..."

"For their sake, not yours." Raising her voice, she demanded. "I need the ship's doctor to see to my footman." Wills laid the stripped Geoffrey at the end of the long line of crewman.

"He isna yours to command," one of corsairs said with a distinct Scottish accent. He wore the same wide pantaloons gathered at the ankles, blousy shirt, and a long open vest belted at the waist as the other pirates, but his apparel shone with rich embroidery. His build was slight, his commanding stance enormous. Below his white silk turban secured by a jeweled clasp, a pair of light eyes glinted. A wicked smile parted his close-cropped, dark blond beard when he saw their astonishment.

Captain Belcher, staring straight ahead, his full cheeks flushed with embarrassment, did the honors. "Lady Flora Longleigh, Duchess of Bellevue, and Lady Thalia Longleigh, may I present Murad Reis, Lord High Admiral of the Bashaw of Tripoli."

"The *renegado*, Peter Lisle, in the flesh," the duchess murmured.

"Aye, your Grace. I sold my soul to Allah and got a pretty price for it: a flagship, a fleet, and his eldest daughter for a wife. The bashaw will be pleased with the prize I bring him today. Those poxy Americans think they have our harbor bottled up, but I can come and go as I please in a xebec. When I heard of this fat merchantman floundering along off our coast, I could not resist."

Captain Belcher sputtered, "But we have a non-molestation treaty."

"I have no plans to molest *ye*, Captain. Once we take your cargo and these fine ladies for ransom, you are free to be on your way."

The footman, Wills, helped his counterpart to his feet. Geoffrey swayed and touched the huge purple knot on his head, but stayed upright. "We go with you, your Grace," he said.

"And I," replied Balfour. "I may not have defended you, but I will continue to serve you and Lady Thalia wherever you might go."

"Scrawny and too plain for the harem. She willna bring much in the slave market," Murad Reis accessed.

"None of them shall go to the slave market. My husband will ransom all of us." Lady Flora showed no fear. "Show no fear," now that should be the family motto, Thalia thought as she imitated her mother, even when the turncoat admiral made his next remark.

"May he redeem ye in a timely manner, but if not, I might have this one as my second wife—or my third. I keep forgetting the one I left behind in London." He pointed the tip of his bejeweled scimitar at Thalia and stepped closer to her. Though she stood taller than he, the pirate raised her downturned face with his fingers. She hoped he recognized defiance and saw no fear in her gaze. "Would ye like that, sweetheart? No? Ye willna get to say yea or nay for the Moslem world is a man's world—as it should be."

Balfour gasped at his words and began to whimper. "Now that one is no prize. Come along then, ladies. Let's load ye with the other contraband."

A steady stream of boxes and chests, their own included, passed from hand to hand and made their way over the side and into the xebec. Herded by the bleeding Turkish sailor with the cutlass to the rail, the women found themselves tossed across the gap and into the grasp of another foreign seaman. Balfour went with a terrified squeak, Lady Flora with her garments aflutter like a small, yellow bird, and Thalia as impassive as the ship's figurehead. Nimbly walking a boarding plank, the traitorous Murad Reis joined them.

He called out to Captain Belcher who had turned to watch him leave. "I've left ye enough water and supplies to make port, Captain. Give thanks and praise to Allah for my leniency upon your arrival and report that I've plucked ye like a green goose. And send along a note to the mighty Duke of Bellevue that a ransom demand will follow."

Murad Reis allowed them shade and water but as an afterthought, had Wills stripped of his livery like his comrade. When the xebec lay low in the water crammed with all the purloined goods it could hold, the Turkish sailors cast off from the *Seahorse,* and jeering at the English crew, set sail close along the coast. After shouting out his orders in Arabic, the admiral gave the ladies his unwanted company for the duration of the voyage and proved to be obnoxiously loquacious. He lolled close enough to Thalia for her to smell his sweat and the spirits on his breath, but she did not move or flinch.

"Ye'll get a chance to see the American fleet as we skim by them in the shallows where they cannot follow. Nay use ye calling out to them. They sit so far off, they willna hear. Arrogant fools if they think they can blockade us. I come and go as I please. Their government should simply pay the price to ransom their sailors and keep off the corsairs like the rest of the world." He called for a jug and drank from it long and often.

"Rum, not for the ladies, or I would share it with ye."

Lady Flora plied her fan to move the warm, tropical air. She formed a retort. "One of the prophet's teachings I have always admired is his prohibition against strong drink. Are you not a convert? My husband says the amount your bashaw asks of the Americans would bankrupt their new nation and so they have invested in warships instead." Her mother's knowledge of both the Koran and current events made Thalia proud.

The admiral shrugged. "The American treasury is not my concern, and I've found it necessary to bend the teachings of the prophet here and there." He bathed his throat in rum again.

How Thalia wished she had not obeyed Miss Thurgood's prohibition on reading the newspapers. "Allow your husband to think for you in these matters and you will be a happier wife," she'd admonished. Mama and Papa were happy and often debated heavy matters of state. She thought Rick would allow her to do the same, but then, they'd taken no time to discuss world events when passion called. She rubbed a thumb across her engagement ring. The gesture caught the eye of their captor.

"How did my men miss that pretty bauble? I believe you owe it to Ali for the slashes to his arm and side."

Lady Flora puffed up like an angry canary. "I gave him that blow to the arm, not my daughter."

"But you wear no jewelry."

"Only a fool travels to foreign parts with expensive jewels."

"I wouldna say that to the bashaw. He canna even ride across town without taking two strongboxes of gold and jewels with him on every excursion, one of his little quirks. I wouldna cross the man as he has more unpleasant habits. He is not a Turk, know ye, but a local boy. Yusuf Karamanli came to his throne by shooting his own brother, wounding his mother who got in the way, and exiling another son. Now off with the ring, Lady Thalia."

She gave up her diamond with great reluctance. "It is my engagement ring from the Earl of Danelagh. Could you not spare it for its sentimental value?"

"I could for sentiment, but not for its great worth." Murad Reis did not call Ali forth to receive it but placed it on his own finger and admired it there. They neared Tripoli, and he called for mint tea to refresh his breath, allowing the ladies a cup each of the same. As the xebec glided into the crescent-shaped harbor, they saw what he'd said to be true. The Americans could not reach them in the shallow waters, more the pity.

The admiral lowered the boats with the ladies aboard and set Wills and Geoffrey to rowing them ashore. When close enough, Murad Reis cursed and cajoled the two footmen into the surf to carry the two noblewomen above the water line, threatening them direly if so much as their hem got wet. Poor Balfour he simply made wade ashore with her skirts held high and her skinny legs showing as he laughed at her struggles.

The massive fortress palace of the bashaw dominated the city of Tripoli, but delicate minarets rose above it and pierced the deep blue desert sky with their ornate tips. Smaller houses, white and flat-topped, squatted beneath clumps of palm trees swaying with the ocean breeze. Were it not for their situation, Thalia thought she might find their surroundings beautiful and exotic. The captives marched along a dusty street where idle men called out greetings to Murad Reis. Their women, wearing heavy black garments that allowed only their eyes to show stared at the lightly clad foreigners and giggled behind their hands, captives in their own way, she believed.

At the palace, heavily armed guards opened huge, iron-bolted doors. Warning barks and growls issued from large dogs wearing spike-studded collars and barely restrained by their handlers who encouraged the beasts to snap at the ladies' skirts. Thalia tried to emulate her mother, who marched along as if the animals were no more than one of her lap dogs, not an easy thing to do.

They descended into a dark tunnel and came out of it blinking into a courtyard filled with the bashaw's janissaries bearing so many types of weapons they might have raided the hall of arms at Battle Hill: sabers, scimitars, daggers, pistols, muskets, and hatchets. The men stared at the women and made what could only be ribald comments, but Lady Flora, Thalia, and even the bedraggled Balfour walked straight-backed, eyes ahead, unintimidated into the maze of corridors within the palace.

Their small group eventually arrived at the reception room and into the presence of Bashaw Yusuf Karamanli. Between thirty and forty years of age, fleshy but highly impressive, the bashaw sat cross-legged and four feet above them on a dais that held a throne inlaid with mosaic and covered in velvet and gold fringe. Small gems glittered in the folds of the cloth and on the diamond-studded belt of his long, silk robe. A great, black beard covered his chest and a turban bedecked with ribbons sat upon his head. Surrounded by guards, he still wore a sword and two pistols in his sash as if he might be attacked personally at any moment. The bashaw gestured them forward across the marble floor and the heavy oriental rugs.

Murad Reis took up a place by the side of the platform. He spoke their names to his ruler and most likely explained their great worth, because the bashaw smiled, showing his teeth in avarice. He held out a hand bearing an enormous sapphire of a blue so deep it might have been a piece of desert sky that had fallen and landed on his finger.

"The bashaw says ye may kiss his ring."

"Thinks he's the bloody Pope," Lady Flora muttered much to her daughter's shock, but the duchess formed her mouth into a pleasant smile, stepped forward and accepted the honor. Thalia followed her gesture.

Balfour would have, also, but Murad Reis waved her aside. "Ye are only a servant. Stay back."

The bashaw spoke again, and the admiral translated. "He says ye will be well taken care of until your ransom arrives and shall stay with the women of the harem. He asks why such beautiful women have no jewels."

Before she thought to stop her words, Thalia said, "Because Murad Reis took my engagement ring."

The admiral laughed and passed along the message. With a curt order, he was obliged to return it. "Och, well. Easy come, easy go."

Then the ruler of Tripoli gestured to his two strongboxes, the ones he never failed to have by his side. A guard assigned to the task unlocked and raised the lid of one chest to reveal a tumble of jewels. "He bids ye choose one each to comfort ye in your captivity. Do not insult him by refusing," Murad Reis recommended.

Lady Flora stepped forward and after some consideration, selected a smaller version of the sapphire on the bashaw's hand. "It will remind me of the desert sky over Tripoli and the generosity of its ruler when I am again on British shores."

If the duchess could flatter the patronesses of Almack's to get their preferment for her daughter, she showed herself to be equally effective in dealing with an oriental potentate. His expression revealed his pleasure at her statement. Thalia's admiration for her mother increased even more. For herself, she chose a diamond of a size similar to the one she wore again on her finger and could think of nothing better to say than "Thank you very much, your majesty." She figured she could give it to Krista if she did not end up being the third wife of Murad Reis.

"The bashaw perceives you must be tired. Ye are to go to the seraglio. His wives and their servants will see to your comfort. Your maid may go along, but the men ye brought with ye must be kept elsewhere. Now back from the room showing due reverence to your host."

Heads down, they retraced their steps to the corridor. Once outside, Lady Flora said, "And now the bashaw would rival the King of England, though I do have to say, King George has never given me any jewels."

Murad Reis chuckled at her comment. "If ye were not past your bearing years, I might fancy ye for a wife as well."

Thalia expected her mother to answer tartly, but instead Lady Flora simply fanned her cheeks, pink with pleasure at the compliment. They proceeded through more corridors until they reached a well-guarded area deep within the palace. The admiral beckoned them to enter when two very solid doors opened onto a short passage leading to a courtyard, but he went no further.

"Enjoy your stay as the guests of the Bashaw of Tripoli," he said and walked away.

Within, they found women of all shapes, shades, and nationalities lounging on well-cushioned divans. None was uncomely. All bared their naked breasts to the sunlight. With so many exposed nipples, Thalia felt as if each had two pairs of eyes to stare at the newcomers, though the orbs set in their beautiful faces were lined with kohl and the other pair rouged to draw the attention of the ruler. The bashaw's beauties basked among pots of red hibiscus and tubs of lemon trees heavy with fruit that very much reminded Thalia of the conservatory at Bellevue Hall—which she might never see again.

Idly, the members of the harem dipped their hands into small, shallow dishes of ripe olives and sweet dates, or peeled oranges, raising the skin of the citrus with the long fingernails only a lady of leisure can possess. When they turned their heads to regard the strangers, the multiple pairs of large earrings adorning them tinkled together like small bells. Fillets of gold and silver fringe held their thick, black braids in place as female servants stirred the air with ostrich feather fans. The scent of jasmine and strong perfumes wafted in the breeze. One, a long-limbed woman black as the Queen of Sheba was said to have been, made a remark that set the others to giggling.

"Do not mind her. She is merely one of many concubines, not a wife." The words came from a lady fully clothed, though her bright, gauzy garments left little to the imagination. She approached with quiet dignity. Her dark hair cascaded to her waist but a thin veil topped with a small diadem covered it. The number of her rings and bracelets she wore greatly outnumbered those worn by the others.

Thalia found herself astonished that any of the women of the harem spoke English, especially with a slight Scottish burr, but Lady Flora said curtly, "I know an insult when I hear it. What did she say?"

"That you are as white as the belly of a fish rotting on the beach."

"I've been called worse. She is simply jealous. You must be the wife of Murad Reis."

The regal woman inclined her head. "That I am. And the bashaw's eldest daughter. Please, I will show you to your quarters. I believe you will find them comfortable. You have only to ask for anything you wish within reason. My father is a generous man unless thwarted."

The princess of the realm escorted them to a spacious chamber with two wide sleeping couches thick with cushions and a pallet on the floor for Balfour who straggled along behind with her damp skirts leaving a snail's trail on the blue and white patterned floor tiles. Their trunks sat along the sides of the walls. From the bits of clothing hanging outside the lids, clearly the chests had been rifled by the pirates.

The wife of Murad Reis pointed out a table bearing a bronze ewer of water and a bowl for washing, a tray of the same refreshments being enjoyed by the women of the harem, and a pitcher of pomegranate juice for their thirst. A window covered with an ornate lattice allowing no one to see inside sat above the low table and allowed some light to filter into the room.

"Rest," the princess said and left them as quietly as she had approached.

Thalia sat on one of the divans and poured small cups of the fruit juice for each of them. She took a sip of hers. "Very good. Mama, you have been ransomed in the past. How long do you think we shall be here?"

"That I cannot answer. My ransom from the Shawnee was more than a year in coming, but the distance between America and England is much greater and ships were slower then. Also, my brother did not put himself out to raise the amount quickly. You can be sure your father will come to the rescue with alacrity. However, I must warn you that captivity can be quite tedious. At least we shan't be required to hoe corn or scrape hides. Here's to languishing in luxury and a quick escape!" Lady Flora raised her cup and chimed its edge against the other two.

Fifteen

Lady Flora soon began petitioning the bashaw for outings. "I tell you, this is like living inside my own conservatory on a permanent basis. Nice for a time but after a while, I would have to break the glass to escape. Unfortunately, we have no windows here, only thick walls and stone lattices. I must say, at least the Shawnee kept me busy." Thalia had to agree with her about dwelling in luxurious boredom.

She soon gained a visit to the bashaw's pleasure gardens outside the city for all of them. He demanded the women be modestly clothed in black robes, their faces half-obscured with a veil, and accompanied by two unpleasant guards as well as their own footmen and maid. There the ladies met some of the captive American officers who were afforded the same privilege, their captain, William Bainbridge, among them. Thalia found them to be gentlemen on a par with any she'd known in England and possibly much braver.

They strolled together past palms and fountains and vivid parrots prevented from flying off by golden chains affixed to their legs, with the duchess on one side and Thalia on the other of the beleaguered sailor. The ladies inquired how his men did in their long captivity in the American Consulate. The captain replied that he kept his officers busy teaching the midshipmen their lessons, but he feared for his ordinary seamen, many of them British, who lived in dungeon-like conditions and did heavy labor daily. The duchess asked what the gentlemen were in need of if it were in her power to provide. He answered that since his men lived on black bread, tough beef and the meat of aged camels, fresh fruit and vegetables would be most welcome. She assured him she would put her mind to obtaining that. As Thalia knew, if her mother put her mind to something, that something would most certainly occur.

"A striking man, don't you think, Thalia?" the duchess said to daughter later. "Six feet tall if he's an inch, and such jetty black hair and large, dark eyes. I find those long side-whiskers and the cleft in his chin very attractive also."

"No more so than Rick," Thalia replied as Balfour helped her out of the stifling robes.

"Spoken like a woman in love. He cannot compare to your father either. Still, I should like to help him. This evening when the bashaw comes onto his balcony to choose his bed partner for the night, I believe we should be found practicing our singing. That is sure to draw his attention."

"I am not certain I want him to notice me. The way his ladies preen to be chosen sickens me."

"He has many to choose from, and I believe he will not molest us. Murad Reis worries me more. However, the bashaw might reward our song with another outing to the market for greens which we can take to the Americans.

"If you think it will work, of course."

Trilling like the caged birds some of the seraglio kept as pets, they blended their voices at the exact time the pasha was known to be watching. Several of his concubines rose up to dance to the music in hopes of being selected, though the innocence of the song and the seductiveness of their movements had little to do with each other.

Shocked at first, Thalia wondered if Godric would be aroused if she did such a dance for him. Most certainly! But their ploy did work. The bashaw was pleased and sent them a purse to spend in the bazaar. Judging by its contents of English coins and paper, the funds had come from their own trunks. He did not approve purchases for the Americans.

They were bidden to buy some ornaments to adorn themselves. So, swaddled in their black robes, they filled their arms with golden bracelets and purchased some ostentatiously heavy neck chains. Using two bracelets to bribe their guards, Hassan and Tarek, Lady Flora and Thalia moved on to the marketplace and traded more jewelry for wholesome foods to be delivered to the American Consulate. In this, they kept the letter of their word. How clever of her mother to find a way to succor the captives. They had bought pretty baubles as directed and had not visited the Americans directly. Eventually, the bashaw learned of their activities whether from the merchants or their treacherous escort, they did not know. Their guile seemed to amuse rather than anger him, thank heaven!

As they stood before him with their heads properly bowed in supposed contrition, he waved his bejeweled fingers and had his daughter translate. "My most generous father says you may visit the American officers if you wish."

"As I hoped," Lady Flora whispered just before praising the sultan for his mercy and kindness to two such weak and helpless women, which nearly made Thalia laugh. She ducked her head even lower to stifle the impulse.

A schedule of regular visits on the mornings of certain days was devised. Stopping first at the market for much appreciated fruits and vegetables, Thalia and her mother went on to brighten the day of the captives with their company. Often, they sang for the men and made their eyes wet with sentimental songs in their native tongue. One day, Captain Bainbridge took the ladies to the roof of the consulate. The city and its harbor lay before them like a map spread upon a table. From the heights, the American blockade seemed very impressive, so many frigates and gunboats to turn back any trading ships.

Ruefully, Bainbridge said, "Commodore Preble does prevent the grain shipments from coming ashore and turns away French and Italian vessels, but the sultan does not starve, only his people. It is true the Tripolitan navy can come and go as they please in their shallow draft vessels. We send out information on our condition and what we spy from here in our messages, but I fear it does little good."

"The bashaw does not prevent this? How do you manage?" Lady Flora's light eyes glittered. Ah, her mother was scheming again.

"We are permitted to send letters home if they contain only innocuous happenings and hopes to be set free, but I have been using lemon juice to write between the lines."

"That old ruse of spies and lovers! The letters fade into the paper and remain unseen until exposed to heat. I should have thought of it myself. I feel quite the dunce. Thalia, we must write your father very soon. I will tell you what must be said and provide a diversion so you may compose in peace. Thank you, Captain Bainbridge."

"No, thank you for your many kindnesses, Lady Flora."

Very excited, the ladies cut their visit short in haste to put their plan into action.

Sixteen

Godric watched Krista ride Pinkerton around the practice ring. The name that came with the white horse was soon shortened to Pinkie by his sister, and she'd tied a bow of the same color to the gelding's forelock. The animal tossed his head to get rid of the ornament which Krista took as a show of spirit. Truth be told, Pinkie had none. He ambled good-naturedly in a circle with Krista on his back and rarely exerted himself beyond a genial slow canter. Krista could not be persuaded to kick her mount sufficiently to get any more effort out of him. Using spurs or a crop—out of the question for the large but gentle girl. Merely thinking of a riding crop made Godric remember Thalia keenly, and he began to go stiff below.

"Enough for today! Bring him in." As soon as Krista turned Pinkie toward the gate, the horse picked up speed, knowing his ration of oats awaited in the stable.

He'd matched them well. The steed stood tall and sturdy enough to make his sister appear more delicate than in reality. He had to admit she looked very striking with her black habit flowing against the beast's white hide. The pink ribbon added a touch of whimsy suitable for a young lady about to venture into the world within a year. By next June, she might have met the man she would marry, a more suitable man than Hugh Grey, though probably not a better one, he had to admit.

Thalia had ventured beyond his control. She wrote often and posted the letters whenever the *Seahorse* came into port so he received a number of messages at once. Godric read most of them aloud to his sister, keeping the portions where Thalia boldly recalled their amorous adventures to himself alone. An account of one of the Barbary apes of Gibraltar snatching Lady Flora's veiled hat as they toured a Moorish tower made both of them laugh aloud. After that missive, no more arrived. He worried. The dangers of travel were many, and some like storms at sea could not be avoided.

Suddenly anxious to see the day's post which must have arrived by then, he led Pinkie to the front of the house, helped Krista from her mount and tossed the reins to a waiting stable boy. While his sister changed clothes, he went directly to the library where Bascom customarily left the mail neatly sorted into three piles: invitations meant to lure him into the social whirl of London, all to be refused, business matters concerning the estate and the shipping interests, and personal letters.

He faced only two stacks today, nothing in the personal pile, not even a note from the Duke of Bellevue, a fairly poor correspondent, perhaps because he'd come to the English language and writing late in life and took no pleasure in putting pen to paper. He thought the man might at least let him know if the covering of Dark Fire by Bellevue's black stallion had gone well. Soon after Thalia left him for her stay in Italy, the mare had shown signs of coming into season. He'd sent the horse off to be bred with the idea of surprising his betrothed with a foal upon her return.

Nothing he could do but turn to the business correspondence and scribble his rejections of the several invitations. A letter from Captain

Belcher immediately caught his eye. Might a communication from Thalia be inside? He eagerly broke the seal but found only a message from the seaman:

I deeply regret to inform you of the loss of our cargo to Barbary pirates. These scurrilous wretches ignored the treaty which costs the British Empire dearly each year. They did, however, leave the ship and crew intact. We were able to make Sicily with ease. I pledge to you that I will fill the holds of the Seahorse with statues of Carrara marble, the antiquities of Rome, the glassware of Murano, and other luxury goods purchased on credit. The sale of these items will more than repay the debt and make a tidy profit for all of the investors in this venture. I swear this on my career and my life.

Damn the man's life and career! What of his most precious cargo, Thalia and Lady Flora?

Most unfortunately, the head corsair himself, Murad Reis, traitor to the Crown, dog of Islam, saw fit to remove the Duchess of Bellevue and your affianced, Lady Thalia Longleigh, from my care with an eye to extracting a large ransom from the duke. Two footmen and a maid, showing their loyalty, went with them into captivity while I was powerless to help. It is my belief the ladies will come to no harm as treasure matters more to the Bashaw of Tripoli than all else except his own family. An amount and letter of demand will follow this letter shortly.

With my utmost apologies, I remain—
Henry Belcher, Capt., The Seahorse

A droplet of moisture marred the end of the letter—seawater, a tear, or more likely a blot from sweat. Godric crumpled the letter in his fist in the same way he wanted to destroy Captain Belcher's fat face and roared out his anguish. Krista came running, so lovely in her new black frock, so alarmed by her disciplined brother's outcry.

"Whatever is wrong?" she asked. "I heard you as I came down the stairs."

"Thalia is gone!"

"Never. She would not leave you for any other man. Tell me she is not lost at sea."

"She has fallen into the hands of a pasha on the Barbary coast. He will desire her. No ransom can ever match her worth."

"And Lady Flora, our men and Balfour?"

"All are being held until the bashaw's demands are met."

An uproar at the front door distracted them from their distress. Bascom appeared at a run and spread his arms wide across the doorway in an attempt to do his duty.

"Milord, the Duke of Bellevue requests..."

"Out of my way, man! I request nothing, but demand to see Danelagh at once." The duke plowed his shoulder into Bascom's back and attempted to bull his way into the library. The doughty butler held the entry until his master gave the sign to stand aside. Dropping his arms, both Bascom and the duke tumbled into the room.

"Good man you have there, Danelagh," Bellevue said as he righted himself and straightened his clothes. "But sometimes a bloody nuisance." He looked at the paper balled in Godric's hand, the expression on the man's pale face. "I believe you know why I have come."

"Our ladies are being held hostage in a foreign land."

"Precisely. I had the details arrive in a diplomatic pouch a fortnight ago, thanks to the courtesy of the Danish ambassador to Tripoli."

"You did not write me immediately!" Godric's blood surged in anger.

"I had plans to make, and you will be a part of them if you give me but a moment to explain. The ambassador has visited the women and assures me they are uninjured and in good health and spirits. But the demands made by this pompous, petty potentate are outrageous. He requires a ransom of forty thousand pounds for Flora and Thalia and another six thousand for the servants in coin, not banknotes. The man does not appear to realize that English nobles do not squat on chests of gold and gems as he does but have their wealth in land and investments. I cannot simply conjure up that sum by calling on a magical jinn to make it appear."

Krista spoke up with more authority than usual. "Brother, you forget yourself. Please do sit down, Lord Bellevue. Allow me to arrange for some tea and refreshments after your arduous journey." Godric raised his white brows at his sister's sudden command of the situation.

The duke apologized. "Forgive my earlier roughness. Tea would be greatly appreciated."

He took the nearest chair, a loose-jointed antique that groaned beneath his size. Krista hurried off to give her orders to the kitchen, and Bellevue eyed the decanter and glasses set on a shelf amongst the sparse collection of books. "While she is gone, some of that brandy would not go amiss."

Godric poured for both of them, and they tossed the liquor down to finish before the more insipid beverages arrived. The Duke leaned back and stretched his travel-cramped legs. The U-shaped chair creaked ominously.

"Exactly what I needed. Now hear me out. The easiest way to raise this ransom is to raid Thalia's dowry of the twenty thousand pounds being held in trust for her. There is a clause allowing the trust to be broken if a dire emergency should occur. Both my solicitor and I say this is such a case. However, though I will try to make it up to her, she might come to you with nothing."

"I would take Thalia for my wife if she arrived in rags without a penny to her name."

The duke grinned broadly. "You are the man I believed you to be. Yes, a Longleigh woman is priceless, as you now realize. I have been wondering how my daughter captured your interest when you seemed to be immune to her charms."

Godric knew his face reddened to the same shade as his scar. "Umm, I found myself manacled in my own dungeon one evening and subjected to what she called the feather torture."

Far from sharing his embarrassment, the duke chuckled. "I know that one well, only the torment is usually performed with scarves tied to the bedposts. I could escape easily at any time but like to see how much I can endure before breaking my bonds and overcoming my wife. Manacles, you say?"

"I believe I was not meant to be set free, but I convinced Thalia to unlock my bonds. That is when we stained the red cloth." Rick bowed his head over his brandy glass unable to meet the duke's eyes. He half-expected to be challenged to a duel for seducing the man's daughter. When the duke laughed heartily, he raised his eyes again.

"Then, my boy, you understand why I must have my wife back. Extraordinary women. However did my daughter get you to the dungeon?"

"I believe Bascom helped. He felt I was dragging my feet when it came to making a proposal."

"And so you were. I've never seen Thalia try so hard to gain the attention of any man. Generally, all she must do is crook a finger in their direction to have them come running. Another reason I like you. You put up some resistance, but in the end we both fell before our ladies. Enough of fond reminiscence. We must discuss the raising of the ransom."

"Tell me what you want of me, and I will do all I can." He meant that. He'd mortgage Battle Hill if he must, endangering both his and Krista's future, all for Thalia.

The duke shifted in the unstable chair and threaded his large fingers together over this hard belly. "Besides using Thalia's dowry, I can also cash in the dowry of my daughter, Iris, and then take ten thousand each from my twin daughters who are only fifteen to share with their elder sisters. In time if my investments pay off, I will restore their funds. Do you think you could manage the six thousand for the servants?"

"Two of them are my responsibility, simply young lads excited to see the world. I am pleased they would not desert our ladies, Balfour also. I will not leave them to be slaves to the Turks even though the cargo was lost and that will set me back."

The tea tray rattling in her hands, Krista spoke from the doorway. "Use my dowry, too. I will have no need of it as I do not intend to marry."

She steadied herself and placed the tray gracefully on a table. A servant following behind deposited plates of biscuits and sandwiches of a size to satisfy a man. She dismissed the maid and poured cups for the men, inquiring how each wanted theirs prepared. Godric observed his sister, so improved in demeanor in the hands of the duchess, though he hoped that lady had not shared her bed secrets with the innocent. One moment Krista was a giggling girl tying pink ribbons on her horse and in another his hostess, making an extraordinary offer without reserve that could blight her future.

"If I accept your offer, I will restore your dowry to its original sum. Captain Belcher swears he can bring home a shipment that will replace our investments with a profit. You need not give up hope of marrying, Krista."

"You have told me Thalia is the only woman for you more than once. The duke feels the same about his wife. Why cannot you believe the only man I will ever love is Hugh Grey?"

Godric set down his tea to take his sister's hand. "Because you are so very young."

"But as true an Erikson as you. Take my money and bring home your bride and our faithful servants. Lord Bellevue, I have ordered a chamber prepared for your stay. Bascom will show you the way when you are ready. Now, I will see what our chef can prepare for dinner in your honor. If you will excuse me." She rose and the gentlemen with her.

"They grow up very fast, faster than boys, I do believe," the duke remarked pensively. "That brings me to another point. I intend to deliver this ransom myself as nothing must go awry, and I will trust no one else with my wife's safety this time. I propose to hire a small ship and sail to Tripoli with the treasure. My staff will see to the children, and my will is in order if I should not return. James is to take over as head of the family in just such an event and care for his younger siblings."

Rick took a turn at grinning. "James? Do you know what he wrote when I informed him of my engagement to his sister? Just two lines. 'I warned you of Queenie's power. I wonder what bait she set to lure you into the prison of marriage and slam shut the cage.' Hardly a man ready to assume the responsibility for nine siblings."

"He will cease his wandering and do his duty if he must, but I was thinking ten children. You might name him as guardian to your sister if you have a mind to join me in this venture. I brought my carriage. I propose Krista visit at Bellevue Hall until we return. Iris is nearly seventeen and thanks to the strict tutelage of that dry stick, Miss Thurgood, very well-educated at home and able to assume some responsibility for running the household even if her head is mostly in the clouds. My own very able butler can assist her. She will enjoy the company of a young lady her own age, though the children remaining in the nursery do provide much lively entertainment. I believe Bascom could see to Battle Hill and its affairs with no trouble at all. Are you with me?"

"I am. I only waited for you to ask."

Seventeen

Thalia observed her mother being the center of attention in the harem for the moment. These spoiled, idle women had so little to do with their time that any small novelty engrossed them for hours. Baring her yellow hair to the rays of the sun, the duchess sat near the center of the courtyard by a small fountain that cooled the desert air with its spray. She and Balfour had removed the crown from one of her wide-brimmed straw hats and pulled her tresses out the top to be laved with lemon juice. The Tripolitan princess explained to the other ladies that this beauty regimen accounted for the beautiful color of Lady Flora's hair. Because they would stoop to any artifice that would make them stand out and win the sultan's favor if only for a night, several concubines waited for Balfour to apply the juice to their own coarse black locks in hope of achieving the same result.

Naturally, they would not. Miss Thurgood always said one must make the most of one's best features, but the gifts of God should not be tampered with to any extreme. Regardless, the treatments were likely to go on for some time. With lemons growing right there in the courtyard, they had no shortage of the tart, acidic juice which also reminded her of Miss Thurgood. Her mother added sugar to life to make it more palatable. Thalia found herself admiring the woman who had given her life and embarrassed her for most of it with her unseemly passion for Papa, her outspoken opinions, and her total disregard for the opinions of others.

In fact, Lady Flora's nimble mind had concocted this diversion. While the women watched the hair treatment, she urged her daughter to compose a letter home. On the surface, the words must be flattering and unctuous when referring to the bashaw and their treatment. The truth of their situation might be written between the lines in the juice of the lemon. Thalia dipped her pen into the ink and began:

My Dear Papa,

I cannot say how graciously we are cared for by the Bashaw of Tripoli and his family. He is most generous with paper and ink and assures us that our messages will be sent directly to you. Even as I write, we sit in a most beauteous courtyard scented with jasmine and a hundred other perfumes while Mama treats her hair with the juice of the lemons that can be plucked directly from the trees in this tropic land. We do not lack for lemonade either.

The bashaw allows us daily outings to the market with our escort of two enormous Turks, our footmen, and Balfour to see to our safety. He gives us generous purses to spend at the shops of Jewish jewelers and insists we return bedecked in baubles superior to anything produced in England. Upon our request, he also lets us visit the captive American officers from the warship Philadelphia who are housed in their old embassy and awaiting ransom which their government declines to pay. We cheer them with song and the gentle presence of the female sex. The American ship's physician, Dr. Cowdery, is permitted to see to our health and also serves the family of the bashaw. How kind is the ruler of Tripoli!

Despite dwelling in a paradise, Mama and I know you will raise our ransom posthaste and send it at once to our genial host, Yusuf Karamanli. We send our love to you, my affianced, and the children.

Your devoted daughter,
Thalia

Casually selecting a new pen as if the nib of the first had broken, she dipped it quickly into a waiting bowl of lemon juice and wrote between the lines:

Mama says you will remember the old deceit of using lemon juice to send invisible messages. In truth, our health is good, and we are being treated well. Not so for the captive Americans. We are not able to visit the common seamen, many of them British, but have been able to provide some succor to the officers by buying gaudy bracelets one day and selling them the next for baskets of fruit and vegetables as they exist mainly on dry bread and camel meat. We bribed our guards to look aside at this, but now have the bashaw's permission to visit the captives openly. We suspect the purses provided to us came from our own baggage, but we would use them for this purpose regardless.

We are at the embassy almost daily from ten in the morning to noon before the day becomes too hot. The rest of the time, we are locked away deep in the castle with the harem. Mama believes you might try a rescue and begs you to be careful. Our guards are most formidable, and we travel about draped in the black robes of the Moslem women and so are not easily recognized when out of doors. Take care. Give all my love to Rick. Mama sends the same to you.

Thalia put that pen aside and picked up the one charged with ink lest anyone take note of her activity, but all eyes stayed on her mother and poor Balfour who sweated in the afternoon sun as she refused to adopt the lighter garments of the sultan's wives and concubines but stuck to her sturdy English cottons and long sleeves. Lady Flora, however, took to the oriental costumes, not baring her breasts of course, but robing herself with gossamer fabrics of bright colors and threads of gold. In fact, she'd had a pair of the scandalous sheer ladies' pantaloons made up and wore them with a wide-sleeved tunic to protect her delicate skin.

This won her great favor in the harem, while Balfour endured mockery she could not understand. When Thalia glanced back at her writing, the sere desert air had dried the lemon juice and caused it to vanish.

She began another letter:

My Dearest Betrothed,

Never fear for our safety. The bashaw treats us as if we were part of his own family and his generosity is great. While we await the day of our redemption, we fill our time with song, poetry, and the study of languages. Two of the ladies of the harem are natives of Italy and glad to assist us in perfecting our speech.

Mama, with her linguistic facility, has taken on the study of Arabic as well. She prepares a scroll of poetry for Papa with the Arabic words written above and the English below. She plans to embellish the edges with a painted pattern such as she might draw for her embroidery designs. A royal princess, the bashaw's own daughter, introduced us to this very ancient Persian poem written by a man called Omar Khayyam. I do not believe an English translation exists, but she gives us the words. I doubt we can do justice to this masterpiece of a civilization so much more ancient than ours.

As for our singing, I practice daily. At times, Mama joins me. This has drawn the attention of the bashaw. We now perform for him often. He rewards us with cups of sherbet and coffee as we sit at his feet, and gives us gifts from his treasure chests. Though we live in luxury, I do beg you to join with Papa in raising our ransom so we can soon be home again.

With Deepest Love,

Yr. Thalia

As Balfour with sweat dribbling from her forehead applied lemon juice to the tresses of the concubines, Thalia seized the pen filled with lemon juice and wrote:

It is true we are well, my love, but time passes most tediously. The Italian ladies have my pity. They became part of the harem to ransom their parents. While they have been forced to accept

Mohammedanism, they tell us, as no others speak their native tongue, that they remain true to Christ in their hearts. Having both borne a child to the bashaw, they will remain here forever. I cannot bear to think that might be my fate.

I do not like the way the princess's husband, the infamous Murad Reis, looks at me when we cross paths. I suspect he watches from a latticed balcony where the bashaw comes to choose his bed mate for the night. How the princess bears the admiral I do not know, for he is coarse and of rough habits. I suspect if Papa has a plan, you will be part of it. Knowing your martial nature, I doubt he could leave you behind. We did fight, Mama and I, but not well enough. Oh, do be careful in whatever comes to pass.

While Mama prefers another stanza of the poem I mentioned, I will leave you with this:

> *Ah love! could you and I with Him conspire*
> *To grasp this sorry Scheme of things entire,*
> *Would not we shatter it to bits—and then*
> *Re-mould it nearer to the Heart's Desire!*

Red streaks appeared in the dark hair of the concubines as Thalia's words faded on the paper. Two of them were wroth because their locks had not turned golden and demanded that Balfour be punished. The duchess let them know only she had the right to chastise her servant. A hair-pulling fight might have ensued to the delight of the bored women, but the princess interceded and suggested both the sun and tempers had grown too hot. All should retire to their chambers for the afternoon nap. She'd told Thalia that, though her own mother had passed away to be replaced by another wife, the princess still held her father's favor and the others deferred to her.

Having risen to come to her mother and Balfour's defense, Thalia sat again and folded her letters. With a smile, she gave them to the princess to post. She only hoped their ruse would fool the censors, pave their way to freedom, and back into the arms of the men they loved.

Eighteen

The sheer tedium of obtaining a ship, preparing for a sea voyage, getting their legal affairs in order, and finding enough guineas to provide the ransom in coin shredded the patience of the Duke of Bellevue, who being a man of action, had very little of it unless he was stalking game on his estate. Here Godric's cooler nature came to the fore. He excelled at list making and deferred desire. At one point, when the duke threatened to break the neck of the solicitor handling the transfer of the dowries because of his slow but meticulous progress, Godric intervened.

"Do not want to make any errors, now do we," the bewigged old gentleman said in a quavering voice as the duke with his large hands squeezing an imaginary windpipe towered over him.

Rick jollied his future father-in-law out of violence by suggesting they remove to a tavern and write James, informing him of his guardianship of Krista and his mandate to care for his younger siblings, see they were educated, and well-married should anything go badly wrong as they sought to retrieve his mother and sister. Over ale, he told the duke tales about the footloose James and speculated how his son would receive the news—with a curse, no doubt. Sobering, the duke said, "We must prevail because we cannot fail in our mission. We need be certain James never assumes these duties."

By the time they returned to the solicitor's chamber, the lawyer had calmed his jangled nerves and in an amazing burst of speed, finished the legal papers. Yes, Danelagh thought he did work well with his future father-in-law. They could now turn their minds to the rescue.

In early July, Krista set off in the ducal coach with Pinkie tied behind as she would not leave her horse. She shed tears aplenty, but at the same time quivered with excitement at making her first visit to a great house other than her own and having young ladies near her age for company. That done, the men traveled to Hull to board the small, swift ship they had chartered and see personally to the loading of the chests full of ransom money. They'd found a small trading vessel called the *Redemption* captained by a man named Featherstone and considered both names to be propitious for the success of their mission.

Besides the treasure, the duke also brought aboard a rather curious box of his own, very plain and greatly battered with wear. When Godric inquired about its contents, Bellevue beckoned him to their cabin. There, he revealed the contents, an actor's many disguises.

"Wherever did you obtain this?" Rick asked as he lifted wigs and opened pots of stage makeup.

Looking a little shamefaced, the duke said, "My father, William 'Billy the Bull' Longleigh, soldier that he was before assuming the title, had a secret penchant for the stage. He performed from time to time under an assumed name and sponsored an acting troop, if you can imagine that waste of money. He left this box behind when he died. The children enjoy playing with its contents, but I thought we might have need of a disguise and brought it from the nursery."

Rick smeared a dab from one container onto the back of his pale hand. It left a dark streak. "If I ever need to play the Moor, this will do the trick."

"Old Billy favored the Bard of Avon and once played Othello, though his favorite role was King Lear. We often clashed in opinion, but my children adored him. A neglectful father, he made up for that with his grandchildren. James might have been his own son he was so proud of the boy. He doted on my many daughters, but always tweaked me about having only the one heir before he passed away. Then of course, I fathered three more. Rarely can we impress our fathers."

"I do know that," Rick agreed.

They closed the chest and went out on deck to watch the casting off from the port of Hull and the slow fading of the view of England's cliffs in the distance. Still, their ship ventured carefully into the channel, rabbiting away from any sail on the horizon should it prove to be a French privateer who would delight in taking their strongboxes of gold. What with running and hiding along the way, their voyage to Gibraltar took in excess of two weeks. During that time, the duke paced the deck very much like the proverbial caged beast. Rick engaged him in saber practice to pass the time and burn off his impatience, but declined to teach him the use of the Mensur sword.

"Mar that face of yours and I would have to answer to Lady Flora," he demurred. "She already blames me for marking her son."

"You do not want Flora to bear you a grudge, believe me," Bellevue said.

However during one bout, he slashed the duke's shirt and viewed firsthand the fabled tattoos inflicted on that broad chest by the Shawnee savages. Many claimed the man bore them but few had seen their likeness. Two stylized red birds ornamented his bronze skin. As Bellevue blotted the scratch he received with the torn fabric, he noted the path of Godric's gaze.

He pointed the tip of his saber at his opponent's face. "Ah, my thunderbirds, symbols of great power. I assure you getting them is more painful than any Mensur scratch, but I, too, did not flinch. My wife finds them very intriguing. In fact, she...no, no, too intimate a detail to reveal about the duchess."

"But I am soon to be family." Rick found the irregularities of the Longleighs endlessly entertaining compared to his strict and puritanical upbringing. No wonder he craved passion.

"Let me just say she bears the figure of a butterfly on a part of her anatomy you will never see. I swear you to silence. Even James does not know nor any of the rest of the children."

"You have my promise."

He and the duke became comrades on that voyage, bound fast as brothers by the time they put in at Gibraltar to gather news and receive messages as they'd written ahead that any communications coming from Tripoli be held for them there at the naval station. Two letters awaited, both in Thalia's hand, the duke remarked with some disappointment. They took them to the ramparts to peruse. Bellevue frowned as he read the missive addressed to him.

"Nothing but how lovely their life is within the harem and the generosity of their host. Ha! Their conniving, treaty-breaking kidnapper she should say. Here, there is nothing in it you cannot read. Yours?" He held out his letter for exchange. The wind riffled the pages as Rick took them.

"Mine is much the same. It is true the bashaw is open-handed with paper—and lemons. Perhaps the duchess could not write as she was having her hair done. Thalia saw no need to crisscross her sentences and left wide spaces between the lines."

"Bah, we have lemons in the conservatory at Bellevue Hall and better quality paper than this. Why write of lemons as if they were some exotic fruit?" He struck his hands together suddenly and caused one of the tailless, brown apes lurking on the wall in hopes of getting a handout of food to bare its fangs.

"Yes, wide spaces! Why did I not see it! We need a candle, a lamp, any source of heat at once. Damnation, simply hold the pages up to the sun."

Rick took a sheet and raised it to the light. "I see sentences between the sentences but cannot quite make them out."

"An old ruse unknown to the bashaw's censors evidently. When away, I frequently sent my wife such messages written in invisible ink lest the children get hold of my letters—not that we have been parted often. Quickly, find a lamp and all will be revealed."

They went immediately to the chamber assigned to them while the ship took on fresh water and supplies and lit a lamp. Gradually, pale brown letters emerged in Thalia's flowing script as the paper heated.

"Do you see, son? Our ladies are not content. They want us to rescue them and have given us the information to do exactly that." A fierce fire lit in Bellevue's dark eyes.

Godric felt he had to lay a restraining hand on the duke's broad shoulder. "Father-to-be, we must consult with the commander here and learn the situation with the Americans first. They blockade Tripoli and even getting a ransom to the bashaw depends of their goodwill. We must plan carefully and measure our words."

"The Yankees be damned! I am not inclined to part with my gold when Thalia has told us when and where we might find our ladies and deliver them from the Turk. Stealth and disguises are called for and plenty of armaments." The duke pounded the sturdy military table with his fist and made the lantern jump.

Rick steadied the lamp before it could tip and set the letters aflame. He planned to keep his always and folded it carefully before placing it in his waistcoat. The duke did likewise but said, smirking at the younger man, "A pretty piece of poetry my daughter sent you, too."

~ * ~

As if some ancient god of the sea plotted to keep them from their destination and raised a gale exactly for that purpose, they had to keep to Gibraltar for several days due to poor weather and wayward winds. The commanding officer warned them of the possibility of more bad seas to come with the temperatures climbing higher as August approached and the winds out of Africa stirred the Mediterranean waters. They might expect to encounter rains bearing mud concocted from the dust and sand of the Sahara. Godric's spirits sank as he learned this news, and he took to cursing the storms and the heat as vehemently as the duke. His control evaporated with each stray gust from the ocean.

To Godric's relief, Bellevue demanded his captain set sail for Tripoli as soon as the skies cleared. Not long on their way, another storm overtook their ship and sent it speeding off course. Far from cowering in their cabin, the duke cursed into the teeth of the gale and lent his strength wherever it was needed. Godric stood by his side, offering another pair of strong arms. Fierce enough to damage the sails and snarl the rigging, the winds finally relented after three days and allowed the vessel to drop anchor in Malta for repairs. Finally, after days that seemed endless to Rick, they arrived in view of Tripoli on August second with the British flag snapping on their mast.

The American ships, newly returned from evading the tempest and undergoing their own repairs, blocked the way. The duke ordered a boat to be rowed to their command ship, the *Constitution*, as spick and span a vessel as ever sailed the seas.

"I am certain their commodore is a man of reason as am I. He will allow us to enter the city either to deliver the ransom or rescue our ladies."

Not nearly as positive as Bellevue, Godric asked to accompany him. As it turned out, Commodore Preble was every bit a match for the duke. The old salt stood nearly as tall and broad-shouldered. Stern blue eyes flanked his hawk-like nose and sat above humorless lips and a sturdy jaw. He combed his thinning brown hair forward much like the little giant, Napoleon, and probably for the same reason, to hide a bald spot beneath his impressive naval bicorne hat. An uncompromising sort, he quickly denied Bellevue access to the city without so much as offering a seat or coffee first.

"Our mission is to deny trade and treasure to the bashaw until such a time as he releases our captured sailors from the *Philadelphia*, over three hundred in number, many of them British nationals. I cannot allow you to augment his treasury with still more ill-gotten gains."

Getting closer to their leader than the younger officers deemed comfortable as they shifted their hands to their swords, Bellevue bared his teeth and said, "Do you know who I am?"

"I do, sir—Pearce Longleigh, the redskin viscount, now a duke. I admit to reading of your youthful exploits among the Shawnee and extend to you a certain admiration. We have much in common, prowess with rifle for one. As you picked off six buffalo in a row from a tree perch, I once shot five swallows on the wing with five bullets. Both of us have the love of a good woman, but I left mine behind in Maine and do not allow her to go traipsing about in dangerous waters and then require rescuing."

The red hue of the duke's face deepened. Glad he had come along to prevent mayhem, Godric laid a stilling hand on the bunched muscles of his arm and said, "But Commodore Preble, if your beloved wife was captured, you would go to her rescue, would you not?"

"Of course, I...to my quarters. Coffee!" he shouted to an orderly. He strode ahead to his cabin and beckoned them to chairs set before a serviceable desk bolted to the floor of the vessel. The gentlemen sat in silence until the orderly returned with cups already poured and a generous bowl of sugar lumps to sweeten the beverage.

"One blessed good thing about this siege, easy access to sugar and good coffee. I admit I've grown as fond as the Turks of taking it thick, black and sweet." The commodore dismissed the orderly, whose exit revealed several young officers lurking right beyond the entry. Godric imagined they regarded the duke as a menace to their commander, but the door shut in their concerned faces, leaving the three men in privacy.

"See here, Longleigh. I sympathize with your dilemma, but you must have noticed we are on the verge of doing battle. Murad Reis has arrayed his gunboats in a line two miles long to protect the city. Tomorrow at precisely one-thirty p.m., we shall begin a bombardment of their fleet and the palace. Word of our intentions must go no further. This is why I must deny you access to the city."

The duke, having sweetened his small cup with two large lumps of sugar, brightened. "Then we have all tomorrow morning to rescue my wife and daughter. Would you permit me to send a message to them about a rendezvous? I will need pen, ink, paper—and lemon juice."

"Certainly. They might gain some comfort knowing you are near, but going into the city at this moment would be lunacy." The commodore laid out the writing materials from his own supply and did not seem at all surprised by the request for lemon juice. He yelled at the orderly who waited nearby to bring that last item.

The duke wrote:

My Dearest Flora,

I have arrived with the ransom but am prevented from delivering it to the mighty Bashaw, Yusuf Karamanli, by the American blockade. Do not despair. I will find a way for the sultan to receive the gold and free you and our beloved daughter. Let her know that Danelagh is with me and will aid in this endeavor.

Yr. Loving Husband, Pearce

When the lemon juice arrived, Preble calmly handed over a clean pen. "We have been communicating with our captive officers using exactly the same method. Their messages have been very informative."

Between the lines, Bellevue wrote:

Go as usual to the American embassy at ten. Be prepared to flee. Danelagh and I will meet you there and carry you back to our ship. Be not afraid, my ever brave Flora. I am coming to rescue you again.

He offered the pen to Godric who added: *Soon we will be together my darling Thalia, very soon. With all my love, Rick.*

As the lemon juice faded into the paper, the duke remarked, "Touching. If you will see to its delivery today, I would appreciate that, Commodore Preble. One more favor if you please. Could you spare us a guide of some sort to show us the way to the consulate where the Americans are held?"

"We have aboard a sniveling Italian who tried to run the blockade and escape the harbor with his cargo. He has proved useful as an intermediary to the bashaw and knows the city. Make what use of him you will, but I cannot be responsible for your safety or that of your women. If one word of our plan leaks out, I shall personally come aboard your vessel and shoot you dead." His stark blue stare did not waver from the duke's face.

"Understood, Commodore. Know that I would receive a thousand bastinadoes on my feet and buttocks and never utter a word if captured. However, since your ships are already aligned against the high admiral's forces across the bay, I do think a coming attack is highly obvious. We will try to return your Italian unscathed." The duke held out his hand.

The commodore shook it. "Right now, the Italian is the least of my worries, Longleigh. Go with God, sir."

As they prepared to debark, a launch bearing a white flag left the *Constitution* and headed toward the line of Moslem gunboats to pass the message to Murad Reis. Godric smiled to himself as the Americans delivered the nervous Italian to their boat and they made their way back to their own ship. For all that was said of the duke's temper, he had just observed a master of schemes.

Nineteen

Taking advantage of the princess's sunny and spacious suite, Thalia and her mother sat embroidering two wide sashes with their hostess, who worked on her own. The needlework certainly helped to pass the tedious days until Thalia might see Rick again. Italy held less and less appeal.

Lady Flora held her nearly finished piece up for approval. A swooping design of blazing golden firebirds ran the length of the crimson cloth, leaving a pattern of orange and yellow flames in their wake. "I believe your father will adore this. He misses gaudy finery now that men's fashions have gone so brown, black and white. This will make an excellent tie for his dressing gown."

"Papa still dresses as if he lives in the previous century—but I do think he will love it. Look what I've made for Rick." Thalia presented her work, a much more subdued creation of silver crescent moons and stars on a bluish-gray background. "Thank you for sharing your beautiful threads and cloth with us, Princess."

The bashaw's daughter nodded her lovely head. "I make this for my husband." She laid out a sash of bright red and green flowers edged in gold.

"Marrying you must have been a great honor for Murad Reis," Lady Flora commented.

"My father needed the loyalty of a superior admiral for his fleet. I was very young and being given to the boldest of corsairs excited me. I pleaded for his advancement after our marriage." She spoke the words as if she wished she had not.

Thalia could not imagine being wedded to such a repellant man, but her fate might be the same. She pricked her finger and quickly sucked away the blood to prevent damaging the cloth.

Appearing like an evil jinn that had been summoned by injudicious speech, the high admiral of the sultan's fleet strode into the chamber and stretched out on the cushioned divan where his wife sat, wrapping around her like a lithe but lethal serpent. Cleopatra and the fatal asp, Thalia could not help but think. He withdrew a letter from his loose white shirt and held it out to the duchess, making her come to him to receive it. "From your husband, madam. Would you care to read it to us now?"

There being little choice, Lady Flora opened the missive addressed to her. "Thalia, good news! Your father has arrived with the ransom and brings Danelagh with him. However, the American blockade prevents him from delivering the gold."

"Do not fash yourself about that, Duchess. Tomorrow, I plan to break the blockade with my cannons and take their flagship for my own. I saw the vessel bearing the British flag anchored just beyond the American line. Wouldna it be a pity if one of my rounds sank it and took your father and betrothed to the bottom of the sea, Lady Thalia?"

Thalia suppressed a shudder. She would not give him the satisfaction of upsetting her.

Murad Reis reached into his shirt tightly belted with a piece of the princess's handiwork and took out a flat flask. He pulled the cork with his teeth, spit the stopper on the floor, and drank heartily. His wife's face darkened with distress.

"My father will be upset if he does not get his gold, my husband. Should you not keep a clear head for the coming battle?" she said in English out of courtesy for her guests.

As casually as if he were taking a tidbit from their tray of refreshments, the admiral raised a suntanned hand and slapped his wife's face. He lay back again and took another swig from his flask. "*Aguardiente*, the local rotgut made from dates, but verra effective. A man must chastise his wife as he sees fit. Woman, I can fish that gold from the ocean floor if need be and make a second wife of this young woman if I so desire. Strong drink has never impaired me in battle or the bedchamber."

Thalia did tremble then, not out of fear but anger that a gentle lady would be treated in such a barbaric way. She vowed to herself if forced to become the wife of Murad Reis, she'd kill him in his sleep even if it meant her own death.

With her embroidery dropped to the cool floor tiles, the princess sat with one hand pressed to her brown cheek. The golden fringe above her kohl-lined, brown eyes trembled. She replied to him in Arabic spoken at such a clip even Lady Flora could not follow.

"Do not threaten me with your father's wrath, wife. The fate of his city lies in my hands. Ladies, ye will excuse us now and be gone to your own chamber. Me and my wife have matters to discuss."

"We should stay, Mama," Thalia said, thinking their presence might prevent more abuse.

The corsair twisted a hand in his wife's long hair. "It will go worse for her later if ye do. Like a dog, a woman must be corrected immediately when she errs. Ye will learn that, too, my lovely Thalia, when the bashaw gives ye to me as a reward for my upcoming victory."

Given no real choice, the women gathered their sewing and left. The cries of the princess accompanied them along the corridor. Thalia pressed her hands to her ears. "I wish we could take her with us when we go, Mama."

"I would wish it, too, but that is an impossibility. Even in the Christian world, women seldom know what they will get in a marriage and cannot escape their fate once they have said their vows. I am fortunate to be married to my heart's desire, my great and gentle bear. I believe Danelagh would consider taking his fists to a woman cowardly, but if he ever should, you must come home at once."

Thalia considered if Rick would take his fist to her and could not envision the possibility. Still, many girls her age probably thought the same of the men who courted them before their marriage. Feeling free to say what she'd thought earlier, she startled her mother by saying, "I would do more than return home. Papa did not teach me to use a stiletto for nothing."

Her mother's gray eyes widened with concern. "I pray none of my daughters have to go so far to escape brutality. That is why I take such an interest in whom you take for your mate. But if your thoughts dwell on Murad Reis, I would do the same."

In their room, they found Balfour taking advantage of the generous supply of paper and ink. She used a small boat-shaped oil lamp ancient in style to illuminate her page.

"Whatever are you about, Balfour?" the duchess questioned.

"Keeping a journal of our stay in the harem, your Grace, but only on those occasions when you do not need my services." The maid hastily gathered her writing materials and put them away.

"If my guess is correct, your journal is about to come to an end." Lady Flora held the brief letter over the flame of the small, clay lamp. "As I suspected, the duke is planning to meet us at the consulate tomorrow. Rescue me again, indeed! The idea was mine. Well, no matter. We should make our plans now. We must leave our boxes behind, obviously. I suggest we wear several gowns under our black robes and take any portable wealth left to us, the bashaw's gems and the gold chains and bangles. He will owe us a new wardrobe."

Eagerly, Thalia suggested, "We should paint our eyes to blend in with the populace as we flee and wear our most sturdy shoes."

"I think we must not enter the consulate. We do not want to endanger the valiant Americans in our escape. We must devise some ruse to linger outside if our men are not precisely on time." The duchess tapped her forehead with one white finger as she thought.

Balfour raised a timid hand. "I can feign the vapors. Between the beggars with their open sores, the heat and the filth of the streets, I often feel faint when we go out into the city regardless."

"Very good, Balfour, quite inventive of you," the duchess commended. She poured three cups from the ever-present flagon of fruit juice and proposed another toast. "To our freedom, ladies."

~ * ~

Before the sun rose on August third, the duke and Danelagh made their own preparations, the greatest of which consisted of staining Rick's skin with the stage makeup and outfitting him in a black wig and short false beard. Having dark skin, hair and eyes, Bellevue pointed out he had little need for any embellishments of his appearance, but chose a great black beard for himself anyway. Their Italian guide supplied two voluminous, gray hooded robes in his possession to complete their disguise, but he could not convince either to give up boots for sandals or felt slippers. Beneath the robes, each man wore his English clothes, bore a saber, and carried a pistol and a dagger for close work. Rick considered them well-prepared to take on the Turks.

With the oars of their small boat muffled, the duke sitting in the stern and the thin, nervous Italian in the bow, Godric rowed them into the harbor, passing through the line of the bashaw's navy like thread through the eye of a needle and ever evading the glimmer of the ship's lamps on the water. They beached their boat in a place the Italian deemed safe and easy to reach upon return.

"Going to be a bit trickier getting back," the duke said, but that observation did not prevent him from following their guide immediately into the warrens of Tripoli.

Godric, thinking ahead, marked each dark doorway they passed with chalk as the paths twisted between tight-packed buildings. His foresight proved valuable when their guide pointed out the consulate building, and running as fast as he could away from the coming encounter with the sultan's guards, promptly vanished onto a side street.

"I have never trusted Italians, Bellevue. They would rather poison a person than fight. You see why I was reluctant to let Thalia live among them."

"You have more experience of them than I. I bow to your superior knowledge and cunning in marking our way." The duke did exactly that, then settled himself with arms crossed over the false beard against a shadowed wall for a long wait. Godric took a place beside him, the two of them mimicking indolent Turks passing the time.

The sun rose. The mullahs climbed their many-stepped minarets and called out the first prayers of the day, waking Rick from a light doze. He felt the tension in the air of Tripoli as thick as Turkish coffee. People began to gather on the flat rooftops for a better view of the upcoming battle, no secret as the duke had said, only a matter of when and who would fire the first shots.

~ * ~

In the harem, the women could speak of little else than the upcoming battle. When the princess appeared, walking stiffly without her usual grace but not outwardly marked, they heaped her with praises for her husband's valor and prayers for his safety. The unfortunate wife of Murad Reis accepted their praises and wishes with a serene nod and took a seat on a cushion. When Lady Flora, dressed in her Arab costume, asked after her health, the princess merely indicated that she was as well as ever. Thalia sincerely hoped the man died today.

Advancing their plans, Thalia suggested they paint their eyes to pass the time. The concubines, happy to share their cosmetics and expertise, supplied a paste of deep blue ground lapis to apply to their lids and aided in outlining the rims with kohl. Even Balfour submitted to the process, though they laughed at her as she screwed up her face while they worked.

"Now you are one of us," the princess remarked sadly.

Thalia leaned near and spoke low. "I have no desire to wed your husband, only to return to my own betrothed."

"After today, you may not have the choice if Murad Reis triumphs."

"Forgive me, but then I must hope he does not."

The duchess interrupted by clapping her hands. "Come, we must put on our robes for our walk to the consulate. Perhaps the Americans will allow us to watch the battle with them from their rooftop."

"Take care, my friends," the princess said.

"And you," Thalia answered as the duchess shooed her maid and daughter back to their chamber.

There, they donned the extra clothes they had discussed, and loaded themselves with the pasha's chains, bracelets, and loose gems. Thalia looked critically at her mother who busily wrapped the sash she had sewn for the duke around the illuminated scroll of poetry and shoved both into the baggy pantaloons of her costume. "Are you going to the ship as dressed as a harem girl?"

"Your father will adore this outfit and the bottom is quite convenient for carrying objects without them falling out. I shall put two of my gowns over it and surprise him when I disrobe."

"Oh, Mama!" What else could a daughter say?

On the other hand, Balfour filled out her meager bosom with the pages of her journal and put her second dress over the top. Thalia chose the gown of jonquil, naturally, and two others. By the time they were done, each looked as if they had gained twenty pounds while in the sultan's care. Their black robes went over the top. Each wore sturdy shoes with a pair of more dainty slippers stuffed inside.

They made their waddling way to the guarded doors of the harem. Their usual escort waited, two enormous Turks heavily armed with daggers, pikes, and scimitars, and the footmen, Wills and Geoffrey, dressed in the garb of slaves and prisoners: a hooded jacket, a plain shirt, pantaloons, and slippers. Early on, the two young men had assured the duchess that, though dressed as heathens, they had retained their English undergarments and would never give them up. Their earnest patriotism made Lady Flora smile and the younger women flush. Both of their blond giants had dwindled in size with lack of food and hard labor, but were no less handsome as the African sun browned their faces and made their blue eyes and light hair even more striking. If left behind, the footmen would bring a pretty price in the slave market. Lady Flora swore this would not happen. As they had not abandoned her, she would not abandon them, she'd proclaimed often enough for them to believe it.

This morning, Wills made Balfour blush again, though little could be seen of it beneath her veil, by saying, "Why Miss, your eyes look very fetching today."

Geoffrey nodded in agreement. He'd never been right since the blow to his head and suffered from headaches and vision problems, but he refused be left behind, no matter how ill he felt when the ladies went into the city. "You never know what these foreigners might try, and I will give my life to stop them," he asserted, knowing their guards had no English.

The loyal footmen had a far harder time of it than the ladies. When asked by the duchess about their trials, they described hauling water for the janissaries, shoveling dung of all kinds from dog to horse to camel, and doing whatever else their captives cared to inflict upon them. Having them accompany the ladies gave them some respite, and so Lady Flora always asked for them every day until their presence became routine.

Today, Wills told her, "They threaten to take our manhood, they do, acting it out like to shake our nerves. One who has got a little English says then we can go live in the harem like the geldings they have there to serve the women."

"Eunuchs?" Lady Flora supplied the dreaded word.

"That's right, your Grace, that's the word. But we don't flinch, Geoffrey and me. I'd kill meself before I let that happen."

The huge Turk with a single long braid sprouting from a topknot on his shaved head, Hassan by name, shouted a command they had all learned meant "Shut up" and gestured curtly for them to get in line. He frequently insulted them in his own language, not knowing the duchess understood his every word. She had repeated the phrases to the princess who reluctantly translated and offered to have another guard assigned. But no, Lady Flora said. Hassan amused her. She did not add that she hoped her husband would kill the guard when he came, as she was sure Bellevue would do. No need to distress the princess by saying so. The other guard, Tarek, very much an underling, was just as big but not as bad. He laughed at his superior's remarks but rarely made any himself.

The procession formed up with one guard to the front, then Geoffrey, the tiny duchess, tall Thalia, the maid and Wills bringing up the rear with the second guard. Their retinue was well recognized outside the palace. Merchants called out friendly greetings and held up their wares as they marched along the twisting streets. Beggars cried out for baksheesh, and Lady Flora, known for her generosity, scattered small coins brought for the purpose. The mendicants fought for this largesse like village curs over offal. They trailed the group until the guards drove them off.

At the consulate doors, Hassan raised the butt of his pike to demand entrance for the ladies. No sign of their rescuers, only two large, bearded locals with raised hoods loitered against a nearby wall. The duchess whispered to Balfour as the women clumped together, "Faint!"

The maid did, putting a hand to her forehead and declaring, "I feel vaporish," before dropping like a stone toward the cobbles. Wills caught her going down, and the other ladies began exclaiming and fanning Balfour's face with their hands. Thalia whispered in her mother's ear, "Do you see the boots beneath those robes?"

Lady Flora nodded and, not daring to let her eyes seek the duke, patted her maid's cheeks. Disgust on their fierce faces, their escorts turned toward the commotion. Hassan made an unflattering comment in Arabic and tried to jerk Balfour upward. It would be his last insult.

Twenty

Casting their robes aside, the duke and Danelagh surged from their resting place. They led with their pistols, but Hassan deflected the duke's weapon with his pike. Danelagh's shot went wide as the guard flattened himself again the wall. Casting the useless guns aside, the Englishmen came on with swords drawn. Hassan attempted to impale Bellevue on the pike, but the duke knocked it aside with his saber and came down hard on the shaft near its head to shatter the blade from the rod. The Turk threw the shaft aside and engaged with his scimitar in one hand and a dagger in the other.

Wills propped Balfour against the wall, seized the discarded rod, and began laying about the Turk's broad shoulders and head. The enemy paid no more attention than he would to a sweat fly buzzing round his head. Thalia stooped, picked up the broken blade, and wrapped it in a fold of her robe to await her moment.

Danelagh took on Tarek, battering at his pike's staff until his blade forced the tip skyward and another blow sent it spinning out of the guard's hand. Quick to draw his own sword, the second Turk defended himself aggressively. Too evenly matched to dispatch one another, they battered away, each waiting for the other to tire. Thalia screamed with all her soprano might, the only thing she could think to do in warning. The shriek broke the warriors' concentration and both glanced aside to see the duke, his boot slipping on a piece of fruit left to rot in the streets, go crashing to the ground. Balfour, who had pulled herself up against the wall, slid down again.

The giant Hassan sprang atop him with dagger raised high. Bellevue strained against the man's weapon arm with a strong hand and pulled against the other to unseat him. Lady Flora threw herself on the man's muscular back and grabbed both his elbows, trying to prevent the fatal blow. Quickly using the flat of his blade to disarm his own distracted enemy by striking his wrist, Danelagh spun to rescue Bellevue with a decisively placed, two-handed blow that cut half way through the Turk's neck and barely missed the top of Lady Flora's veiled head.

Balfour took in the sight of spraying blood and fainted dead away at Thalia's feet. Considering her mother's valor, Thalia felt nearly as useless as the maid. Geoffrey put himself in front of her and the fallen woman as Tarek charged at them. Dagger gripped in his teeth, he bodily lifted the unarmed footman and flung the man into Danelagh, the rising Bellevue, Wills, and little Lady Flora, taking them all down. Ignoring the maid, he pulled Thalia tight against his chest with a thick arm around her shoulders and his dagger poised to slit her throat. He spat out an order. All action ceased.

The duchess, huddled against her husband's bloody chest, translated the obvious. "He will kill her if you do not surrender."

Danelagh and Bellevue dropped their swords. Tarek grinned like a shark at a sea full of drowning men and made a gesture is if he would cut the woman's throat after all now that his enemies were disarmed. Thalia's arm jerked hard, deflecting the knife. Godric threw himself forward, but before reaching her captor, the Turk's eyes widened. He dropped his weapon and staggered back. The blade of the broken pike protruded from a spurting wound deep in his groin. Balfour newly awakened, fainted again as the blood showered over her.

"Good work, my daughter, true to the Longleighs," the duke said as he gathered his sword and tossed Godric his own bloody weapon. With her own robe spattered, Thalia stepped aside and braced herself against the wall. She had nearly killed a man and would not falter now. Her men impaled Tarek more or less simultaneously, putting a fast and final end to him.

"Get the weapons. You, revive Balfour and haul her up. We must move before the guards inside the consulate figure out this is not a diversion to make them open the doors for the Americans to escape," Bellevue ordered. "Splendid," he said, helping himself to the foot-long dagger with a carved ivory handle that had almost dispatched him.

Geoffrey, a bit wobbly himself, knelt to pat Balfour's cheeks, and that failing, hoisted her upright. She blinked her kohl-lined eyes. "Is it over? Did I miss the fight?"

"Afraid so, Miss. Brief but victorious."

Godric retrieved the pistols, scimitars, and remaining dagger, leaving the broken pikes behind. "We must assume our robes again and try to make our way to the boat as normally as possible. At least they will cover the blood stains."

"Not on me, but wearing black has always been useful to hide spills." The duchess brushed against the front of her dark robe. Her hands came away red, and Balfour sagged against Geoffrey. "While she is out, hand me that dagger, my dear."

"Must you, my blood-thirsty darling?"

"He tried to kill my husband." She sliced off the long, braided queue from the nearly beheaded Turk, but did not take the skin with it.

As usual, the duke told her she had not scalped the man correctly, but she shoved the braid up her sleeve. Her parents—Thalia never knew what to expect of them next, but in this moment, she was grateful to have both alive.

The duchess calmly suggested they leave. "You and Godric go first like Arab men leading their timid wives and with Wills and Geoffrey walking behind as our obedient slaves. Walking in that order we should not arouse suspicion."

She took her place behind her husband, but Thalia moved forward to help Rick settle his robe over his shoulders. With one hand still wrapped in her robes, she adjusted the black wig that had come askew with the other hand and kissed his lips right there for all to see. "You make a very handsome Arab, my love."

"And you are worth all the women in the sultan's harem."

The duke cleared his throat. "None of that now. We must march. Getting away will be difficult enough in broad daylight without any more delays."

With Wills and Geoffrey supporting Balfour until she grew steadier on her feet, they followed the chalk marks until they nearly reached the beach. It seemed all the populace had taken to the roofs to await the battle and only themselves and the beggars still roamed the streets. A blind flower seller sitting under an awning still offered his bouquets as he had nothing to see and women might want to purchase posies to toss at the heroic troops after the victory. Bellevue and Danelagh paused nearby to recharge their pistols and distribute a scimitar to each to the footmen now that they no longer had to pose as slaves. Thalia held out her hand for the ornate dagger. She would not go unarmed again and intended to hold her own if their boat was boarded.

Godric gave the orders to his servants. "We must go as quickly as we can across the beach. Wills and Geoffrey, you row. Bellevue and I will have our pistols at the ready. Go around the near side of the Turkish fleet. They are looking seaward, and we might get past before any notice. I doubt if they will want to waste a cannonball on a boat filled with women. We must simply take our chances."

"Wait, I have an idea," said Lady Flora. "Do not groan, my dearest. You have not heard it yet, my dear! Allow me to buy some flowers."

"Flora, darling, we haven't time for horticultural souvenirs. We need to get to our ship before the bombardment begins."

"If we are noticed by Murad Reis' men, I propose we shower them with flowers while shouting *Allahu Akbar*, Allah is great, as if offering them tribute. While they are bemused, we row away."

"Isn't that blasphemy, your Grace?" Balfour said with a trembling voice.

"Only if the Archbishop of Canterbury is in the boat with us, and I do not think any of us will tell him later. Deceit and cunning are part of warfare."

"Buy your flowers, my little general. I pray we don't have to use them."

Lady Flora found her most valuable Turkish coin and pressed it into the flower seller's hand. He fingered the size and the imprint and blessed her many times over as she thrust large bouquets of tropical blossoms at Thalia and Balfour. Admiring her mother's cunning, Thalia took hers with a slight smile.

The duchess used her Arabic to urge the blind man to stay inside today, and having made a considerable amount on one sale, he took her advice and began closing shop. His unexpected customers moved onto the beach and, thank God in heaven, found the boat exactly where it had been left.

The men helped the women wearing their bulky attire into the small vessel and pushed it into the water. Obviously, the duke and Danelagh had not expected three rather slim women to take up so much room as they were quite crowded. The footmen climbed in and took the oars to hold the boat steady while Godric and Bellevue took seats in the bow and stern to balance the load. Their small vessel surged forward as Wills and Geoffrey rowed the length of the harbor and passed under the bow of a Tripolitan gunboat. The hour neared noon and once past, no shadows hid the little, overloaded boat. A Turkish seaman called out and drew the attention of his fellows. Several raised pistols in their direction.

"Now ladies," the duchess said. "*Allahu Akbar!*" she cried and strewed her flowers into the water. Thalia did the same with great enthusiasm. Quaking as if she put her soul in mortal danger, Balfour complied with less vigor. For good measure, Lady Flora used her Arabic to tout their bravery and say simple prayers for their welfare. The dark-skinned sailors grinned beneath their turbans and shouted back less than polite invitations for the women to come aboard. Seeing their painted eyes and escorts large enough to be the muscle men at a house of ill-repute, some asked at which brothel they could be found after the battle.

The duchess did not translate their offers but continued to throw flowers until a few of their adversaries realized the boat skimmed nearer to the American line than theirs. The Turks shouted warnings at first, then realizing they had been duped, sent a barrage of shot at them. With Wills and Geoffrey leaning into the oars as it their lives depended on it, which it did, the balls of lead fell short. They crossed the open expanse of water toward where the *Constitution* lay at anchor. The duke threw back his hood and used his stentorian voice to hail the American ship. The commodore issued a command for all aboard to hold fire and offered Bellevue a smart salute as their boat moved past the frigate and on to the British ship awaiting them beyond. Their own crew, very aware of the mission they'd undertaken, raised a cheer and lowered a rope ladder.

"Ladies, can you manage the climb?" he asked.

"I am uncertain," Balfour said shakily.

"Geoffrey, can you take her on your back?" Rick suggested.

"I know I wasn't much use in the fight, milord, but this I can do." The footman pulled in his oar and braced himself on the first rung of the ladder.

Hesitantly, Balfour put her arms around his neck and hung there. The duchess spoke up, "No, you silly goose. You must wrap your nether limbs about him as well."

"Oh, oh my!" Flustered, the maid gathered her robes and hoisted her herself around Geoffrey's waist. They progressed slowly up the ladder without mishap.

"Flora, will you climb or ride upon me?" the duke asked his wife.

"You know I could climb but always prefer to ride," she said coyly.

Thalia sighed. Even here, having barely escaped with their lives, her parents continued their love play. Instead of experiencing the usual flush of embarrassment, she discovered herself wishing she and Rick might act the same at their old age and still be besotted with each other.

Quick and agile, the duchess climbed onto her husband's broad back. He expelled a small "oomph" and said, "Flora, exactly how many of the sultan's dates did you eat?"

"Beneath these robes, I carrying a great deal of baggage, and it is not due to an excess of flesh. Onward and upward, my dear." She kicked his flanks as if she expected him to jump aboard in one great leap like a hunter taking a fence. They made short work of the climb.

"Now our turn, dearest Thalia. Climb or ride?" Rick asked with a smile that hid his scar.

How she wished she could answer as lightly as her mother, but instead, she took her right hand hidden all this time in her robe and revealed a deep gash across her palm. As the fabric fell away, the wound began bleeding again.

"I am afraid I am the first casualty on our side of the battle. I did hold the blade wrapped in my garment but had to thrust with such force to inflict damage, it cut through to my hand."

"Is there a problem?" the duke shouted from the deck.

"Yes, Thalia has injured her hand very badly. Wills, go aboard. I am taking her back to the *Constitution*. They will have a superior surgeon to sew her wound."

Before any could protest, he left Wills hanging on the rope ladder and claimed the oars. With deep and urgent sweeps, Rick crossed the distance between the two ships. Hailing the *Constitution*, he stripped his Arab robe, the ridiculous wig and beard, and asked permission to bring a lady aboard in a chair. He climbed alongside her and once on the deck, ignored Commodore Preble's glare. Rick drew off her black robe and announced, "My newly rescued affianced is in need of medical care. She slew a Turk, or very nearly so, and was injured in the process." While Thalia's hand throbbed, her heart swelled at Godric's pride in her.

Preble softened. "Then she deserves the best of care. Carry on."

Rick took her directly to the ship's doctor. They found him in his surgery preparing for the wounded to come with cauterizing irons in the fire, bone saws at the ready, and baskets of lint to pack the injuries. As proper and cleanly as the rest of the ship, he washed Thalia's hand with seawater, making her hiss in the process.

"Deep but no tendons cut. Still, you will bear a scar, but I shall use my most delicate stitches to sew you up. Seldom do I get to operate on such a lovely hand. Once the palm heals, you must work to regain its full use by exercising it. Do you play the piano? I suppose all young ladies do."

"Yes." She bit her lip. "I suppose I will never play Mr. Beethoven's sonata with great passion again."

"You might in time by stretching the hand." The surgeon offered her a bottle, one of many standing ready for use along with tincture of opium for the worst cases. "Whiskey for the pain before we begin."

"Drink it and never think about Beethoven again," Rick said.

He held her unharmed hand in his and put the bottle to her lips. She took two large gulps. Rick urged another on her. The fiery burn did distract her from the first of the stitches in her palm, but did little good after that. She squeezed Rick's hand nearly hard enough to break bone and held back her tears until the work was done and the wound wrapped with a bandage. Then, one drop overflowed from the corner of her eye and made its way down her cheek carrying a black line of kohl with it. She wiped it away with her good hand.

"I am no longer physically perfect."

Rick kissed her bandage. "Your scar, like mine, is a badge of honor to be displayed proudly. And you know I do prefer the blasted pine," he jested to ease her pain. "I must take you back to our ship. Time grows short."

Having heard part of the tale, the American sailors lowered her gently into the boat tethered to the end of the rope ladder. Rick climbed down and took up the oars again. He offered his back for transport aboard the *Redemption,* and she wrapped herself around him as they clambered up the side of their ship. Though her hand still throbbed, the dose of whiskey made her sleepy and a trifle amorous. She nuzzled her lover's neck and whispered small endearments as they went. Once over the rail, she slid off and into her mother's arms.

"She shed nary a tear," Rick reported as Lady Flora examined the bandaged hand.

"Because she is a Longleigh," the duke said with even more than his usual pride in his eldest daughter.

Though she still wore her eye paint, the duchess, looking more herself with her black robe, jewels, and all but one gown put aside, suggested, "Now that we are all together, we must set sail at once before the bombardment begins," the duchess declared. "No more talk. Off to Italy."

"I am inclined to stay and see how the battle goes," the duke countered.

"I would like to offer my services to the Americans," Rick said so offhandedly it took a moment for his statement to catch hold.

"No!" the women answered together.

"I should have thought of that myself. We do owe them for Thalia's care," the duke said with a small flicker of fire showing in his eyes.

Lady Flora stamped her small foot on the deck. "You owe them nothing! They impeded the delivery of the ransom with their siege."

As if he were always the voice of reason, the duke replied, "However, they did allow us to cross their line and enter the city to rescue you, and we still have our gold. Yes, we should go to their aid, Danelagh. Splendid idea!"

Rick placed his hands on Thalia's shoulders and looked directly into her dark eyes. "I have trained all my life to be a warrior and have never gone into battle. Do you understand why I want to do this, my love?"

"I have no wish to understand, but you will go without my permission. I ask that you keep safe and return to me whole by the end of this day."

"War does not allow for such promises, but I will do my best." He kissed her bandaged hand and then her lips.

The duke attempted to do the same with his wife, but she drew away, her arms folded across her chest. "Now, Flora, do not send me off with anger and ill words." He pressed his mouth to her disheveled golden curls.

Her arms moved around his waist, and she buried her face against his chest despite the dried blood that crusted it. "I thought I needn't be brave any longer...now this."

"You are always valiant, dearest. You wanted an adventure. Allow me mine."

"I love you, Pearce Longleigh. Never forget that!"

The men parted from their ladies, went over the side and into their boat once more, taking themselves to the *Constitution*. The duchess and Thalia watched them all the way.

"To think Captain Bainbridge of the *Philadelphia* must lose his command and his career once he and his men are freed because he surrendered rather than risk all their lives. Other men will die today because of his decision," Lady Flora said as she shaded her eyes to catch a last glimpse at her husband's wide back as he boarded the American flagship.

Thalia answered her. "I believe the wives and children of Bainbridge's sailors will bless him, no matter what others say." The afternoon sun shone hotly on Danelagh's white-blond hair for a moment, and then she could see her lover no more.

Twenty-one

Commodore Preble did not precisely welcome the extra hands aboard. He eyed Bellevue from his scuffed boots to his sweat and blood-stained coat and shirt. The commander's uniform embodied the word "immaculate" with its shining brass buttons, spotless waistcoat, and blue jacket. "You are in disarray, sir. What do you want now, Longleigh? Have you more women who need rescuing or a splinter in your thumb that needs pulling?"

"We have come to offer our services in the upcoming battle."

"Really? You would fight for the United States of America?"

"In this instance, yes."

Preble took a second, deeper look at the duke. "We are of nearly the same age, and boarding enemy ships is a young man's business. Your white-haired lad might be of some use if he is skilled at arms and brave of heart."

"I am both," Godric declared. "I come with my own sword and pistol and know how to use them."

"Very well, add one of our hatchets and a pike to your armaments. Join Lieutenant Stephen Decatur's command. His second division will be attacking the north end of the bashaw's line. Make haste! I will be giving the command to advance shortly."

Danelagh picked up his equipment and ferried to a waiting gunboat. Bellevue, who appeared to be forgotten as Preble gave the order to advance, prompted, "I am not so old as to be useless."

"Then stand near me and you will have danger enough. Do as I tell you without question."

"You have my word upon it."

~ * ~

Godric manned a sweep as the cumbersome gunboat heavy with cannons and overloaded with men began to move forward under both sail and oar. For an hour, the slow vessels maneuvered into position. Murad Reis and his navy waited. The signal to attack came at two-thirty. Shells burst over Tripoli. The gawking populace disappeared from the rooftops and took shelter. The bashaw's shore batteries opened fire none too accurately, but their strength lay with their admiral whose ships began to close confidently on the Americans as if expecting them simply to fire once and retreat.

They did not. Instead, Stephen Decatur and his men, brandishing their edged weapons, boarded the nearest enemy gunboat. Shrieking like wild Indians, they cut down a crew desperately trying to reload their pistols. Godric's strong arm split a head with a tomahawk and his sword took down another enemy. The Turkish captain fell and the remainder of the Turkish crew jumped overboard or surrendered.

Towing his prize, Decatur's gunboat moved on. His men boarded its next target with the same ferocity. Decatur took on the enemy captain with his pike, but the burly Turk simply wrenched the weapon away and turned it against him. The American shattered his cutlass against the shaft and then unarmed, threw himself bodily on his adversary, taking a cut to the arm in the process.

Godric saw it all but, engaged with his own enemy, could do little to help. A scimitar wielded by another of the bashaw's sailors rose above the struggling Decatur's head. Danelagh tried to disarm his enemy as he had to save the duke and go to the rescue, but this seaman possessed more skill than Tarek and parried his attempt. Fortunately, a wounded American sailor saw and threw himself between Decatur and the deadly blow. The scimitar missed, cutting the man's scalp and sending a shower of blood over both the fallen men, but neither Decatur nor his savior died, as a third American shot the wielder of the crescent sword dead in his tracks. Working loose his own pistol, Decatur discharged his gun into the back of the Turkish captain. Godric suddenly found himself without a foe. At the death of the leader, his opponent leapt overboard. Others held up their hands in surrender.

Smiling with savage joy, Decatur hailed another American gunboat as it came near. He expressed his desire to share his victory with his brother, James, in charge of the other vessel, only to learn his sibling lay dying from a wound to the head given to him by an enemy captain who had supposedly surrendered. Bloody, exhausted but filled with anger, Decatur asked who would go with him to avenge his brother. Eleven seamen and Godric Erikson volunteered to pursue and punish the devious Turk. They caught the ship before it could hide behind the rocks of the harbor and boarded it with mighty yells. Decatur himself slew the captain who'd put his brother on his deathbed, and those who were left after Godric drove a pike through one and severed a hand from another surrendered.

~ * ~

The *Constitution* moved forward and let loose a blast from half her portside cannons and then another broadside from the others. Within the city, a minaret crumbled as if it made of sugar instead of stone. The crew cheered, the duke along with them. The bashaw's batteries answered and shot their main yardarms away. Another ball lodged in the *Constitution's* mainmast. A cannon beneath the quarterdeck exploded and sent shards of wood and iron arrowing through the air. The duke, standing near the commodore, sustained a small cut to his arm, a nearby marine an injury to his elbow, and Preble a mere tear in his uniform.

Regarding the rip, Preble remarked, "Dangerous enough now for you, Longleigh?"

"Quite."

The battle ended before five o'clock. Glad not to find Danelagh among them, the duke lent his strength to hauling the wounded, more of them Turks than Americans. When Decatur reported to the quarterdeck, Bellevue found Godric, blackened and bloodied but grinning, standing behind his valiant lieutenant who saluted and declared to Preble, "I have brought you three of the enemy's gunboats, sir."

"Three, sir! Where are the rest of them?" the commodore replied with the greatest ingratitude. "At least a dozen of Murad Reis' gunboats have escaped!"

He commanded the *Constitution* to be moved six miles out for repairs. The duke asked to be transferred to his own ship on the way, but Godric stayed behind to pay last respects to his leader's brother who lingered, but would most likely not last the night. "Explain to Thalia," he asked Bellevue.

"As best as I can explain to any woman why you don't immediately rush to her arms after a battle. You know, the Shawnee had a period of purification after the warriors returned. I've often thought that might be the best idea for all societies, a transition from battle back to peace away from others."

Regardless, the duke expected his wife to be waiting with open arms on the deck, but only Thalia appeared. After telling his distressed daughter that Godric would remain the night aboard the *Constitution*, she informed him that the duchess awaited him in his cabin. Strange, as Flora was always most exuberant in greeting him. Stinking of smoke and the stench of bodily fluids from the injured he'd carried, he sought her out immediately. The sight that greeted him when he opened the cabin door would ordinarily have pleased him very much.

With her white breasts exposed, the bashaw's gold chain dangling between them, and her nether limbs encased only in filmy pantaloons that left nothing to the imagination, Flora lounged on the box bed. She fluttered her painted eyes at him. "I am your prize of war," she said seductively.

"My dear, I hope I will say this only once in my life, but I am simply too tired for bed sport."

Her disappointment showed for just an instant in her large, gray eyes. She made it vanish with an understanding smile. "Then shed your clothes, wash, and lie beside me all night. It has been too long since we've had even that."

Twenty-two

Godric returned to the *Redemption* the following afternoon. Washed clean of the Arab makeup and the soot from the cannons, his skin and hair gleamed white, but shadows haunted his mind. Decatur himself had given him fresh clothes in which to attend the brief service for the lieutenant's brother. Commodore Preble spoke the words over the corpse and gave a fine report of the young man's conduct and brave demise. James Decatur had died a sailor's death and went to rest wrapped in canvas and weighted with shot to the bottom of the Mediterranean Sea.

Wearing the gown the color of jonquils, Thalia waited for him looking like spring had arrived after a bleak winter. She greeted him sedately with a kiss to the cheek and inquired if he needed food or rest like any considerate hostess, as if she no longer recognized him.

"No, I slept from exhaustion last night and dined with the officers before returning. Do not be angry with me, dearest."

"I am not. Once I knew you were well, I got over my disappointment that you did not return to me immediately. Would you like to tell me about it?"

He led her to a recess where she could sit out of the sun. "I cannot explain going into battle. It is both exhilarating and terrifying. Once we boarded the enemy ships, each man had to take care for himself yet fight bravely. I killed several, lost count after the first two. Stephen Decatur would have died if another sailor hadn't come to his aid. I was not quick enough, and it would have been a great loss if he had died." He found talking to her helped.

Thalia touched his cheek with her bandaged hand. "And a great loss to me if that distraction had cost you *your* life. Would you do it again?'

"Yes, if called upon by my country, but not so heedlessly as this. I've learned war is not a student's game of swords. I have you and my sister to care for now. I am the last of the Erikson name and must be sensible of that. Life can end in a second as it did for James Decatur. Thalia, I am not inclined to wait until the jonquils bloom again to marry."

"Nor am I."

Half-hidden in their shady recess, Rick bent to take her into a more passionate embrace, but the duke's boisterous voice shouting from across the deck halted him midway. "Ah, there you are, Danelagh. I see the top of that white head."

Thalia whispered, "Mama and Papa kept to their cabin all morning and only appeared at dinner looking remarkably pleased. I'm not sure if it was nausea over the way they fawned on each other, envy, or worry about you that put me off my food."

Her father joined them far too quickly. "What news from the *Constitution*, my boy?"

"The Americans caught a French privateer trying to sneak from the harbor this morning. Preble plans to use him as a go-between to the bashaw. He is offering an exchange of prisoners and fifty thousand dollars to free the captives from the *Philadelphia*. Do you think the offer will be accepted?"

Lady Flora, only a few steps behind, joined them. While she seemed a bit fatigued, her gray eyes free of the harem's adornment held a delightful sparkle. "Not by the Yusuf Karamanli we've come to know. The man thinks himself king of the world rather than simply a ruler of one small sultanate."

"I'm of a mind to wait and hear the results. It might be some days, though. Keeping your enemy waiting during negotiations is an old ploy," the duke replied.

"No!" the ladies said.

"We were promised Italy, and all we have gotten is a long stay in Tripoli," Lady Flora pouted.

The duke hugged her to his side. "A finer adventure than going to Milan, I'd say. Wouldn't you like to be here to see your American friends released and join in the celebration?"

"Of course, but Thalia and I have wardrobes to replenish and want to see Venice at the very least before we move inland. We will hear the news in Italy."

"Come now. Only a few more days. What difference can that make? Thalia, are you willing to indulge your old father in this?"

"You will never be old, Papa. I suppose I can wait a while, but I want you to know you are delaying my nuptials. Rick and I have decided to wed as soon as we set foot on land."

"Oh my, no!" her mother objected. "We must find an Anglican priest and have the banns read properly. I suppose there will be one in Venice despite all the papists there. While we wait, we will have a new gown sewn for the occasion and must prepare your trousseau. We should send a message to your brother, James, and urge him to attend the ceremony. He can stand up with you, Godric."

"Flora, Flora, you have convinced me that a few days here at anchor are very preferable to going on to Venice at once. We remain until the bashaw gives his answer. It can do no harm." The duke had made up his mind, though Godric would have had it otherwise to possess and marry Thalia as soon as possible. He'd also gain opinionated in-laws and must defer to them.

~ * ~

One day passed, then two. With no way of knowing if the Frenchman's head sat on a pike outside the palace or if negotiations continued, Commodore Preble spent his time repairing his ships and making plans for another assault. Aboard the *Redemption,* the women fretted to leave, and the men allowed their cuts and bruises to heal beneath the fierce August sun.

Sword practice and sea bathing passed the time for the gentlemen. They retained their undergarments and kept to the far side of the ship when swimming for the sake of the ladies aboard, and in Rick's case to ward off the effects of the sun on his fair skin. The ladies without even their needlework to keep them occupied read what books there were, played at chess and draughts, and walked the deck for exercise. Lady Flora appropriated a large, straw hat from Godric and trimmed it to her satisfaction with a tie of gauze from her harem pantaloons and an assortment of seashells offered to her by the sailors. In the evening, she happily adjourned to her husband's cabin.

The two footmen slung hammocks with the crew and declared themselves more comfortable than they'd been in months. Thalia and Balfour stayed across from Godric's room. On the second night of waiting with the maid snoring lightly nearby, Thalia could contain herself no longer. Wearing nothing more than her chemise, she crossed the narrow hall and scratched on Danelagh's door.

"Rick, let me in!"

He opened at once. A lantern hanging from its gimbal still burned within, and he closed the door quickly but softly. "At last you've come. Since you are bedding with Balfour, I could hardly..."

"I know. We must be quiet with Mama and Papa in the next chamber."

"Why? They kept me awake much of last night with their thrashing about." He made short work of removing her chemise and she of getting rid of his shirt. Naked, they fell into the box bed.

"But they are married, and we are not. It is a matter of propriety."

"Propriety be damned! Your father knows of the feather torture and has decided not to hold my actions against me. As soon as you left, I knew I would never last the year without following you."

"You and Papa have a great deal in common. Kissing...now kissing is a very quiet activity."

"It can be."

They set out to prove that, but kissing led to the stroking of tongues, of breasts, of Godric's hardened shaft, and on to low moans until they discovered the built-in bed had never been intended for sharing between a large man and a tall woman. He tossed a blanket to the floor and took her there, withdrawal at the last moment just barely possible after so many months. After resting from her spasms and sleeping for a while, Thalia took a turn on top, careful to watch for the signs of his climax. She would have her time to study opera in Milan without fearing a pregnancy even if they wed in Venice. All of her dreams were about to come true. They stayed in her mind as she arced over Rick's strong, white body, collapsed against his chest, and slept in his embrace.

~ * ~

A small, graceful xebec as swift as a gazelle hound sailed from the harbor of Tripoli. It swung wide of the American fleet during the darkest hours of the night and crept up upon the ship bearing the British flag. A grappling hook bit into the *Redemption's* railing, and Murad Reis, hand over hand and braced against her side, hauled himself aboard. He snorted softly at the lax security. Because the vessel was neither warship nor merchantman and lay at anchor near the great guns of the *Constitution,* only one guard kept the watch. That one nodded in his sleep and woke to find a blade at his throat.

"Tell me where the English women are kept or die this second, ye worthless wretch."

"Down the near hatch, second cabin on the right."

Murad Reis sliced across the sailor's windpipe in punishment for his negligence and in need of silence. The high admiral slipped the body overboard and made his way to the indicated hatch. Moving down the narrow steps, he slunk to the second cabin on the right and silently opened door. Only one woman laid asleep there, the scrawny bitch of a servant. Rage surged from his stomach to his throat in a tide of black bile. He wanted to kill her where she rested for not being Thalia.

His father-in-law had expressed great unhappiness over losing the ladies and their ransom on the same day the Americans raped his fleet and left it tattered and torn. Losing a few gunships came to nothing, but the inner harbor had suffered great damage from the *Constitution's* bombardment. They had ravaged his reputation as well. If he could retrieve even one of the women and let the bashaw demand all the ransom for her return, he was redeemed. Unlikely the mighty sultan would care what he did with her either, since both ladies had abused his splendid treatment. He chose to take Thalia, naturally, but where did she hide?

A prick of his cutlass woke the maid who opened her mouth to cry out but closed it at once on his orders. "Shut your trap, ye blathering sheep. Where is Lady Thalia?"

"Across the way," she sniveled. "At least I think so."

With the tip of his sword, he rooted through their small pile of belongings and found a long, handsome sash embroidered with the moon and stars, Thalia's work he recognized, that would serve to bind the annoying female's hands to her feet. A wad of paper shoved deep into her mouth ensured her quiet, that and a threat to come back and kill her later if she did not comply. Done, Murad Reis moved from the cabin and out into the narrow companionway again. He tried the handle and found the door latched from the inside. Sliding his blade through the crack between frame and door, he lifted the light bar that blocked his way and entered.

There she lay in the flickering light of a lamp guttering from lack of oil, a wanton goddess spread across a man every bit her equal in physical beauty but marred by a scar upon his cheek. He'd seen this soldier, easily distinguishable by his white hair, through his glass during the battle as the huge warrior cut down man after man. As much as he could admire that, anyone who possessed Thalia other than himself must die. A shame her lover would do so in his sleep rather than in a duel to the death, but so be it.

He took a single, stealthy step forward. A board creaked beneath his feet. A pair of gray eyes sharp as a blade of Toledo steel snapped opened.

~ * ~

Rick rolled Thalia behind him and guarded her with the protective wall of his body. So many years of practice, so often ambushed by Bascom to keep his skills sharp—and his sword hung on the wall and the dagger he had taken from the Turk did no good beneath his thin mattress. He should have leapt up immediately upon hearing the slight noise, but the corsair who stood over them had already placed the curve of his cutlass against the root of his penis.

"Quiet, the both of ye," the pirate said. "A fine picture ye make. I'd gladly turn this lad into a pretty eunuch of for taking what I should have. I must believe he is the betrothed ye told the princess about so proudly and not just some marine ye gave yourself to because he impressed you with his manliness, eh, Thalia?"

Thalia did not dignify that remark with a reply. Godric felt her left hand move under his arm and splay across his heart as if she wanted to keep him from death. Suddenly, he knew who had him pinned.

"You are the traitor, Peter Lisle."

"There ye are wrong. I am the bashaw's high admiral, Murad Reis, these days. He wants the girl back and the ransom. The first would do for me. She's ruined for a wife now ye've been inside her, but what a fine concubine she'll be once I convince the sultan that the Duke of Bellevue won't pay for a dishonored daughter. Cover yourself, lass. We must be going." The cutlass pointed toward the discarded chemise.

Seizing the moment, Rick flipped over and made a grab for the man's ankles, hoping to bring him down, but Murad Reis, light on his feet, jumped back and planted the cutlass firmly between his shoulder blades.

"I dinna get to be admiral by falling for such simple ploys. Dress, my lovely, or go on deck bedecked in nothing but your lover's blood."

Covering her nakedness as best she could with her hands, she crawled from behind Rick and donned her single, thin garment with her back turned from the corsair. "Will you allow me to go to my chamber and dress more fully?"

"No, my darlin' girl. Ye left clothes enough behind in the harem, and as ye will be taking a little swim, less is better."

"But I cannot swim."

"No need to be concerned. My men will scoop ye from the drink soon as ye land and enjoy doing it. Go above now and make not a sound if you value this man's life." Not to be fooled twice, he did not bother to make a gesture but kept his blade against Godric's back this time.

"You will kill or maim him if I go."

"And so I will if ye do not. He isna exactly dressed for pursuit and does look the fool lying there like so much useless meat. I might spare him as I've seen his work with arms and do appreciate it, but have yet to make up my mind." To emphasize his point, the admiral of the Bashaw's fleet drew a thin, bloody line down his rival's back. Godric lay perfectly still.

Thalia inhaled as the blood welled red against his white skin. "I am going. Please spare him, and I will owe you my gratitude for my entire life."

"Your gratitude is not what I want."

"Whatever you want for however long."

"We will discuss the possibilities later. Off with ye."

Her bare feet barely making a sound on the flooring, Thalia left the cabin. Her light tread went up the stairs. Murad Reis poised his blade on Godric's neck.

"I did not want her to see this as it might turn her against me."

"Am I allowed last words?" Godric said. When the blade did not move, he went on talking. "She will always be against you, and you vastly underestimate her. Thalia is capable of great surprises. I hope she murders you in your sleep."

A dull pounding noise sounded across the way causing both men to turn their heads toward the doorway. Murad Reis spat out, "Christ's balls, that silly cunt of a maid is trying to raise a warning. Now I have no time to kill you properly." Rick rolled and caught the blow at an angle on his left shoulder, but before he could rise the admiral had gone, following Thalia swiftly above.

Godric surged to his feet, grabbed his saber and pulled the dagger from under the mattress. The ancient Celts fought naked and according to the duke, the Shawnee warriors took on their enemies wearing nothing more than a breechcloth. What did he care for modesty or the humiliation of being caught helpless in the nude? He raced after them, barely passing Bellevue's cabin when that door opened.

"What the devil's arse is going on?" the duke, attired only in his shirt, said.

Rick answered only, "Thalia," before he mounted the steps taking him out on deck. Thalia had moved far away from the hatch to the side opposite the grappling hook that held the xebec to the side of the *Redemption,* making it harder for Murad Reis to force her overboard in the proper place for retrieval. Far from cowering, she stood tall by the far rail, stately as a figurehead on a man-of-war, with her hands behind her back. The pirate made for her, but Godric's voice caused him to stop and turn.

"Peter Lisle, will you fight me for her?"

The corsair grinned, showing his coffee and rum-rotted teeth through his light beard. "Come on then. That shoulder wound gives ye a weak left side, I imagine."

"Imagine what you like. That does not make it true."

Saber clashed with cutlass. Knowing his bleeding injury would tell in time, Godric pressed forward, making each strike a hard blow. He had a height and weight advantage over the much smaller admiral, but the man had experience and agility on his side. From time to time, the corsair made a feint at Danelagh's exposed genitals, but he was not fooled and fought on without flinching. Murad Reis circled round a mast and reversed their direction. Rick saw the duke in his nightshirt with pistol poised at the enemy's back but knew Bellevue would not be able to draw a bead on their always shifting position.

Also armed with a pistol, Captain Featherstone appeared from his cabin. "Where's the watch!" Glancing at the blood on the deck and railing, he knew the answer to his question and moved to clang the ship's bell, rousing the sailors sleeping below. Never taking his eyes off Godric, Murad Reis shouted out in Arabic. Two more grapples sailed over the rails and tightened as his men answered his summons.

Curls tousled, Lady Flora came above wearing her harem pants and one of the Duke's large shirts covering her nearly to the ankles. Balfour stumbled after her, but covered her eyes at the sight of so much nakedness. Three Turks climbed over the rails. The duke bade both women to go back below and planted himself and his pistol before the hatch. He shot the first of the enemy that came his way, and Featherstone took down another. Godric no longer fought alone.

Immoveable, Bellevue reversed the pistol and prepared to use it as a club. A metal grip pressed against his other hand, and he looked down to see his wife delivering his sword. He snatched it up in time to hold off a double-edged scimitar slashing his way. Bringing pikes and cudgels, the British sailors, with Wills and Geoffrey in the forefront, climbed from their hatch and began pushing the Turks into the sea, smashing their heads as soon as they showed above the rail. More pistols discharged. The moonlit night grew hazy with their smoke.

Murad Reis pivoted again in a move that would take him back to Thalia and put the oncoming Turks between himself and Danelagh. Fearing the bashaw's admiral might use Thalia as a shield if he got to her first, Godric pressed harder. His affianced's long, graceful arm moved suddenly from behind her back and tossed a belaying pin under the feet of the pirate. He tried to jump over it, but the obstruction was so unexpected, he caught his forward foot and fell back on the deck. Godric's saber bit into the wood where the corsair's head would have been had he not crabbed backward, bunched, and sprung up again like a warrior sown from dragon's teeth. Another belaying pin slung by Thaila sailed toward the admiral's head. As he ducked and protected his skull, Godric took a piece out of his side.

"You see, Lisle. She is full of surprises."

"Keep the damn bitch then!"

The corsair backed off into a cordon of his men. They made for the railing and dove overboard. The xebec cut free of its grapples and pushed away with its dripping admiral barely aboard and a few of its crew swimming in the wake. The *Redemption's* sailors, roaring with triumph, tossed the bodies of his dead and dying after the high admiral.

"Not bad for a mere small trading vessel," Captain Featherstone said. "An extra rum ration today." That brought on more cheers, whether for the compliment or the additional grog was hard to say.

Lady Flora's white hand shoved another item from the hatch. The duke held up a pair of trousers. "For Danelagh," she said without climbing any further. The man in question stood wrapped close in Thalia arms with the muscular half-moons of his buttocks gleaming with sweat in the moonlight.

Godric felt a tap on his uninjured shoulder. "Put these on before you embarrass yourself," the duke said.

"Too late for that."

"Regardless, you have an appointment with the surgeon's mate."

That taken care of and not dressed much more herself, the duchess popped up bearing a blanket to cover Thalia from the eyes of the sailors. Enwrapping her daughter, she led her away to privacy below while her husband saw that Danelagh got his shoulder properly sewed up and bandaged. Wincing, Godric could only admire Thalia more for her stoicism when having her hand stitched. What a woman he loved.

~ * ~

In Thalia's cabin, the women shared round a bottle of wine Balfour had demanded as a restorative from the ship's stores. The maid drank rather more of it than the other two.

"I've never seen the like," she said. "A stark-naked man battling with a sword. Shocking, but rather magnificent really."

"A Greek god carved from Parian marble," Thalia answered with her dark eyes gone almost as dreamy as those of her sister, Iris.

"Yes, yes, from what I observed, outstanding. However, I still prefer the version done in bronze," her mother answered.

Twenty-three

The duke sent a report on the *Redemption's* night attack over to the *Constitution* containing the information that Danelagh had injured the high admiral and expressing the sincere hope that the wound would fester and kill the man, though he doubted the tough corsair could be so easily slain. Commodore Preble replied that word had come through the French counsel from the bashaw concerning the proposal to free the *Philadelphia's* crew.

With characteristic bombast, Yusuf Karamanli replied, "I would rather bury myself under the ruins of my country than basely yield to the wishes of the enemy."

Bellevue read the letter to the others after dinner while they lingered over coffee and the captain and his mates had gone about their duties. "There is to be another bombardment of the city tomorrow. We should be able to watch it quite safely from here."

"We *should* be on our way to Venice," his wife insisted. She eyed Thalia and Rick so engrossed in each other they paid no attention to anyone else. "Some of us are running out of restraint."

"Ah, yes, restraint. Just one more bombardment and then we shall go. I promise."

"On the word of a Longleigh?"

"Yes."

"Very well, then I agree to one more day and only one." The duchess lowered her voice and spoke for her husband's ears alone. "I do not want my first grandchild to be born prematurely."

The duke raised his voice loud enough to break the rapture of the starry-eyed lovers newly aware of how much they meant to each other. "Did you hear, Danelagh? Flora says we may stay for another bombardment if the two of you promise to stay in your own cabins."

Thalia buried her face in her hands. "Oh, Mama!"

"I said no such thing. Your father puts words into my mouth."

With her face covered, Thalia did not see Rick's grin. "I would take pleasure in another bombardment, especially if the Americans reduce the palace to rubble and bury Murad Reis in it, so I will be on my best behavior—but I cannot vouch for your daughter."

Thalia glared at him. "You are as bad as they are!"

"Or as good."

"My, yes," the duke said. "I never thought to like a son-in-law quite so much.

~ * ~

The bombardment began at 2:30 p.m. sharp on August seventh with a salvo from every American vessel sent soaring over Tripoli. All aboard the *Redemption* gathered on deck to watch. Captain Featherstone lent his glass to the duke and Danelagh and would have done the same for the ladies, but they declined. As plaster and stone sprayed from the walls of the palace, they fretted over the women in the harem and worried for their safety. When Murad Reis' gunboats attempted to slip from the harbor and do some damage, the *Constitution* drove them back again. Clearly, the high admiral was still in command and had not gone to hell as yet. A pity, all agreed. By 5:00 p.m., the battle ended. Bellevue found it highly satisfactory.

As agreed, the *Redemption* prepared to set sail for Italy in the morning, but not before the duke sent a congratulatory letter to Commodore Preble on the mighty performance of his navy. A curt reply was returned.

My Dear Sir,

I appreciate your words of praise and confidence, the more so because I have been relieved of my command. During the bombardment, an American vessel arrived carrying the orders for my dismissal, citing the loss of the Philadelphia *and my inability to free the prisoners. It stings, sir, it does sting, but I will continue to do my duty until my replacement arrives. I ask that you keep this to yourself, though it will soon be known to all.*

Yrs. in Friendship,

Edward Preble, Commodore, U.S.N.

Telling no one, not even his beloved Flora, Bellevue placed the letter amongst his belongings to be carried back to England and added to the treasures of the Bellevue Hall library.

~ * ~

The duke did try to dicker. "Negotiations are under way again to free the prisoners for ransom, but I am sure there will be another bombardment after the bashaw's defiant remark. Flora, would you not like to remain to see your friends freed at any time now?"

The duchess stared her husband down with those large, gray eyes of hers. "Your word as a Longleigh," she reminded him. "I am quite tired of washing out the same set of undergarments and hanging them in the cabin to dry so as not entice the sailors."

They set sail for Venice.

Twenty-four

Fair winds and good fortune sped the *Redemption* to its destination. As the duke feared, when the ladies reached land, they embarked on a spree of buying new gowns made of luscious silks and sumptuous velvets for colder weather along with the more practical linens and cottons. This extended to new uniforms for Balfour plus a Sunday frock and the replacement of the gold and black satin livery for the two footmen and advanced on to purchasing bolts and bolts of drapery material to be taken back on the *Redemption* for the refurbishment of Battle Hill. While some of the expenses came from the sale of the bashaw's gifts, all but the diamond and the sapphire being placed into settings by the skilled jewelers of the city, a great deal more of the funds came from the ransom money immediately banked for safety. The duke reminded them Thalia could do as she wished with her twenty thousand pounds, but the rest must be returned to the dowries of Iris and Krista. That slowed the ladies down a bit.

The greatest priority of all was given to finding an Anglican priest among all the papists. Located in a small but lovely chapel, the local vicar agreed to begin the publishing of the banns the coming Sunday and set the date for the wedding four weeks hence. The duke dispatched a message to James Longleigh in hopes he still lingered in Heidelburg and requested his presence for the marriage of his sister and his good friend. Letters from Lady Flora, Thalia, and his soon-to-be brother-in-law added entreaties. To their astonishment, the errant James did arrive the day before the wedding without ever having replied.

The duke embraced him heartily. As they stood together, their resemblance from their height and thick, straight black hair to the broad shoulders and bronzed skin marked them as father and son, the major difference being James' gray eyes, darker than his mother's but very striking against his dark complexion. With a reproachful glance at Godric, who stood aside awaiting his turn at greeting, Lady Flora kissed her son's cheek and ran her finger along the slight scar high on his cheekbone.

"Do not fret over it, Mama, nor place any blame on Rick. It has made me very popular with the ladies."

"Any special lady?" she queried.

"No. I won't be placing my foot in the parson's mousetrap anytime soon. I did warn my friend about Longleigh women, especially Thalia, but he fell anyway."

Thalia stepped up to deliver her kiss. "Your advice made it very difficult for me."

"Merely delayed the inevitable," Godric said as he offered a firm handshake.

"I understand my duty is to witness your wedding and indeed, to make sure you show up for it. But if you change your mind, Rick, I am considering an escape to Greece or perhaps Egypt very shortly. You may seek adventure with me instead of settling in to be a husband and father."

Thalia yanked a hank of her brother's black hair much as she used to do in the nursery when he defied her. Though he wore his cropped in the latest style, enough grew over his collar to allow her a good handful.

Laughing with his strong white teeth showing, James merely pulled her wrist away and held her hand. He turned it over and looked at the still red scar crossing her palm. She tried to clench her fist to hide it, but he spread it wide with his thumb. "Rick wrote me how you got this."

"I am no longer perfection," she said, glancing away.

"My new brother and I agree on many things. One of them is that perfection is boring. This scar tells a story of courage while the whitest hand in all the ton says nothing of the character of its owner. Besides, it makes you much more bearable. If I needed another brother, as if three were not enough, I would choose this man for you. I wish you both well, Thalia, well and happy."

Her ordeal in Tripoli had caused her to shed only a single tear, but Thalia blotted her eyes with a new handkerchief at his words. She sniffed, then said, "Wait until you see my gown for the wedding. It is a pale jonquil yellow. The color is a favorite of Rick's, and we've had it adorned with Venetian lace. I shall have a veil of the same rather than a bonnet, and Mama has found daffodil bulbs and forced them into bloom at exactly the right time for my bouquet."

"Really? Jonquil yellow is your favorite color, Danelagh," James said drolly to his friend. "I never knew."

"You shall never know why. I propose that as my best man, you take your father and me to the nearest tavern and pay for a round in celebration of my wedding."

"Yes, let the ladies get on with their preparations," the duke agreed. "Tomorrow morning is the big day."

~ * ~

When Thalia walked down the short aisle of the chapel in her pale yellow gown, her large, dark eyes and red lips framed by white Venetian lace, Godric knew he had found the perfect woman, perfect for him. The scent of the jonquils simply tied with a bow filled the small space and made his mind wander from the wedding vows to the wedding night. Keeping their word, they had stayed apart for over a month. Denial of the flesh promised to make the evening spectacular. He placed the gold ring on Thalia's finger, and they left the building as man and wife with the two footmen in the gold and black Danelagh livery clearing the way of onlookers and Balfour in Sunday dress coming behind carrying the lacy train of the wedding gown.

They hadn't far to go before stepping into one of the fabled gondolas that carried the wedding party to an old palazzo where the nuptial feast awaited. Through courses of prosciutto and melon, pastas and fish, beef and veal and at last, a very rich cake, he waited to claim his bride. The wines of Italy accompanied every dish. Toasts offered by James and the duke began with the serious and moved forward on a tide of robust reds and sweet whites to bordering on the bawdy. Thalia's cheeks reddened. Lady Flora called an end to the dinner and a beginning to the couple's married life.

"A bridal chamber is prepared for you in this very house. You will have absolute privacy for as long as you wish. Your father and I have hired a gondola for the remainder of the day. We intend to glide the canals."

"Yes, one of the old, broad vessels with a private compartment curtained in red velvet. The gondolier swears his craft is very stable, and he will serenade us as we—go along," the duke assured them. "What will you be doing, James?"

"We are in Venice, Papa. I imagine I can find some interesting company."

"In the morning, a boat will come to take you to dry land and the hired carriage. Then off you go to Milan. Stay the winter. Practice your voice lessons, Thalia, and neither of you have a worry for Krista or Battle Hill. We shall see to both. Now in the old Roman tradition, the wheat, Balfour."

Lady Flora opened a small pouch, and she and the maid showered the couple with grains for prosperity and fertility. Ducking beneath the deluge, Godric noticed Balfour scooping some of the wheat kernels that bounced off the bride, clutching them in her hand, and looking hopefully at Geoffrey, the man she was told who had put his body between her and the Turk after her faint, and now stood at attention across from Wills by the doorway. He would amuse his bride with this observation at a later time.

Playfully, the duchess threw a handful at her husband and son. James jumped aside so quickly to avoid being hit, the kernels might have been the arrows of Cupid. Godric laughed at his friend, but the duke smiled and encompassed his small wife with his great arms.

"Flora, I believe we possess prosperity and fertility enough."

While sharing one of their always inappropriate public kisses, the older couple completely missed the escape of the just married to their secluded chamber.

~ * ~

Her mother had chosen well, Thalia thought. A large and lavish bed filled the room. Its covers were silken and strewn with the yellow petals of a late summer rose. With the sheer pleasure of lying naked upon them, they failed to turn down the bedclothes before beginning. Pale bars of sunlight seeped through the closed shutters and crisscrossed their bodies, but they had no intention of waiting until dark to enjoy themselves. Already knowing each other in the most intimate way, no shyness or false modesty impeded them.

"Do you know, I think I prefer love in the afternoon to all other times of the day," Thalia told her new husband as she toyed with the pale hair on his chest. "And rose petals are much more pleasant than jonquils to lie upon."

Rick stroked her breasts and brought them to his mouth to enjoy like ripe fruits. Thalia ran her hand tenderly over the healing wound on his shoulder, and if her own hand ached, both soon forgot any minor pain as her fingers traveled down to cup his firm, white buttocks. Wherever he touched, she tingled. They were together again, man and wife now, and would never part.

His hand wandered down the curves of her body and into the nest of dark curls between her legs. Unsurprised, he found her wet and waiting for him. Still, he took his time, making sure she bucked and writhed and had her pleasure before he sought his. Mounted over her, she urged him on by clutching his waist and rising to his rhythm. As she began to pulse again, he forced himself free, turned over, and left the dark stain of seed on the golden silk covers.

With his face half-buried in a pillow, he said, "That becomes harder each time, but I am determined you shall have your stay Italy without having to carry a child."

Thalia folded herself against his turned back, her legs locked behind his, her arms encircling his shoulders. She kissed his nape. "Few men would care enough to do this."

She coaxed him onto his back and went to rest with her head against the beating of his heart for a time. Then, she smoothed the scar upon his face and lavished his lips with a deep kiss. One by one, she licked his nipples and worked her way downward to lap at the very tip of his penis. Already hard, it moved against her hand. She took him inside her body and began her ride with the ringlets of her black curls tickling against his chest until she arched back to enjoy him the more, to see him the better.

"Enjoy and trust me to know when to dismount," she whispered. "Let the restraint be mine this time."

When his breathing became labored and his pale eyes closed, when his steady rhythm and upward thrusts began to go wild, she left him and brought him home with a few firm strokes of her hand. As he lay there recovering, his eyes still shut, she stroked his white hair and teased his lips with a fingertip until he smiled for her. Touching both sides of his face, she bent to kiss him and murmured, "Do you know, I believe I have found perfection in a husband.

Epilogue

The Longleigh family always provided the members of the ton with a goodly supply of outrageous gossip, most of it true. The publication of *Life in the Harem and a Daring Rescue from the Hands of the Turks by an anonymous Lady* set them twittering again. Some thought the Duchess of Bellevue responsible for the book, but she denied this. The dedication, *To Lady Flora Longleigh, Duchess of Bellevue, and Lady Thalia Erikson, Countess Danelagh, without whose wisdom and courage this volume would not have been written* seemed to support her disclaimer, but one never knew with the Longleighs.

Those who read it to learn of a foreign culture found it informing. The ones who had a prurient interest expressed sharp disappointment. They had no interest in how the women of the harem dressed, but only in their frequently being bare-breasted. No revelations of their sexual dexterity made it into print. The majority found *Life in the Harem* to be a jolly good read and an exciting adventure.

Balfour had begged to accompany the duke and duchess home to Bellevue Hall rather than remain in Italy. Several months later, she approached Lady Flora with her handwritten manuscript of their time in Tripoli and eventual escape. The duchess looked it over carefully. Other than rather enhancing the maid's own contribution to their adventure, she felt it to be fairly accurate. Being unconscious for most of their battle with the guards, Balfour freely admitted to using accounts she had transcribed from the memories of Wills and Geoffrey on the return voyage to England. Lord Danelagh had sent them back to Battle Hill to see to their health after their captivity. Both maids and footmen could be hired in Milan.

Of course, the publisher insisted on several changes, among them that Thalia must be said to have stabbed the heathen Turk in his heart rather than the groin, which was far too indelicate. Their men got no credit for finishing off the guard, but the artist hired to illustrate the book more than made up for this by showing Godric completely decapitating Hassan and holding the head up by its long braid now in Lady Flora's possession. The editor declined to mention Lady Flora's cutting off the guard's queue for a trophy, but that lady willingly showed it to any who asked about their escape.

The duchess rather enjoyed the frontispiece of herself attired in her tunic and harem pants, the illustrator having added a turban with a feather to sit atop her curls. This started something of a vogue in styles, especially at fancy dress balls, which pleased her even more. Her husband continued to enjoy the topless version in the privacy of their bedchamber where he wore only a dressing gown and his sash embroidered with firebirds. They played sultan and harem girl beneath the scroll she painted for him while in captivity. It read in both Arabic and English:

A Book of Verses beneath a Bough,
A Jug of Wine, a Loaf of Bread—and Thou
Beside me singing in the Wilderness—
Oh, Wilderness were Paradise enow!

The duchess thought she would like to translate the rest of Omar Khayyam's verses, but considered her Arabic lacking. Someone else more adept would have to do it at a later date. Besides, however would she find the time with two girls seeking marriage to bring out in the spring?

Speaking of courtships, when Balfour began receiving income from her book, she soon resigned her post to become Mrs. Geoffrey Johnson. Despite being some years older than the footman, the former maid and authoress regarded the frail but very handsome young man as her savior. Lady Flora, who believed herself gifted in such matters, thought she had scented the sweet smell of romance between the two on the long voyage home. As usual in affairs of the heart, she was right, though which one of them had made the proposal remained a mystery. Awed by Balfour's intellectual accomplishments as he could barely read, and assured of a position for life at Battle Hill in one capacity or another for his services to the new countess and her mother, Geoffrey determined to settle down in a nearby cottage with his somewhat older wife and never travel abroad again. On the other hand, Wills applied for and received the next army commission awarded by the Earl of Danelagh and went forth to seek his *fortune* in the military. A great step up, he called it.

The tongues of the ton set to wagging again when the jonquils came into bloom the following spring, and Earl and Countess of Danelagh returned from their Italian sojourn. The Duke and Duchess of Bellevue had announced their daughter's August marriage in Venice immediately after arriving in London. No amount of assurance by Lady Flora that the young couple had chosen to marry abroad because the dramatic rescue enhanced their love and appreciation for each other sufficed to stop the gossip, so she let society speculate. Many a matron expected the earl and his lady to return with a child who already walked and spoke despite a claim of being only nine months old. Others said surely the lecherous Bashaw of Tripoli had taken advantage of the beauteous Thalia and the babe would be born with the dark skin of an Arab, darker even than Bellevue's countenance. How gallant of Danelagh to wed her and save Lady Thalia from disgrace.

To their great disappointment, neither prediction proved true. At a gala reception for the couple, Thalia Longleigh Erikson, Countess of Danelagh, performed two arias for the company. She stood before the assembly, her tall form as perfect as ever with her gloved hands clasped before her and sang with such emotion that tears sprang into the eyes of the more sensitive listeners. Later, she played a few piano pieces toward the end of the evening after the majority of the crush dispersed. Those who stayed to hear found her skill at the instrument diminished somewhat, but as Lady Thalia had married so well, she no longer needed to keep up her accomplishments, now did she?

Danelagh and his countess stayed on at Bellevue House in London for the season to be feted by numerous friends of the duke and duchess and to lend their aid in finding perfect matches for Iris and Krista.

On a late June day so clement, so free of damp and full of sun that Lady Flora and Thalia carried their needlework into the small garden behind the house, the duke took his newspaper outside to sit with them on the pleasantly shaded benches. Back from a ride in the park, Godric soon joined the small gathering. Knowing his wife's hand often ached because she wanted her embroidery to be as flawless as before, he took her palm in his and massaged away the cramp with such tenderness, with so great a softness in his usually stern gray eyes, that the duchess immediately made a supposition.

"Tell me my dear daughter, are you *enceinte*?"

Thalia's dusky cheeks bloomed with rose. "The child will arrive at the end of the year. We could not restraint ourselves through another jonquil season."

"Do you hear, Pearce? We are to have our first grandchild!"

The duke folded over his paper to a particularly interesting article. "Yes, yes. I suspect we shall have a great many, given our ten children. There is more news you will like to hear. Captain Bainbridge and his sailors were released by the Bashaw of Tripoli on June fifth for a ransom of sixty thousand dollars and the exchange of a handful of prisoners. You say the captain did all he could for his men and endured his captivity nobly, but he will stand before a court martial regardless for losing the *Philadelphia*."

"I pray he will be acquitted."

"I pray our navy will never have to go up against the likes of Preble, Decatur, and this Bainbridge in the future because the outcome might be in doubt. Good men, very good men."

The doors to the garden opened, and the two debutantes who had slept very late after dancing until the wee hours at a ball came down the steps to join the rest of the family enjoying the pleasant weather. Krista guarded her creamy complexion, highly praised by her suitors, with a wide straw hat. Iris, tawny and black-haired like her elder sister but without the curls or the height, did not give a care.

Bursting to tell someone who might have more enthusiasm for the expected baby, the duchess announced to both girls, "You are to be aunts come December."

Delighted, they lavished hugs and kisses and congratulations on Thalia and Rick. Once their youthful joy subsided, the young ladies perched on a bench and fanned themselves as the day grew warm.

"Tell me," Thalia said as she leaned her head against her husband's broad shoulder and smiled with contentment. "Have either of you found a man as fine as mine to be your husband?"

Folding her fan, Krista glanced down at her gloved hands. "No, but I shall look forward to being an aunt to your children."

"Me neither," Iris claimed, but a blush belied her words.

None of them knew another Longleigh scandal loomed over them like a storm cloud about to break open with bursts of thunder and lightning. For now, all was perfection.

Afterword

I rarely use real historical characters in my books as there are too many pitfalls in portraying them, but since I allowed the Longleighs to become entangled in the battle of Tripoli, I thought it only fair that I sort out the real from the fictional characters. Though editors dislike epilogues, I always love when an author tells me what became of the people she created. I thought you might want to know a bit more about the true historical figures.

To begin with Commodore Edward Preble, he was every inch as starchy and irritable as portrayed and in general is credited for setting the standard for the newly emerging United States Navy. While his interaction with the Duke of Bellevue is entirely fictional, his expressed disappointment in Stephen Decatur's only capturing three gunboats is true. He later apologized to the young man who would become one of America's great naval heroes. Our story ends in June, 1805. Preble did not survive much longer. He died at the age of forty-six in August, 1807, of consumption, now called tuberculosis. He expressed his greatest regret in dying of a "stinking" disease rather than gloriously aboard a ship in service to his country.

Stephen Decatur is a well-known military figure. He served gallantly in the War of 1812 and the Second Barbary War, which eventually broke the power of the pashas of the Mediterranean coast and ended piracy in the area. Quite a dashing man but often critical of other naval officers, he died in a duel with a fellow naval man at the age of forty-one in 1820. The home he built in Washington, D. C. still stands and is called Decatur House. His most famous quote was offered in the form of a toast to "Our Country. In her intercourse with foreign nations, may she always be right. But right or wrong, our country!" It has come down in history as "Our Country, right or wrong."

William Bainbridge was acquitted of misconduct by a Naval Court of Inquiry upon his return to the United States. He went on to command with great success the *U.S.S. Constitution*, known today as *Old Ironsides,* in the War of 1812 against the British. The ship still sits in Boston harbor to be visited by tourists. Unfortunately, the later part of his life was tainted by a suspicion that in acting as a second for Decatur in his fatal duel, he manipulated the man's death because of a long-held grudge. Nevertheless, he became a commodore and served out the rest of his life with distinction, dying in 1833.

As for our interesting characters, Yusuf Karamanli and his High Admiral Murad Reis, the Second Barbary War broke the Bashaw of Tripoli. Without a flow of riches supplied by his corsairs, his rule crumbled. Forced to abdicate to a son in 1832, he spent the remainder of his life with only three wives left to service him.

Murad Reis, the notorious pirate Peter Lisle, fell out of favor with the bashaw after viciously attacking another American ship and causing an international uproar. He went into exile in Egypt for a number of years. Recalled to court to act as a translator, he eventually regained much of his power. Known to be a hard drinker and quick with his fists when in his cups, he might well have beaten his wife, the bashaw's eldest daughter. I regret I was unable to discover her name. Murad Reis came to his end after a flamboyant career as a corsair during the coup of 1832 when he was hit by a cannonball, a far better fate than hanging for piracy.

LS

Meet Lynn Shurr

Lynn Shurr grew up in Pennsylvania Dutch country but left to wander the world shortly after getting a degree in English literature. After living in several states and Europe, she picked up a degree in librarianship. Her first reference job brought her to the Cajun Country of Louisiana. Eventually, she became director of a library system. For her, the old saying, "Once you've tasted bayou water, you will always remain here," came true. She raised three children near the banks of the Bayou Teche and lives there still with her astronomer husband where she writes, paints, and studies history.

Other Works From The Pen Of
Lynn Shurr

Lady Flora's Rescue – Book One of the Longleigh Chronicles. Lady Flora follows the man she loves into the American wilderness not knowing he plans to remain there. Will he choose love over his own liberty?

A Taste of Bayou Water - a prequel to *Blessings and Curses*. When Celine Landry refuses to leave Cajun Country to marry billionaire Jonathan Hartz, what else can a brilliant techno-geek do but try to become Cajun?

Blessings and Curses - Adrienne and Pete—is their love real or are they the victims of an old traiteur's love potion?

The Courville Rose - Can four souls find love in two bodies?

A Place Apart - A wounded warrior and a society girl both seek seclusion on the same deserted island. Sparks fly!

Letter to Our Readers

Enjoy this book?

You can make a difference

As an independent publisher, Wings ePress, Inc. does not have the financial clout of the large New York Publishers. We can't afford large magazine spreads or subway posters to tell people about our quality books.

But, we do have something much more effective and powerful than ads. We have a large base of loyal readers.

Honest Reviews help bring the attention of new readers to our books.

If you enjoyed this book, we would appreciate it if you would spend a few minutes posting a review on the site where you purchased this book or on the Wings ePress, Inc. webpages at: https://wingsepress.com/

Visit Our Website

For The Full Inventory
Of Quality Books:

Wings ePress.Inc
https://wingsepress.com/

Quality trade paperbacks and downloads
in multiple formats,
in genres ranging from light romantic comedy
to general fiction and horror.
Wings has something for every reader's taste.
Visit the website, then bookmark it.
We add new titles each month!

Wings ePress Inc.
3000 N. Rock Road
Newton, KS 67114

www.ingramcontent.com/pod-product-compliance
Lightning Source LLC
Chambersburg PA
CBHW070642100726
47907CB00007B/2071